THE INCUNABULUM OF SHERLOCK HOLMES

AIRSHIP 27 PRODUCTIONS

TM

The Incunabulum of Sherlock Holmes

"The Adventure of the Substitute Detectives," "The Adventure of the Second Heir," "The Adventure of the Giant's Wife," "The Woman Who Collected Sherlock Holmes," "The Case of the Fourpenny Coffin," "The Angel of Truth" © 2021 I.A. Watson

Cover & interior illustrations © 2021 Rob Davis

Editor: Ron Fortier
Associate Editor: Fred Adams Jr.
Production and design by Rob Davis
Promotion and marketing by Michael Vance

Published by
Airship 27 Productions
www.airship27.com
www.airship27hangar.com

ISBN: 978-1-953589-01-9

Printed in the United States of America

10 9 8 7 6 5 4 3 2 1

The Incunabulum of Sherlock Holmes

by I.A. Watson

Contents:

The Incunabulum of Sherlock Holmes

I.A. Watson

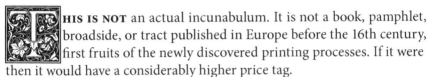

CAVEAT LECTOR:

A FOREWORD WARNING FROM I.A. WATSON

THIS IS NOT an actual incunabulum. It is not a book, pamphlet, broadside, or tract published in Europe before the 16th century, first fruits of the newly discovered printing processes. If it were then it would have a considerably higher price tag.

Nor is it a set of linen swaddling-bands used to strap an infant into a cradle to prevent the baby from falling out, from which the Latin *in-* and *cunae* for "in the cradle" give us the word *incunable* that was popularised in 19th century literary commentary as a replacement term for the earlier *fifteener*, meaning a 15th century "newborn" print edition.

What it *is* is a trap for pedantic but lazy critics who might see the title of this volume and, not bothering to read this introduction, loftily display their cleverness by crowing how "I.A. Watson appears to not even know the actual meaning of the word 'incunabulum'." So *caveat criticus* too.

It's not easy to find a good name for a new collection of stories about Sir Arthur Conan Doyle's most famous creation. Most of the obvious ones were used for his own anthologies: *Adventures of Sherlock Holmes*, *Memoirs of...*, *Return of...*, *Case-Book of...* Even *His Last Bow* was subtitled *Some Later Reminiscences of...* Others have contributed *The Apocrypha of Sherlock Holmes* (several different volumes with different contents), *The Exploits of Sherlock Holmes* (John Dickson Carr in collaboration with Adrian Conan Doyle, 1954), *The Final Adventures of Sherlock Holmes* (ed. Peter Haining, 1981), *The Further Adventures of Sherlock Holmes* (anthology, 1985), *Les nombreuses vies de Sherlock Holmes* ("*The Many Lives of...*" anthology, 2005), *Encounters of Sherlock Holmes* (Paul Magrs, 2013), and a good deal more. Google in your own time.

But *incunabulum* can also more generally be applied to a primitive or old-fashioned collectable, something hand-crafted with authentic materials, put together in a traditional fashion. In that sense, a story might be such an item, if it is assembled with care and affection for its sources, with respect for the proper techniques, with an intention to create something to delight. Let's borrow the term for a couple of hundred pages, may we?

A while ago, sorting through old files, mostly-but-not-quite finished

Holmes stories, tales printed once in prestige-run anthologies but never collected together, adventures that did not fit editorially-fiatted word counts, it became clear that some kind of compilation volume was indicated. Just a little work (the author fondly and naively believed) and there would be a compete book ready to launch.

All the stories save one in this incunabulum meet the proper criterion for Canon-compliant Holmes stories. Here are accounts that Dr Watson never passed to Dr Doyle for editing and publication in *The Strand Magazine*. Other, lesser literary agents must recover the rest from those notes crammed into a trunk at Cox's Bank, and several of I.A. Watson's reconstructive efforts feature in this volume.

Since incunabula tend to be early efforts, two of the stories selected for this book cover the first part of Holmes and Watson's association. "The Adventure of the Substitute Detectives" was originally written for *Sherlock Holmes and Doctor Watson—The Early Years* volume 2 (Bellanger Books, 2019), with a brief to detail some early case from the mostly-unchronicled first five years at Baker Street. "The Adventure of the Second Heir" has never seen print anywhere and shows the friends' growing understanding of each other and of the unique role a 'consulting detective' might play.

"The Adventure of the Giant's Wife" appeared in *The MX Book of New Sherlock Holmes Stories—Part XIV: Whatever Remains . . . Must Be the Truth (1881-1890)*, which collected stories wherein Holmes *apparently* encountered the supernatural. "The Case of the Fourpenny Coffin" debuted in *The MX Book of New Sherlock Holmes Stories—Part XIV: 2019 Annual (1891-1897)*. Both these volumes raised funds for the Stepping Stones School and property at Sir Arthur Conan Doyle's Undershaw estate.

"The Woman Who Collected Sherlock Holmes" is another case new to this book. It features the return of Miss Alexandra Doré, who first appeared in *Sherlock Holmes, Consulting Detective* volume 13 (Airship 27, 2019) as "The Woman Who Collected Queen Victoria"; her obsession has now found a new focus. This narrative offered an interesting technical challenge for I.A. Watson since Holmes was thought dead at the time this adventure is set. Is it still possible for a story to be *about* Sherlock Holmes, to actually *be* a Sherlock Holmes story, if he isn't available to appear in it? Read and find out.

Finally this edition includes "The Angel of Truth", commissioned by editor Christopher Sequeira and published in *Sherlock Holmes and Doctor Was Not* (IFWG Publishing International, 2019). This is the one exception to the Canon rule, since the high concept of that collection was "what if Holmes and Watson never met, but Holmes encountered some other famous doctor from literature or history?" Of the list of suggested possibilities—Dr Moreau, Dr Jekyll, Dr Curie, Dr Doyle, Dr Frankenstein etc.—the one that seemed oddest was Dr John Dee, Queen Elizabeth I's philosopher and conjurer, who lived from 1507 to 1608/9. I could not resist finding a way for him to collaborate with Sherlock Holmes; hence this final story in our incunabulum.

The collection of incunabula has long been an obsession of discerning gentlemen and ladies.[1] I hope that you, the discerning reader, will feel happy to add this book to your collection.

IW
Surrounded by post-incunabula
May 2020

---

1   Lord Peter Wimsey listed collecting incunabula amongst his hobbies, and was frequently consulted for his expertise on questions of literary scholarship.

The Adventure

of

The Substitute Detectives

IN MY EARLY months in residence with Sherlock Holmes my experience of his caseload was rather sporadic. I was slow in recovering from the wound I had taken at Maiwand Pass and a subsequent fever at Peshawar when my life was despaired of. I took constitutionals, visited the Army and Navy Club, and wrote a little, but not much else. I was gradually drawn into my flat-mates' odd world of crime and detection, piece by piece.

Some of my experiences were comprehensive, as was my introduction to the career of a consulting detective—that is, an expert to whom other investigative professionals refer when a matter is too difficult or baffling. The demise of Enoch J. Drebber was a salutary revelation about the science of detection, so much that I made copious notes for a planned essay on the affair.[2]

On occasion I played a role or was an observer in Holmes's other investigations. I saw first-hand what the detective could accomplish in the Adventure of the Impossible Coin,[3] the Murder of the Amorous Balloonist, the Significant Misfortunes of a Malarial Thespian, and other singular events.

At other times my involvement and understanding of Holmes's cases was incomplete and second-hand. I cannot with authority describe the Problem of the Inverted Pygmy, the Mystery of the Baboon's Heart, the Second Death of Reverend Mayhew, the Disturbing Matter of the Wrong Wedding Cake, or the scandalous snooker tournament[4] that led to the near-detonation of Woolwich Arsenal. Those enquiries will likely remain unrecorded forever.

Holmes and I were coming to know each other. We discussed his cases in confidence and I gradually came to understand something of his methods. I became familiar with some of the wide cast of informers, specialists, and agents he had gathered, and with the Metropolitan Police officers

---

2   This would eventually become *A Study in Scarlet* (1888), Dr Watson's first published account of the great detective's work.

3   Recounted by I.A. Watson in *Sherlock Holmes Consulting Detective* volume 15 and *Sherlock Holmes Adventures* volume 2.

4   Snooker was then a very new game, derived from Indian officers' cue-based pastimes like pyramid and black pool, and codified in 1884 by Sir Neville Chamberlain's published rules. Snooker was originally military slang for a 'rookie' or first-year officer.

who were his most regular applicants. Of the Scotland Yard men, the most prominent were Inspectors Gregson and Lestrade, rival investigators to whom the most difficult investigations were awarded. It seemed to me that both men's first action in any case was to turn to Mr Sherlock Holmes.

It was Tobias Gregson who called at 221B Baker Street on a blustery October morning, shaking the rain off his coat and stamping over to the hearth.

"I told him that Mr Holmes isn't here," our housekeeper protested to me, hovering at the doorway. "He said he'd see you, Dr Watson."

"Thank you, Mrs Hudson. Would you send the girl up with some tea?"

The formidable landlady disfavoured Gregson with a last sniff and retreated to prepare refreshments.

"Holmes has been absent for several days now," I instructed my visitor. "I have not seen him for almost a week."

"Where is he?" Gregson demanded. "He is needed."

"I have only his note warning me that his work has taken him away, and that he may be gone for some time. This is not the first occasion when Holmes has vanished on some investigation."

The jowly, portly Detective Inspector growled. "He is a very inconvenient fellow."

"You appear to find him of use," I noted. I confess that my voice carried a note of criticism; Gregson and the other Scotland Yarders received the credit for the cases that Holmes helped them solve. The injustice of it niggled me, and I was determined that one day I would set the record right.

"He has a mind that works in odd ways," the Inspector allowed. "It sometimes comes at a problem from a different angle. That's why I need his view on the work I have in hand."

"I will be happy to pass word to my fellow lodger that you need to speak with him, or to give him any note you might wish to leave."

Gregson warmed his hands on the fire, uncomforted. "That's no good. The Commissioner is breathing down my neck now, before the papers catch hold of what's happening. If once the broadsheets get their teeth into it... well, I need to get to the truth." The Inspector's eyes sparked with venal inspiration. "Holmes keeps note-books about the criminals of London, doesn't he? Long lists of which men are coiners and which men are confidence tricksters—and who the best cracksmen are. If I could look through those journals..."

"I'm afraid that would be an unconscionable breach of privacy," I insisted. I have no doubt that five minutes' glance at the pages of Holmes's

index would have enhanced Gregson's career significantly, but I had no intention of allowing such an invasion. "Also, Holmes is careful to obscure his information by means of codes and abbreviations, to protect his sources and ensure anonymity for those who require it."

"But there must be a file somewhere that details the most skilled thieves, the sort of men who can enter a locked premises, open the best safes on the market, and depart again unseen without leaving the slightest trace!"

"You are referring to the Kirby Jewellers robbery," I surmised. That crime at least had made its way into the press. Five nights earlier, somewhere between eight and six, a packet of uncut diamonds valued at two thousand guineas had been extracted from a sealed strongroom without witness or sign of forced entry.

"That's one," Gregson confessed. "There are three others, the details of which have not yet been made public. The first was ten nights back, when a thief entered the premises of the stockbrokers Lumley & Chayne and abstracted Swedish bearer bonds valued at three thousand krona—eleven hundred pounds. Since the break-in at Kirby's there has been an assault on Hepple's Currency Exchange, where foreign notes to the value of almost two thousand pounds were taken, and most recently, just last night, another outrage. An heirloom tiara of the O'Tierney family was being maintained and polished at Esperson's Jewellers and was removed from their new combination safe. The security guard saw nothing."

"That does sound like a case that might interest Holmes," I agreed. "Unfortunately, I have no way of contacting him and no idea what he is doing. I'm not even sure he is in England."

Gregson's beefy jaw worked as he struggled with this setback. "We know they were the same criminal," he confided in me. "Look at these."

He handed me four deckle-edged calling cards, each containing but a single word in copperplate font: One, Two, Three, and Four. Hand-inked beneath the printed script were the word "Rec.d" and then the recorded sums of money equivalent to the value of goods stolen.

"The fellow is leaving receipts?"

"He is laughing at us," Gregson hissed. "Laughing at Scotland Yard!"

I had to confess that the thief seemed to be mocking his hunters. "I will certainly let Holmes know of the problem when he appears," I promised.

Gregson was clearly under serious pressure to get results. "I cannot wait. If you will not allow me to check Holmes's books then you must help me some other way, Dr Watson. You have gone about with him when he has chased his prey. You must know whom he would go to, who he would ask about things like this. You must have seen the secret of how he finds felons."

"I have some little acquaintance of certain individuals, but I am certain they would not receive me as they do Holmes. There are some who speak with him because they owe him favours. Others because he pays them well. Still others are informers because they fear Sherlock Holmes's closer attention to their own affairs. I cannot approach these men as Holmes would."

"There must be something you can do. The matter is urgent."

I reviewed the resources that the world's only consulting detective might call upon. My eyes strayed to the rug upon which the inspector stood, and I recalled a very different visitor who sometimes occupied that space, ragged cap in hand, trousers torn at the knees, grubby-faced and mischief-eyed. The young rogue's name was Wiggins and he led an irregular troupe of street-urchins who sometimes served as Holmes's eyes and ears.

"I will make some enquiries," I told Gregson. "I cannot promise success."

"Anything is better than nothing," the policeman responded. "There was no sign of how the burglar got in, none! Four perfect robberies in less than two weeks. When the news breaks, so does my career!"

He agreed to return the next day to hear if I had uncovered any word. After I saw him out I resorted to Mrs Hudson to discover how Holmes alerted his street Arabs, and to set them on.

That afternoon I received another call from the forces of the law. This time the querent was Inspector G. Lestrade, Gregson's great rival for the public's laurels. Thin where his opponent was stout, rodent-faced where Gregson was jowly, sallow rather than florid, Lestrade was in many ways the temperamental and intellectual opposite of his fellow officer.

"The two of them are the best that Scotland Yard can offer," Holmes had once told me, in the tones that a medical man might use to impart the need to sever a limb to save the patient. "Gregson is marginally the brighter but Lestrade the more persistent. Gregson is the fox-hound, hasty and boisterous, Lestrade the terrier, temperamental and implacable. One believes everything, the other nothing. Between them they manage to occasionally catch the right man. But they are the best."

"Where is Sherlock Holmes?" Lestrade demanded as Gregson had before. "There is a case that would benefit from his review."

I explained again that the detective was gone away, beyond my means to contact him.

"That won't do," the inspector protested. "What does he mean sneaking off like that when there are matters of public importance to address? I have a dead soldier and a mysterious fakir, and a note from the Foreign Office demanding to know what has happened!"

"You have my sympathies," I condoled. "However, I cannot produce Holmes for you. You might have to address this case by yourself."

Lestrade shook his head. "You don't understand..." Then he paused and looked at me speculatively. "Or you might understand. You were an army doctor who served in India, were you not?"

I confessed to holding such posts in the 5th Northumberland and the Berkshires.[5] "I was out on the Sub-continent for a little under two years, although the last three months of it were in a hospital bed thanks to a Jezail bullet."

"Then you must know about these Indians and their magic men."

"I've seen a fellow do the rope trick and some snake-charming, if that's what you mean."

"And the rest? They say that the Indians invented thugs."

"The Thugee? They were suppressed thirty years ago, Lestrade. It's history now."[6]

"Is it? Because I've heard sailors on our wharves speak of such killers. They wear a yellow sash, don't they, that they can use as a strangling cord? And they carry a special dagger, a personal weapon for ritual murder."

"That's how they were sometimes described. The old laws of the Mughal

---

5   Holmes historians generally reconcile different references in Watson's military career by assessing him as first being an assistant-surgeon to the 5th Northumberland Fusiliers, dispatched to India at the outbreak of the Second Afghan War, and then being attached to the 66th Regiment of Foot, the Berkshires, before the Battle of Maiwand on 27th July 1880.

6   The Indian Thugees and Dacoits were organised criminal fraternities that survived by robbery and ransom. They traditionally perpetrated ritualised mutilation and murder on their victims. Ziau-d din Barni's *History of Firoz Shah* (c 1356) includes an account of Sultan Jalaluddin Khilji arresting and deporting one thousand Thugs, and reads as if the organised criminal fraternity was already a matter of common knowledge. The power of the gangs was finally broken by the British administration's *Thuggee and Dacoity Suppression Acts*, 1836–48, which increased the penalties for Thugee crimes, and by military action.

Empire awarded death sentences for murderers who shed blood; strangulation is a bloodless death and allowed a legal loophole. Hence the *rumāl*, the yellow headscarf, which could be a throttling cord. Their status weapon was the *katar*, a short blade with a strange H-shaped grip. Their drug of choice was datura,[7] a nightshade, which makes its victims sleepy."

"So you do know about them," Lestrade celebrated.

"I know *of* them. Enough to tell you that they are long gone. India has its troubles, but not Thugee."

Lestrade was not satisfied. "The dead man is a retired Colonel, Logan Fisk. He was attached to the British force in Bangalore."

"I can't say I know it. Bangalore is in Kamatarka, in the southeast of the Sub-continent. My experience was up the west coast and across into Afghanistan. India is a vast place, Inspector, thirteen times the size of Britain, and it has many different terrains and cultures within it."

"This Fisk, he was found burned in the ruin of his house, but it is clear from the remains that he was cut up first. Tortured, perhaps?"

I was out of my ambit. "If Holmes were here, I'm sure he could..."

"But Holmes isn't here!" Lestrade interrupted. "So we must do the best we can. You are a doctor. Won't you come and examine the body? You've had some martial experience so you know knife wounds, and you've accompanied Holmes to coroner's inquests and autopsies."

"That hardly makes me a substitute for Sherlock Holmes," I protested.

"Doctor Watson, this Colonel Fisk was only recently returned from India. Several men testify to the presence of a mysterious fakir or hindoo Thug lurking around his home. The mandarins of the Foreign Office expect answers about the murder. You are the only fellow I know who has experience of the place where Fisk spent ten years in military service and who knows something of the people out there. And you understand forensic investigation. Won't you help agents of your Queen and country solve this mystery?"

This was an appeal for which there could be no denial.

---

7   *Datura stramonium* is also known as Jimson's Weed, Jamestown's Weed, Devil's Snare, Devil's Trumpet, Devil's Weed, Devil's Cucumber, Thornapple, Moon Flower, Talolache, Hell's Bells, Tolguacha, Stinkweed, Locoweed, Pricklyburr, and False Castor.

What would Sherlock Holmes do? I was acutely aware of my lack of experience in his investigations. I felt like a sham accompanying Lestrade to Logan Fisk's recently leased and re-named Cubbon Lodge[8] on the Upper Thames, and raking over the remains of the burned-out shell.

"The fire was discovered about three-twenty this morning," he told me, as if I was Holmes. We shouldered our way through the police firefighters who were tidying away their pump-engine and coconut matting. "The house-boy gave the alarm, being woken by the smoke. The flames began in the gun-room, we think. That's where we found Fisk's body. The domestics all got out through the back."

There were four servants, huddled miserably in blankets as they must have been since early morning. They were a cook and gardener couple, a housemaid, and the alert page boy. All had been in service only three weeks, hired when Fisk had first taken the cottage upon his return from Bangalore.

I heard what they had to say on the mysterious Indian. Each had been separately approached while they were away from the lodge-house by a tall swarthy turbaned foreigner with good English who had tried to question them about their employer. Money had been proffered. His questions had been about the layout of the house, about what visitors Fisk had received, about the Colonel's daily routine, and about when and where he went when he left Cubbon Lodge.

None of the staff admitted to taking a bribe and supplying the stranger with answers. All of them had reported the approaches to Colonel Fisk, who had questioned them closely about the Indian. Fisk had found it significant that the fellow had worn a yellow neckerchief.

"It wasn't just them that were questioned," Lestrade told me. "Fisk's luggage and furniture came back with him on the boat, of course. It seems that the same foreigner accosted some of the crew who unloaded it. That's where accounts of the weird dagger come from, those meetings on the docks. And this fellow disappeared without trace when somebody tried to follow him, which is why they thought him a hoodoo-man."

We viewed the body, but it was a charred ruin. The best I could offer was to confirm that, yes, there were signs that some cuts had been made to the epidermis pre-mortem, and they were consistent with cruel knife-

---

8   Fisk presumably named his house after Lieutenant-General Sir Mark Cubbon KCB (1775—1861), the British Commissioner of Mysore state, or more likely after Cubbon Park (now Sri Chamarajendra Park) in the heart of Bangalore, named after the administrator.

work. I suggested that the body be examined for poisons, though I didn't know if any such traces would survive a roasting. Holmes would know.

It occurred to me to ask the servants the same questions that the Indian had. They revealed that Fisk was an employer of irregular habits. He left the house without notice and was sometimes gone overnight; the gardener thought there might be a woman involved. His only visitors were four military men, old comrades who had retired with him. All of them had shipped home together at the end of their service. They had come to dinner on four occasions. One or two of them had called at other times.

A uniformed constable drew Lestrade's attention to something the fire-fighters had spotted. On the charred wall of the former gun-room were the burned ash rectangles where a series of Fisk's framed pictures had hung. The servants confirmed that these were old prints from the Colonel's Indian service and daguerreotypes of people he had known there. We were able to trace three gaps in the burned silhouettes, where nails were knocked to hang pictures but no frame had burned.

"They were removed before the fire was set," I realised.

Nobody could remember what those particular images had been.

"I wish I could be of more help," I assured Lestrade when we had finished pacing the ruined cottage and questioning the survivors. "I suppose you have a watch set for this supposed fakir?"

"Of course. But you know the docks. London Basin is the busiest port in the world. At any time there are hundreds, probably thousands, of mysterious foreigners teeming about there. Plenty of them wear turbans and dress strangely. How can we tell one from the other?"

"Perhaps you should go back to the Foreign Office fellows who set you on?" I suggested. "Why are they so particular to have this crime solved? I mean, yes, one wants to catch the fellow who murdered a retired soldier, but what draws so much political attention?"

Lestrade reluctantly agreed to brave the superiors who had placed him on the case. He did not relish exposing his lack of progress to them.

So pitiable did he look, stood in the ashes of Cubbon Lodge, that I agreed to discuss the matter again with him tomorrow. It was the least comfort I could offer.

Perhaps Holmes would have returned by then?

I was checking Holmes's volumes of *Hart's Army Lists*[9] regarding Colonel Fisk when Gregson appeared the next day. The inspector was even more ruddy-faced than before, giving me concern for his health.

"A letter has been received by the O'Tierneys," he revealed. "A ransom note of sorts. If they do not purchase back their family tiara it will be cut up for its gems and gold and sold separately."

"The thief is bold," I admitted. "How would such a fee be paid?"

"In uncut gemstones, delivered to a distinctive rock on the coast and left there. It is a well-selected spot, bleak and open, which would make it difficult to lie in wait for the criminal."

"Everything else that he stole is untraceable," I observed. "Bearer bonds, foreign currency, and small diamonds. Now he converts the one notable piece of loot into something that cannot be tracked either."

"It means he needs no intermediary to 'fence' the plunder. The chap is devilishly cunning."

"Is there any further development on how he might have accessed the sealed rooms and safes?"

Gregson looked sullen. "Ordinarily I would look at the man who holds the keys. But four such dishonest stewards? And three of them family men who were at home during the times of the thefts, attested by kin and servants. And yet somehow the burglar defeated the finest locks, even a combination safe, and came away with his prizes, all unseen."

"The night-guard at Esperson's?"

"Wide-eyed and vigilant, he says. He seemed credible enough when I questioned him." The inspector scowled unhappily. "Have you been able to discover anything through Holmes's contacts?"

Wiggins had reported to me only an hour before, but the street-urchin had not relished the idea of answering to the Scotland Yard officer in person. "The burglar's deeds are known amongst the criminal classes, if not by the general public. There is much discussion in low quarters as to his identity. The consensus is that he must be new in town, some outside talent. Quiet enquiries are being made by the villainous fraternity, either to recruit or remove him."

"Not one of the regulars, then?"

"If there had been a fellow of such talents on the loose in London for long, would we not have encountered him before?" I pondered. "And don't

---

9   These annual and quarterly lists of the members of the British Army and their accomplishments began in 1840 and continue to the present day. The original format has never altered through two hundred editions.

forget the numbered calling cards, the receipts. That is something new."

"Then… he might not even be *in* Holmes's indexes." Gregson sounded crestfallen. "We *must* find Holmes."

I had learned much of my fellow lodger's habits in our months together. "Holmes has a talent for disguise, sharpened by some time as a thespian, and an ear for accents. He can pass as a barrow-boy or old tar, as a grumpy major or a gullible toff. He can vanish into the *demi-monde*, hearing and seeing all but never raising suspicion. He knows the back alleys and hidden courtyards of London as well as any man alive. He has many contacts, aides, allies in every walk of life, cultivated to assist him with whatever endeavour he undertakes. We are unlikely to be able to discover him."

Indeed, I had ventured to suggest that Wiggins and his Irregulars might locate Sherlock Holmes, but the ragamuffin had refused. "If Mister 'Olmes is 'iding out then 'e's got good reason for it," Wiggins assured me. "'E won't go thanking us for givin' 'im away."

"And if he isn't hiding?"

"Then why is them fellows watching 'is 'ouse?" the lad challenged me.

"What fellows? Where?"

Wiggins had pointed them out to me, a surly-looking brute selling bootlaces along the far side of the street and an idler with a newspaper who wandered past every ten minutes or so.

I had suggested accosting the blighters and seeing what they were about. Wiggins advised against it. "If Mr 'Olmes don't want 'em to know 'e's onto 'em, it's best to let them bide, sir. But the lads'll follow 'em when they goes off and see where they ends up."

For this reason I did not mention the surveillance to Gregson. Indeed, bootlace vendor and pavement reader had both vanished while the Scotland Yard man was visiting.

The choleric detective was still unhappily baffled. "Something must be done. I need some break in this case—before it breaks me!"

"Holmes would study the scenes," I considered. "He might inspect the locks for signs of scrapes where tools were used, and from that deduce the distinctive technique of the cracksman. There may be some tread-mark, some disturbed object, some grease-smear or lost thread that opens up lines of investigation."

"Well *he* might," Gregson grudged, "but he isn't here to do that, is he? We've been over the sites many times, pulling everything apart for clues. There's nothing!"

I imagined Holmes's comments on the police searches. But in the great detective's absence, what else was there to do?

I was at a loss, but felt I must make some suggestion. "There may be another burglary. If so, then seal the scene. Bring in a scent-hound to discover any trail. Seek witnesses from people whose business takes them out at night—the cabbies and night-soil collectors, even the streetwalkers. Perhaps you might even find some old criminal who has served his time for burglary and see if he can suggest how the deed was done?"

Gregson snorted at the idea of resorting to housebreakers and harlots, but he was become desperate. Whatever reply he might have made was interrupted as the page announced another visitor.

Inspector Lestrade had arrived. He and Gregson eyed each other like dogs who disliked intruders on their territory. Gregson was by the hearth so Lestrade took position by the bow window.

"Holmes is not here," Gregson deigned to inform his fellow officer. "Still."

Lestrade' sharp close-together eyes glowered. "I see that. I'm here for Dr Watson."

"You're still no further with the Fisk murder, then."

"And you're stuck on the burglaries."

"I have a number of lines of enquiry."

"So do I."

Gregson shrugged, as if his rival was not worth his time. "Thank you for your comments, doctor. I must be off. *My* case was given me by the Chief Constable himself."

"Mine came by fiat of the Foreign Office," Lestrade topped him. "Colonel Fisk was a man of consequence, well known to several senior civil servants to whom he had directly reported during his time overseas."

I remembered the army lists. "Fisk led a small unit of detached men on intelligence operations. He spoke the native tongue well enough to pass as local. He was commended for his work during the riots and uprisings of the Madras Famine."

I shuddered as I spoke. No-one could pass through India as I had and not hear of the great famine that had struck during '76 to '78 in the southwestern provinces of Madras and Bombay, and in the princely states of Mysore and Hyderabad. The shortages covered 257,000 square miles, starved 58,500,000 people. Five and a half million died. And yet during the famine, the Viceroy Lord Lytton exported a record 6.4 million hundredweight[10] of wheat to Britain, and the supposed Famine Commissioner

---

10   320,000 tons.

for the Government of India made harsh cutbacks in who received aid.[11] It was hardly the Empire's finest hour.

"I don't know what he was up to out there, but it got him a medal and it means that there's important people paying attention to this case," Lestrade insisted.

Gregson relented enough to allow one mildly sympathetic glance at his fellow officer. "They don't realise how tough it can be to crack some investigations," he admitted.

"Has the coroner done his work?" I ventured.

Lestrade looked discomfited. "Yes. There was something in the colonel's blood and stomach—datura. The Thugee's drug."

"Your fellow was poisoned then, not stabbed to death," Gregson suggested.

"Datura doesn't usually kill," I enlightened him. "It makes one delirious, perhaps to hallucinate. A man might seem drunk or lunatic. Soldiers sent to quell a 17th century rebellion in Jamestown, Virginia, famously made a salad of it without realising its properties, and spent several days as naked madmen."[12]

---

11   In 1878, the Famine Commissioner for the Government of India Sir Richard Temple imposed stricter qualification standards for relief, and more meagre relief rations. The "Temple wage" for a day's hard work in the Madras and Bombay relief camps was 1lb of grain plus one anna (1/16th of a rupee) for a man and a slightly reduced amount for a woman or working child. Viceroy Lord Lytton supported Temple against critics, arguing that "Everything must be subordinated to the financial consideration of disbursing the smallest sum of money."

By early 1877, Temple proclaimed that he had put the famine "under control". Critic William Digby noted that "A famine can scarcely be said to be adequately controlled which leaves one-fourth of the people dead." In the second half of 1878, an epidemic of malaria killed many more who were already weakened by malnutrition.

The long-term consequences of the mishandled situation included migration of many Indians to British tropical colonies as indentured labour and to the foundation of the Indian National Congress, which began a new generation of Indian nationalism and eventually led to independence.

12   Watson is referring to Robert Beverly Jr's *The History and Present State of Virginia, Book II: Of the Natural Product and Conveniencies in Its Unimprov'd State, Before the English Went Thither* (1705), which describes the 1676 "Baker's Rebellion". His colourful account reveals that:

"...some of them ate plentifully of [the weed], the effect of which was a very pleasant comedy, for they turned natural fools upon it for several days: one would blow up a feather in the air; another would dart straws at it with much fury; and another, stark naked, was sitting up in a corner like a monkey, grinning and making mows [grimaces] at them; a fourth would fondly kiss and paw his companions, and sneer in their faces with a countenance more antic than any in a Dutch droll.

"The substance was used to incapacitate, then. Or to make Fisk vulnerable to questioning."

"But the method of his death, the slow knife-torture, was the mark of the Thugee," Lestrade insisted.

"You have not found your inquisitive Indian, then?" I asked.

"Indians we have found, and plenty of them. The one Indian we especially seek... who can say? We may have questioned him and let him slip away again."

Gregson's compassion was exhausted. "I daresay a proper search will turn the fellow up, and then the full story will come out. My own mystery is a much harder nut to crack."

"Your mystery? The only question is how long you will flounder until Sherlock Homes turns up!"

It was clear that no more was going to come of the discussion, so I threw the detectives out and returned to my own work.

A little after five that same afternoon I received a note of hand from a small girl who knocked anxiously at our back door to deliver her missive. I recognised one of Wiggins' barefoot accomplices and tipped her a half-crown for her efforts.

The letter was hardly more than a note, an edge-scrap torn from some pocket-book, but I recognised Holmes's handwriting: *'Walk south along Baker Street at 7pm sharp. Jump into the cab that stops for you at Portman Square. Speak to the person to whom the cab delivers you—S.H.'*

Intrigued by those odd instructions, and reasoning that the precaution was to abstract me from Baker Street without my being traced, I followed Holmes's directions to the letter. As the hall clock struck seven I parted from Mrs Hudson and began my perambulation.

I immediately saw the bootlace merchant, still lurking in a doorway across the way. He was stooping to disguise his height, as Holmes often

---

"In this frantic condition they were confined, lest they should, in their folly, destroy themselves—though it was observed that all their actions were full of innocence and good nature. Indeed, they were not very cleanly; for they would have wallowed in their own excrements, if they had not been prevented. A thousand such simple tricks they played, and after eleven days returned themselves again, not remembering anything that had passed."

I recognised one of Wiggins' barefoot accomplices...

did, but this fellow was broader, stockier. Upright he would have topped six foot. He kept a workman's cap pulled well over his brow.

As I followed the pavement I became aware of the man with the newspaper, idling along behind me. There was also a covered dray standing further up the road, with a suspiciously alert-looking driver.

My shoulder blades tingled, as they did in the Maiwand Valley when some murderous Afghan was aiming his Jezail rifle at my back. It was not a comfortable walk.

A smart two-wheeler rattled down behind me, swerving round the parked dray, and pulled up featly beside me by the green garden of Portman Square. "Cab for Doctor Watson!" the driver called.

I leaped aboard. At once the coachman shook his reigns and set the cabriolet[13] surging forward at speed. The dray sprang after us, confirming my suspicion that it was also part of the watch.

I checked the cabbie who cornered us into Portman Street to see whether it was Sherlock Holmes in disguise, but was disappointed. Unless the dedicated detective had shaved his head and pulled out several teeth he was not the madman driving this hansom.

"Jus' 'old on, sir, an' I'll 'ave these fellers off a us in no time!" he promised. He slid the cab round a tight turn into one of the old cobbled service roads behind George Street. The narrow alley had back gardens on one side and stable blocks on the other and was scarcely wide enough to pass. The larger pursuing dray would have had even more trouble, but as it began to navigate the passage one of the stable doors opened and a resident began to navigate his trap out, completely blocking the vehicle that followed us.

"That was deliberate," I recognised. "Holmes set it up."

"Yus, sir." The cab drew away from our thwarted pursuers. We swerved across Oxford Street, down Park Street where we blended with dozens of other cabs taking people on their evening constitutionals, and onto Piccadilly. "Mr 'Olmes says you are to 'op off 'ere," he told me as we pulled in beside Green Park. "You're to 'ead along Queen's Walk, all the way into St James's Park. Go to the Blue Bridge and wait in the middle. Talk to the fellow what comes to see you."

"Not to Holmes?"

The cabbie shrugged. "That's as I were told, sir."

---

13   In Victorian taxi terminology, a hansom cab or cabriolet was a two-wheeled vehicle, while a Clarence or growler was four-wheeled with an enclosed cabin. These were all hackney cabs; a hackney coach was a six-seater.

"And I don't suppose you were told who those men watching in Baker Street were? Or what they wanted?"

The driver had no further useful information, except that he was to continue on through the city as if he were still conveying me, to further frustrate pursuit. I tipped him, slipped onto the kerb, and passed into the heavily-treed Green Park where my passage would be screened from the road.[14]

It was a fine autumn evening and the park was well populated with promenaders. I made my way along the straight footpath of Queen's Walk, trying to apprehend whether I was being watched or followed. There were too many bypassers to have any real chance of knowing. I wondered whether Holmes was also watching me—there was a limping newspaper vendor there, a portly doorman, a shabby tinker, a strolling ostler. Was I the bait to let him spy out some enemy who was spying on me?

I slipped from Green Park across the newly-opened Mall[15] into St James', leaving the path and threading through the trees onto the lawn, to better get an idea of anyone who was following me. I cut down to the lake, trying to look like any visitor who wished to go and visit the pelicans.[16]

There were people crossing the suspension bridge, of course, and quite

---

14   Of the connecting chain of four parks that run northwest to southeast across the heart of London—Kensington Park, Hyde Park, Green Park, and St James's Park— Green Park is the only one that contained no memorials or buildings in Watson's era; earlier monuments had been removed and buildings demolished. The park consists almost entirely of mature trees rising out of turf and the only flowers are naturalised narcissus. It is bounded to the south by the road called Constitution Hill, which divides it from the grounds of Buckingham Palace; this is the site of Edward Oxford's 1840 attempt to assassinate the four-months pregnant Queen Victoria.

15   The famous ceremonial route was installed along the north edge of Green Park as part of royal architect John Nash's 1826-7 renovation for the Prince Regent (later King George IV), but was not opened to the public for sixty years. The Mall had therefore only been available to general traffic for two years at the time of our present narrative.

16   The 57-acre St James's Park includes a lake with two islands, Duck Island and West Island. The Blue Bridge crosses the water and affords spectacular views across the lake to Buckingham Palace to the west and eastward to Horse Guards Parade and the Westminster Palace Clock Tower (where Big Ben is housed; the tower is nowadays called the Elizabeth Tower) . The original 1857 iron suspension bridge was replaced by the present bridge in 1957.

Although the park has long since ceased to be the royal zoo where King James I (1603) kept camels, crocodiles, an elephant, and an exotic bird aviary, a colony of pelicans donated by a Russian ambassador to Charles II in 1664 still thrives there today and is a key feature of the lake.

a few idlers tossing bread to the birds. I positioned myself halfway across and waited for contact.

After ten minutes I was beginning to wonder whether something had gone amiss. The whole affair seemed slightly ridiculous. Was this a prank? But then a well-tanned barrel-chested fellow approached me and asked, "Doctor Watson?"

I admitted to my identity. "And you, sir?"

"Sergeant Farnley, sir, late of the _____shires."

That was Fisk's regiment. "You have recently come from India," I surmised, feeling a little like Sherlock Holmes.

"Yes sir. I was with the garrison at the Bangalore Cantonment.[17] I returned home just a short while ago, after discharge."

"On the same ship as Colonel Fisk?"

"The *Homer*, sir, yes." The retired sergeant paused, looking stiff and uncomfortable. "I was instructed to give you my testimony, sir."

I realised that on the bridge in full view of the evening strollers we could see any approach and were as anonymous and private as if we had met in some club; perhaps more so. "Instructed by Sherlock Holmes?"

"Yes sir. Mr Holmes tracked me down at the boarding house where I had taken lodgings and was kind enough to fund my removal to a different one. He asked me to repeat to you the account that I gave to him of some events in Mysore last year."

I noticed that the old soldier was keeping a careful watch on the lines of approach, much as my orderly Murray used to do back in our service.

"You knew Colonel Fisk?" I ventured.

Farnley nodded. "I was one of the staff in his headquarters, the Intelligence Office. The Snoopers Shop, we called it."

I wondered how much Farnley was allowed to tell me about such matters. My limited experience of those spy-wallahs was that they liked to keep their secrets.

Something odd occurred to me. "Fisk returned to England with four

17   From 1806-1881, the Bangalore Cantonment was a 13-square mile military base extending from the Residency on the west to Binnamangala on the east and from the Tanneries in the north to Agram in the south, the largest military garrison in South India. Stationed in the cantonment were three artillery batteries and regiments of the cavalry, infantry, sappers, miners, mounted infantry, supply and transport corps, and the Bangalore Rifle Volunteers, along with their families and support staff. The area was a small city in itself and included clubs, churches, bungalows, shops, and a hospital. It was directly under the governance of the British Raj rather than the local Durbar of the Kingdom of Mysore as Bangalore city was.

brother officers. Were they all Snoopers?"

"Yes sir. Colonel Fisk and Captains Levett, Shackleman, Dennis, and Selby."

"And how many others were officers in their unit?"

"No others, sir. That was all of them. The unit was closed down."

That seemed stranger still. "They were all commended, decorated, for their effort during the Famine, for work against rebels in the hills of the Western Ghats."[18]

"Aye, sir, we were."

"You were there? You'd better tell me what Holmes wanted you to repeat."

"Yes sir. Well, you know how the famine hit the south west. People like skellingtons, too weak to even brush the flies off their eyes. Thousands dying, and others turning to banditry and raiding to survive. It were a busy time for the Intelligence Office."

"Your chaps would pass themselves as natives and go amongst the crowds listening and watching. Visiting informers."

Farnley nodded. "And a bit more than that, sir. The Snoopers liked to get ahead of trouble if they could, by making it happen a bit early."

I frowned. "You mean they fomented rebellion so as to weed out the troublemakers?"

"Well, maybe. It weren't my bit of the job. We NCOs just took out the squads what did the arrests. I wasn't part of the interrogation team."

Another aspect of the intelligence division that I disliked was their use of what, in other circumstances, would be described as bloody torture. I doubt that Her Majesty would be pleased to know that such things were done in the name of Queen and country.

"Well, sir, one of the prisoners blabbed about an organised cell of rebels over in the Animali Forest—that's up in the Ghats, forty miles east of Madurai, something over two hundred miles off Bangalore. There'd been quite a bit of trouble there, including some railway lines pulled up to stop the trains. These rebels were better organised than most, it seems, and they'd holed up in some old temple or stronghold from the Thugee days."

"Had they now?"

"Yes sir. And they were better equipped too than the raggedy desperates who were raiding the farms and granaries, which meant they had

18   The Western Ghats or Sahyadri (Benevolent Mountains) run 990 miles north to south along the western edge of the Deccan Plateau, covering 62,000 square miles with an average elevation of 1,200 feet, rising to the peak of Anamudi at 8,242 feet.

money behind them. Proper weapons and a bit of leadership, those were bad signs."

I agreed that they were. "What did Colonel Fisk do?"

"It took a bit of time but he eventually worked out where they must be. There were some old accounts in journals from the time when the Thugs were suppressed, that gave him clues, evidently, and I know some natives were brought in for hard questioning. Eventually, just a month before rainy season,[19] we set off with an expedition to Animali, the five officers and about a hundred of our company for support. And me."

"To hunt these bandits in a former Thugee stronghold."

"We had a devil of a time finding it, despite the old diaries. You know the terrain, sir, with no track lasting longer than a season. I don't know if you've seen the hills there, with thick forests and stalking tigers and venomous snakes, but it's hard going even if you're sure of your route. We lost three men in there just to reach the site. But at last we found this old ruin, something of a stone temple maybe judging by some carvings that showed some right goings-on. The place was half-reclaimed by the jungle, but it was a rebel camp all right."

I thought back to the scant line of information in Fisk's *Hart's* entry. "The Colonel led an attack."

"He did. We came in by night and took them just as dawn came up. But they was expecting us—it being hard to sneak a hundred men through that sort of terrain—so it all became a horrid mess. I suppose we weren't used to going into prepared positions that were held as well as any proper fortress. Those rebels were properly armed too, with Pattern 853 Enfields— not the Indian Service ones we gave to our native regiments after the Mutiny, that were deliberately less good, but the proper British versions.[20] We ended up in a right old firefight."

I could well imagine it, that confused exchange of lethal shots where all semblance of co-ordination and order was lost and there was only may-hem and death. I had seen it and survived it—barely.

---

19   India's monsoon season begins around the end of May and continues until early October. It is particularly vicious in the area around the Western Ghats, making some roads impassable.

20   After the Indian Rebellion of 1857, the native regiments' Enfield rifles were replaced with the Pattern 1858 Indian Service version which reamed out the rifling of the Pattern 1853 and replaced the variable distance rear sight with a fixed sight, which greatly reduced their effectiveness. The weapon's increased bore gave it a tendency to explode. British troops retained the previous superior 1853 model.

"We won in the end," Farnley told me. "It was a heavy butcher's bill. We lost forty-three men and nineteen wounded as eventually recovered. Captain Dennis was hit in the shoulder but he survived. But we killed close to two hundred rebels, in the fighting or by execution after. We caught their leaders too, including some princeling with an Eton education and ideas above his station."

"So Fisk was commended for suppressing the dangerous bandits but censured for the heavy cost in lives," I supposed.

"Well, that too, sir. But when they questioned this prince chap about where the money came from, I mean money to buy all those guns—and they had a field piece as well, though it was never used—well, after some persuasion with hot tools his 'ighness revealed that there was a Thugee loot cache in the old temple. There was actual treasure hidden in a secret room!"

I raised my brows. "Did you discover it?"

"Well, the officers tried to keep it quiet, but you know how troops are. There were guards in on the interrogation and soon news was all around camp. But Colonel Fisk kept discipline. 'There's procedures about this, boys,' he told us. 'There'll be a prize share for all when we bring this back to the Cantonment.' And then we found the secret door, to a room no bigger than a cupboard really, but there was gold and silver, jewellery and gems, like a maharajah's store!"

There had been no record of that in *Hart's*. "What became of it?"

"We took it back, of course, under strict guard. Captain Shackleman, he said he thought it must be worth fifty thousand pounds, and three-quarters of that would come to the men who found it. The NCOs would be in for a tenth, and by then there was just two of us still alive, and even the privates would get maybe four hundred pounds apiece.[21] We all thought as we'd be rich men."

"I take it that was not the case?"

Farnley shook his head bitterly. "I don't know the full story. Politics, I suppose, but this princeling was somebody important, and it didn't go down well with the Indian posh-knobs that he'd been tortured, killed, and robbed. Things was already tricky with the famine and that, and by then the government back in England was looking closely at how things were being handled. So in the end the treasure wasn't confiscated by the army and divvied up with prizes like it should have been. It was handed back to

---

21   £50,000 in 1881 would be around £4.4 million in modern currency. £400 then would be worth £35,400 today. The standard wage of a British private solder in 1881 was around £30 per year before stoppages (£2,625 in today's currency).

this prince's relatives, to shut them up I suppose."

"How did Fisk take that?" I wondered.

"Not well, according to camp gossip. Cut up rough, he did, and evidently made threats to the higher-ups, saying he knew things that they'd want to keep quiet and that. I suppose he did. The Snoopers knew where all the bodies were buried. But it didn't do him no good. Within months he'd got his discharge papers and all his cronies with him—and the rest of us, because we might be 'disaffected'—by which they meant sore at being cheated of spoils of war we bled and died for. And so we were shipped home on the *Homer* and here we are."

"So there might be Indians, wealthy and powerful Indians, with reason to dislike Colonel Fisk?"

"I reckon so. Him and his buddies. But I'm not waiting around to see what happens next. Mr Holmes has arranged for a train ticket to be waiting for me at Paddington, and then I'm gone from London for good. I'm not hanging about to get tortured to death."

"You think the man who killed Fisk might hunt for others? For you?"

Farnley shrugged. "I don't know who killed the Colonel. But I know his pals are dangerous men, and angry ones. When we was on the *Homer*, Captain Levett had a quiet word with me. Did I want to make some money when we got back home, to make up for what was owed us, what we'd had stolen from us? There was a place for loyal men with proper training and discipline if I cared to try my hand. Well, I didn't care to try it and said so; it sounded very dodgy to me, sir."

"They were planning something illegal?"

"I didn't ask for details, sir. The Snoopers aren't squeamish about burying loose ends. I just said no and determined to lie low until I could vanish. When I heard about the Colonel I was frightened worse. And then Mr Holmes found me, and if he could then the Captains could. So… that's my story, sir. And why I'm off and away, while I can."

"Did the Captains talk to anyone else returning on the *Homer*?"

"I don't know, sir. If they did they'd be quiet about it." He glanced along the bridge, as if nervous to see Snoopers creeping up on him. "I need to be off, sir."

I thanked the fellow and let him go. As he hastened away towards Horse Guards I pondered his remarkable testimony. I began to see why Holmes might have felt it better to disappear; four well-trained and experienced intelligence agents on some kind of spree might well object to a competent investigation into their present activities. The watch set on Baker Street suggested that they knew of his interest.

I wondered why Holmes might have needed me to hear Farnley's story. Was my friend worried for his life and wanted another person to know what he had discovered? Or...

The revelation came to me belatedly. A squad of well-trained Snoopers, versed in infiltration and all kinds of dirty deeds, were now loose in London. Lestrade was investigating the murder of their former commander. Gregson was hunting some likely-new gang of burglars who were performing incredible heists and leaving receipts for the cash they took. Were they seeking to steal fifty thousand pounds-worth of compensation?

Somebody in the Foreign Office had presumably made the decision to return the Thugee horde to that princeling's family for political expedience. Somebody there knew what the discharged Snoopers were capable of. Gregson had been set on to the hunt but had not been warned of the tigers he was stalking.

Holmes was warning me to warn the Scotland Yard men. They faced not two cases but one.

"Levett, Shackleman, Dennis, and Selby," Gregson repeated. "Where are they, Lestrade?"

"Vanished," the other detective inspector answered. "We assumed they were hiding from this mysterious fakir. Instead they may be out there plotting more crimes."

"These were men accustomed to passing amongst the people of India in native dress," I pointed out. "Any one of them might be the fakir."

"Why would they kill Fisk, though?" demanded Gregson. "Did he try and stop their burglaries?"

"This sergeant that Dr Watson spoke with feared for his life enough to leave London," Lestrade noted. "Farnley presumably knew what his officers were capable of."

I revealed another worry. "If the Snoopers really feel that they are owed fifty thousand pounds by an ungrateful nation then there is plenty more thievery to come."

"And we still have no proof that Levett and company were actually behind any of it, the thefts or the Cubbon Lodge fire," Gregson complained.

"Still, now we have suspects we can begin to…"

"To search in all the places this Thugee fellow has already searched!" Lestrade interrupted him.

The two detectives glared at each other across the length of the Baker Street fireplace. They shared the same frustration but not much else.

"It occurs to me that Holmes's disappearance has not prevented him from investigating this case," I observed, to keep the peace. "His absence is likely entirely due to his involvement. The watchers on this house—gone now, so we cannot question them—are a sign that these felons wish to get Holmes before he gets them. And yet Holmes was able to locate Farnley, the man whose testimony links your two mysteries together. Surely even now he is working to bring your cases to resolution."

The idea both comforted and annoyed the Scotland Yard men. "I don't doubt but that proper routine work would have come to the same conclusion in the end," Lestrade sniffed. "Holmes is merely unhampered by Judge's Rules and judicial oversight."

"This is all theory anyhow," Gregson criticised. "These officers were behind the thefts? That does not explain by what magic they walked through locked doors and came unseen into top-rate vaults. These off-the-books soldiers might have skills, yes, but why would they be taught safe-cracking?"

"And why drug and torture Fisk before he died, to resemble a Thugee execution? Or burn his house?"

I had no answers for those questions. I was fumbling for something else placatory to say when Mrs Hudson rapped on the door. She entered looking a little pale, and our maid and page were with her.

Behind them came three strangers, all of a military aspect despite their new civilian clothing. They carried .422-calibre Beaumont Adams service revolvers like my own and they ushered our staff to join the Inspectors and I in our sitting room.

"I'm sorry, sirs," Mrs Hudson apologised as if there had been a spot on our breakfast tray tablecloth. "These gentleman were insistent to come up here and see you."

Lestrade saw the guns and would have charged the intruders anyway, but Gregson held him back. "Steady," he advised his rival. "There's no chance."

I had come to the same conclusion. The trio had spread out around the room, one by the door and the others covering us from opposite corners. They held their weapons like professionals and looked exactly as deadly as one might expect from a crack military unit.

"What's the meaning of your intrusion, sirs?" I demanded.

One of the men levelled his pistol at me. "I think the conclusion should be fairly obvious, Dr Watson. You have picked an unfortunate fellow-lodger with whom to share your chambers."

"And you are pointing firearms at members of the Metropolitan Constabulary," Gregson warned them. "Do you think we don't know who you are, Snoopers? Levett, Shackleman, Dennis, and Selby... where's the fourth of you?"

One of the intruders sneered at the florid policeman. "Selby? Selby's dead. Selby had second thoughts about our retirement operation."

"Another murder to your name!" Lestrade accused them.

The speaker amongst the renegade officers seemed to find that amusing. "What's one more, Inspector? If you know those names then you know about Animali, about what we endured there. And about how we were betrayed by our superiors and our government."

"Soldiers sometimes suffer," I admitted. "It's no licence for mutiny, or for crime."

"Is it not? We'll have to disagree. We are owed, for service to our nation, for the blood of comrades, for the stupidity of our leaders. You're an old India hand, doctor. You saw the poor choices that were made in the retreat from Kabul, the bloody mess at Maiwand. We saw the greed and ambition of politicians and of generals who might as well be politicians kill millions of the natives of Madras and Bombay. What now of our moral claim that we British are better suited to rule the Sub-continent than the indigenous princes? We did our murder more efficiently, I suppose. But in the end we faltered and appeased the princes and maharajahs, though it was not the great and noble who paid the cost. It was men like those you see here, and the common troops under us."

I could not tell whether the man was condemning the Empire for its behaviour or for flinching from absolute tyranny.

I indicated that Mrs Hudson and our maid should take seats on our couch. "I apologise for the disruption," I told our housekeeper.

"It's not your fault, Dr Watson," she told me resolutely, and cast a scorching stare over the invaders on her domain. "I imagine Mr Holmes will deal with them right enough."

"What do you hope to accomplish by coming here?" Lestrade demanded of the soldiers. "Even if you silence us—especially if you silence us—you will never escape."

"That's true," I agreed. "Holmes is on to you. He is closing in."

"He got to Sergeant Farnley," our captor agreed. "That was annoying. But you three haven't worked out yet how we managed our robberies."

"I'll take your confession," Gregson assured them. "Anything you say will be taken down and used in evidence against you."

I glanced at each of the three armed men who occupied our home. "This is how you did it," I realised. "No lock-picking necessary! You simply came to the houses of the men who had the keys, who knew the guard routines. You held them at gunpoint while one of you visited the business premises and perpetrated the theft. Did the families even know that they were hostage for your successful burglaries, or was it just the key-holders themselves? Did you make those men fear for their loved ones if they ever admitted what you had done?"

Gregson's lips pulled back in a snarl. "You forced them to be your accomplices!"

"Of course!" Lestrade spat. "These aren't house-breakers. They're spies, torturers, and strong-arm bullies. That's how they did their jobs—by threat of force."

"If you like," our captor agreed. "But it's worked well for us so far, and we have much more to raise for our retirements before we're done. The quiet men in the Foreign Office who did us dirty will bitterly regret their weaselling. And threat of force will work for us again here, now."

"He wants to hold us 'ere until Mr Holmes turns himself over to them," Mrs Hudson guessed. "They couldn't find him so they'll make him come to them."

"Holmes set a watch on this place just as we did," another of the soldiers spoke—I learned later that it was Levett. "He had those tramp-children on lookout. He'll know soon enough that we came here, and if he's smart he'll know better than to involve more police."

"I regret for the necessity," their leader told me. "Especially I apologise to you, Dr Watson. I'd have preferred not to harm a brother officer. But we must be ruthless. Holmes cannot be allowed to carry on hunting us. Already our men are unnerved by the Thugee spectre."

My head jerked up. Of course Holmes would adopt a disguise to pursue these renegades. What better way to obfuscate identification than to assume an identity that suggested the vengeance of that princeling's family, or the vengeful last remnant of the suppressed Thugee? Holmes's delight in the theatrical sometimes got the better of him.

"Then the fakir did not kill Fisk," Lestrade concluded. "It was you men."

Another smirk from the Snoopers' leader. It was enough confirmation.

"Nobody killed Fisk," I suggested to the intruder who'd done most of the speaking. "*You* are Fisk. You killed Captain Selby. You drugged and murdered him when Selby cavilled at the plan, and chose the method of death to turn the manhunt on the Indian who was chasing you. You burned your own house down to cover your tracks, keeping only certain prized mementoes that you could not bear to sacrifice."

The Scotland Yard men's relentless accusing gazes grew harder yet.

"We also had to know if Selby warned anyone about our plans," Levett added.

I sneered at Fisk. "You are no brother officer of mine. You're a disgrace to your regiment and to the service."

"The regiment and service disgraced themselves first," Colonel Fisk snapped back.

There was a rap on the door, and a deep Cockney voice called out, "Oy, in there! I'm sent up by Captain Dennis, to bring you this 'ere Indian bloke!"

Fisk gestured wordlessly to his comrades. I was impressed by their instant and co-ordinated response. Levett checked the window then took position covering all of us hostages. Fisk and Shackleman flanked the door, covering anyone who entered. Only then did their leader call, "Come in."

A scarred pugilist of a docker pushed the fake Thugee through the door. The Indian wore a turban and a long coat over native fig and a yellow scarf. The prisoner looked as if he had taken a heavy blow to the head; he swayed from side to side, only kept upright by the bruiser who held his bound wrists.

"Captain Dennis says this is the fellow what you put out that reward for," the wharf-scum crowed.

Fisk grabbed the Thugee by his coat lapels and pushed him roughly to the floor. "Mr Sherlock Holmes," he crowed.

"Actually, no, Colonel Fisk," said the docker in quite different tones. "That would be me."

He produced from his coat a small round bomb with a burning fuse and tossed it directly at Logan Fisk's feet.

"Grenade!" the soldier shouted, diving for what cover there was behind Holmes's work-table. Levett and Shackleman moved almost as quickly, trying to find places to evade the spraying shrapnel of the deadly gunpowder-filled sphere.

"Now, Watson!" Holmes called at me. He jumped over to Fisk and downed the distracted fellow with a perfectly-positioned haymaker.

I launched myself out of my chair and caught Levett amidships, recalling my rugby days and having no mercy. The soldier tumbled down still grasping his gun, so I rattled his teeth for him and stamped hard on his radius until it snapped.

Lestrade and Gregson were slower off the mark, but as Shackleman comprehended that the bomb was a dud as fake as the fakir that the disguised Holmes had led in, the Scotland Yard men swarmed the last rogue and brought him down with fists and boots. His Beaumont Adams skittered across the floor; Mrs Hudson halted it under her shoe.

Less than a minute after Holmes's entry, the Snoopers were pinned down and Lestrade and Gregson were holding them quiet with the guns they had dropped. "There's a fourth man who was keeping watch outside," Holmes advised them. "I incapacitated Dennis first. A number of my Irregular assistants are sitting on him."

Lestrade looked at the Indian who was getting up from the rug and wiping fake blood from his face. "And who is this?"

"An old stage associate from my day on the boards. He consented to play the role of the Thugee for this performance, since I had to star as the brutish dock idler. Mr Crowther, thank you for your portrayal. Here is your fee. Please do not drink it all at once, old chap."

"You knew they were coming for us," I realised.

"Yes. I apologise to you all for that. I had underestimated their ruthlessness and how little they would care for the conventions of civilised England. It seems that I still have things to master in this consultancy business. Once I knew of their intent I had to act quickly to thwart them."

"They'll get the reward they deserve from the Empire now," Lestrade promised, "at the end of six feet of noose."

"I regret little," Fisk told us. "Only that I didn't kill you in time, Sherlock Holmes."

"A regret I trust you will share with many others in the years to come," I told him.

"You do not then regret your choice of friend, Watson?" Holmes asked me, with the slightest note of trepidation.

"I consider myself privileged to uphold the honour of our nation and the rule of law," I assured him, "and to have your confidence that I would act when the time was right."

"Sturdy fellow! Inspectors, you have your men, and they will lead you to their lesser accomplices and their ill-gotten gains. This matter is effectively closed, and is no longer of interest to me. I require a change of clothes, a good shave, and a good bath, and then another problem. Mrs Hudson, I apologise again for this unwarranted interruption in your domestic routine."

I reviewed the array of captured criminals in our sitting room and recognised that my recovery days were unlikely to be always idle. There are worse forms of therapy than thwarting traitors to crown and country.

"Yes, well," our landlady replied to Sherlock Holmes, "I'd better see about getting a fresh pot of tea sent up. That one will have gone quite cold."

The Adventure

of

The Second Heir

HERLOCK HOLMES WAS the world's only consulting detective, but he was hardly the only detective. Other investigators, public and private, referred to him in the same way as a doctor in general practice might call in some specialist when a particularly knotty or unusual medical case presented itself.

He was a man of swelling reputation in those early years of our residence at 221B Baker Street, and fully a third part of the clients through our doors were policemen or private enquiry agents, and another third were people who had been sent to Holmes by baffled professionals. If the cases appealed, if they presented some interesting twist or unique feature, Holmes would consent to take them on.

Mr Daniel Hanvers was one such occasional visitor. I had been introduced to the legal investigator soon after I had learned of Holmes's unusual occupation. Hanvers ran a one-man enterprise tracking down litigants for solicitors' firms or locating missing people. I had never sat in on any of his consultations with my roommate, yielding the parlour to allow them discreet privacy, but I gather that Holmes had offered helpful advice on tracking difficult quarries; helpful enough for Hanvers to return again each time he was baffled.

No case that Hanvers brought was ever of sufficient interest, though, to tempt Sherlock Holmes to leave his armchair. It took Hanvers's death to do that.

"I had no idea that you knew and liked him well enough to attend his funeral," I admitted as I accompanied my friend after the hearse.

"I would not usually have attended such an occasion, Watson. Hanvers was an unobjectionable fellow, a mostly-competent functionary for routine work, reliable but unimaginative. Our relationship was purely professional. But when such an investigator is murdered I grow intrigued."

"Murdered?" I had heard nothing of that. No reference had been made at the chapel funeral service.

"The coroner has ordered investigation of organ tissue samples. Material has been sent to Sir Alwyn Cresset of your old alumnus, Bart's."[22]

---

22   That is St Bartholomew's Hospital, London, founded 1123, the oldest hospital in Britain still providing medical services, at which John H. Watson studied and served during his qualification period as a doctor.

"He is a specialist in poisons," I noted. "He has published several articles on the detection of toxins."

"His work is rigorous and innovative," Holmes complimented Sir Alwyn; there are few more complimentary terms in Holmes's encomium.

"The Coroner forwarded the samples at your recommendation," I realised.

"When a healthy man of thirty-four perishes suddenly after stomach cramps, vomiting, and watery diarrhoea, I am inclined to notice. If that man is a private investigative agent whose profession requires him to track down men who would prefer not to be found then I am especially interested."

The black-plumed horse drawing the hearse passed under the churchyard lych-gate. The parade of mourners followed towards the grave.

"You examined the body," I surmised.

"The mortal remains of Danny Hanvers exhibited certain signs of the application of flowers of arsenic—arsenic trioxide. Further investigation was indicated."

"You suspect murder, but the facts are not yet publicly known."

"I am certain of murder, doctor. The evidence was incontrovertible. I may have had to draw the legal coroner's attention to salient points—when will certifying doctors be given competent training in discerning the application of poisons?—but even a complete bumbler could not deny the results of simple observation. The advice of Sir Alwyn and the results of independent analysis are purely formalities to set the judicial process in motion."

The minister gathered us at the grave-head and informed us that the Lord was the Resurrection and the Life. The mourners clung together, some dabbing their eyes with handkerchiefs. A range of family members and friends had turned out for the funeral. Holmes watched them carefully.

Then I realised why we had attended the committal. Holmes was not there to pay his last respects. He had come to observe the mourners, to note who had come and what their attitude was.

Holmes was hunting a killer.

I looked again at the crowd gathered at the graveside. Close to two score people clustered there. Hanvers's mother wept openly, supported by a woman who might well be her daughter, Hanvers' sister. A young man in a Navy rating's uniform looked enough like Danny Hanvers to be a brother. I recognised a couple of faces of other enquiry agents that had visited Baker Street in their time. Beyond that was a mass of people of different stations and backgrounds, but I could discern little more about them.

I knew that Holmes would, though. That keen mind was absorbing every detail about them, from the footwear and clothes that betrayed their professions and recent movement to the language of their bodies from which he read their dispositions and affections. He knew which were sincere in their grief and which were merely professing sorrow for appearance's sake, which were perplexed and stricken by this sudden loss and which calculated benefit from it.

Holmes's attention seemed particularly focussed on one well-dressed man in a black Burberry and pork-pie hat. The fellow wore generous sideburns and carried a soft-leather brief-case. He seemed almost as interested in who was present at the funeral as Holmes was.

When the service ended, as mourners were passing to drop soil or flowers into the burial plot, Holmes strode through the throng and approached the chap who had interested him. "Mr Cleremont?"

The whiskered fellow regarded Holmes with surprise. "Do I know you?"

"We have never met. I wish to ask you some questions regarding the late Mr Hanvers—and I suspect you have questions about him also."

Cleremont's eyes narrowed. "How do you know my name, then?"

"It is embossed upon your brief-case, sir. You are one of Hanvers's clients, from a legal firm operating in the Southwark area somewhere near Bermondsey Spa Gardens judging by the splashes on your spats. You are concerned by his sudden demise and you are worried that it was not from natural causes."

"This is Sherlock Holmes," I supplied to the concerned solicitor. "He advised Mr Hanvers on his more difficult cases. I am Dr John Watson, Holmes's friend and associate. If you are worried, then there is no better fellow to take counsel from than this man."

Cleremont's eyes flickered with recognition. Holmes was not then as famous as he would become, but evidently his name had appeared as an additional expense on some bill proffered by Danny Hanvers. "You believe that something may have happened to the detective? Something sinister, I mean?"

"I know it," Holmes assured us. "May we repair to your chambers and discuss the matter further, Mr Cleremont?"

"This is Sherlock Holmes."

Cleremont's legal practice was indeed in Bermondsey, on Alscot Road overlooking the pleasant Spa Gardens. It was a family firm that specialised mostly in conveyancing, wills, and property management, and the solicitor confessed himself at a loss to cope with his present problem.

"This is confidential," he insisted to Holmes and I.

"Much of my work is," the consulting detective assured him. "You may lay the facts before us with no concerns on that count."

Cleremont was evidently convinced—or desperate. "Like many solicitors' firms, we retain statements of last wills and testaments, lodged safe with us until the time comes for their disclosure. Such was the will of Mr Edward Blanchard, younger son of the famous old campaigner General Sir Theodore Blanchard; it was lodged with us a little under a year ago, nine months before Edward Blanchard's demise. It was this document which has... caused the trouble."

"The will is contested?" I ventured.

"More than that," the solicitor confessed. "The document is held to be fraudulent. Litigation has begun, and the police may be involved in the matter."

"The details," Holmes insisted.

Cleremont nodded and forced himself to calm. He produced a file from the top drawer of his big oak desk, and laid a document out for our inspection.

"A brief holographic note of hand," Holmes commented.

The single sheet read:

'This is the Last Will and Testament of me, Edward George Blanchard, born on the Twenty-Seventh day of June, 1822, of Stonehampton in the county of Shropshire, made this the twenty-eighth day of May in the year Eighteen Hundred and Eighty-Three. I hereby revoke all former Wills and codicils made by me and declare this to be my last Will.

'I appoint Mssrs. Cleremont, Allan, and Staley of Alscot Road, London, to be the executors of this my Will.

'I devise and bequeath all my real and personal estate whatsoever and wheresoever to my son Alistair Blanchard.

'In witness whereof I have hereunto set my hand this twenty-eighth day of May in the year Eighteen Hundred and Eighty-Three.

'Signed by the said Edward Blanchard as and for his Last Will in the joint presence of himself and us who at his request in his presence and in the presence of each other have hereunto subscribed our names as witnesses: Revd. Tobit Galliard and Arthur Hoag, Mansvt.'

"This is a rather brief statement for a man of such substantial holdings," Cleremont admitted, "but quite legal and proper. We were surprised to receive it, having not previously had any contact with the Blanchard family, but we were evidently recommended by a trusted friend."

"It is said to be a forgery?" Holmes queried.

The solicitor's brow furrowed. He produced another document, this one an albumen silver print[23] reproduction of another single-page will. "Here is a different version, signed and witnessed one week before the testament you have before you."

I leaned in to examine the photograph. The two documents looked similar, of almost the same length and almost the same content, save for some minor bequests to household staff, but the earlier one was dated 23rd May and named Revd. Galliard of St Swithin's, Stonehampton as executor. Most critically, the principal benefactor was someone other than Edward Blanchard's son Andrew.

"His nephew," Cleremont supplied, "Only child of his late sister, Lady Charlotte. Adam Ellis is presently in the Caribbean colonies.

Holmes bent forward and looked closely at the wills. He produced a small magnifying lens and ran it over the text with a professional eye. "I see that Reverent Galliard wrote out both the old man's Wills for him—supposedly—and bore witness each time as one of the two necessary countersignatories. The handwriting on the two testimonies is remarkably similar but differs at a few minor points. The terminal of the 'f' and the ascender of the 'e' are erratic on the later document. The 's' curls differently and some cursives lack a flair. But the tittle above the 'j' and 'i' remain consistent, which is hard to forge, and the legs of the 'k's, 'q's and 'r's are identical. One writer has taken some pains to simulate the script of the other."

"That is the assertion, yes," Mr Cleremont admitted.

"The paper and ink used for the documents appears to be identical. Chemical tests will be required; paper and ink have signatures also."

"They seem to have come from the same source," I admitted.

"The signatures differ," Holmes went on. "The pen was held differently to make the marks, and less pressure was placed upon the nib for the second signature on the more recent document."

The handwriting looked identical to me, but I took Holmes's word that there were differences. "What does the Reverend say on the matter?" I asked.

---

23   A photographic print from a glass negative, using egg whites to bind the photographic chemicals to the silver nitrate-soaked paper; this was the prevalent and most popular method of producing photographs in the latter half of the 19th century, succeeding the daguerreotype, ambrotype, and tintype methods.

"He attests to the verisimilitude of the former will, the one that names the nephew as beneficiary of all. He did briefly visit the ailing Blanchard on the day that the second will was drawn up—apparently drawn—but he did not transcribe any document for him. Indeed, he testifies that the invalid was scarcely conscious and his visit did not last more than five minutes, in the presence of servants."

"What was the honourable gentleman's recorded cause of death?" I wondered.

"I believe it was accounted to congenital heart failure. General Blanchard evidently passed away of the same condition. Edward Blanchard's holdings come from his father's legacy bequest to him, but of course the greater part of that fortune was entailed[24] to the older brother."

"What was the statement of the second witness?" Holmes asked, back to the point. "This family retainer, Hoag?"

Mr Cleremont twitched unhappily. "The manservant is illiterate. He can sign his name as a mark, but he could not read the contents of documents that were put before him. He is able to confirm that his master signed a paper on the 23rd ult., for he saw him set pen to paper, and placed the mark you see on the Will there. He claims not to have marked a second document. He cannot tell us more."

Holmes's fingertips joined together as if he were in prayer. "Unhelpful," he muttered, but he also seemed interested.

"What of the late Daniel Hanvers?" I enquired. "How does he come into this affair?"

"Mr Hanvers has carried out many enquiries for us," Cleremont reported. "He is—was—one of our most frequent and reliable agents. He was well-versed in serving summonses, tracing documents, verifying identities. When we received notification from the Court of Probate[25] of a

---

24   That is, legally bound to be inherited whole via a particular method (usually to the eldest male heir), with restrictions to prevent the estate being separated up or sold. This was the method by which British great estates were preserved intact and passed down through many generations.

25   Technically, after the *Supreme Court of Judicature Act* 1873 merged the Court of Chancery, the Court of Queen's Bench, the Court of Common Pleas, the Court of Exchequer, the High Court of Admiralty, the Court of Probate, the Court for Divorce and Matrimonial Causes, and the London Court of Bankruptcy into one Supreme Court of Judicature, the matter would be referred from the Probate, Divorce, and Admiralty division of the High Court of Justice. *The Administration of Justice Act* 1970 renamed the Probate, Divorce and Admiralty Division as the Family Division.

challenge to Edward Blanchard's will, we naturally wanted to discover the truth of the matter."

"You had not yet met Mr Andrew Blanchard?" Holmes checked.

"Not then. He has visited these offices since. He claims no knowledge of the former will. He says he has always assumed his inheritance. Indeed, had his father died intestate, all lands and investments would have descended to him naturally by default."

"How close does he stand to the inheritance of his grandfather's entailed estate?" I checked.

"He is presently the third heir, presumptive.[26] Sir Edward's older brother predeceased him but left two sons. One of those died without issue but the other has a small boy. Title descends after any male branches are exhausted to Lady Charlotte's son, the one in Trinidad."

Holmes shifted restlessly, as he sometimes does when something is bothering him. "What did you retain Danny Hanvers to do, Mr Cleremont?"

"Why, a background search on young Andrew Blanchard," the solicitor confessed. "Cleremont, Allan, and Staley is a respectable firm. We do not wish to be tangled up in a sordid forgery case. On the other hand, we have a professional duty to ensure that a Will entrusted to us is properly disbursed. I wanted to get a feel for this younger Blanchard before we responded to the Court of Probate."

"Something that you discovered alarmed you," I surmised.

Cleremont shifted uncomfortably. "Mr Hanvers' initial report of Andrew Blanchard's character was not favourable," he admitted. "The young man had something of a reputation as a gambler at cards. There was a rumour that he had been found cheating and ejected from some club."

"He had debts?" Holmes wondered. I knew he would soon find out.

"If Blanchard junior owed money…" I ventured. I decided not to speak my speculation out loud.

Holmes had certainly noted the motive for Hanvers's poisoning. "You retained Tommy Hanvers to find the truth," he observed to the solicitor. "Do you now wish to engage me on this matter?"

---

26   That is, 'presuming none of the heirs in front of him in the queue have more children, who would then take precedence before he would be the inheritor'.

Andrew Blanchard aimed a fist a Holmes's nose and lunged in. Holmes deflected with a swift left and gave the young sprig a buffet on the ear that sent him spinning. The would-be pugilist came back for more. Holmes feinted right, came up under Blanchard's guard, and knocked the wind from him with a belly jab.

"Must we continue?" the detective asked the red-faced young man. "Your technique is sadly deficient. I can continue to pummel you until you fall over, if necessary."

Blanchard wheezed and leaned his hands on his knees. "I won't have you spreading lies about me like that!" he growled. "You…"

I frowned at the string of profanities. "You have begun your drinking early today," I noted, seeing the empty whisky bottle overturned on the mantel.

"I shall do as I like!" the drunkard snarled. "You come here, calling me a thief and a cheat and…" He sprang forward again, evidently deciding to renew the fight.

Holmes hooked a leg from under him and pushed him backwards to topple into an armchair. "Try not to make such a fool of yourself, Mr Blanchard. It does not speak well for your character and is hardly befitting a gentleman."

Blanchard might have risen to battle again but his legs failed him and he slumped back miserably into his seat. "You have no right…" he objected. "No right…"

"I would point out that we have made no accusations regarding your honesty or propriety," Holmes reminded him. "We called at your chambers seeking to interview you upon the matters to which you allude, but levelled no charges. We came to hear your testimony before forming judgement."

"So far you are doing yourself no favours, young man," I scolded the sprig.

Blanchard laid his head in his hands and groaned. "It doesn't matter. I'm done for anyway. I might as well take Cauldwell's advice."

"Cauldwell?" I asked.

"Old school chum of mine. Came to see me after word got out about… well, he called. Don't know as he believed me about not doing anything wrong. But he told me… he said plain, I'm over. Ruined. Dishonoured. He advised me to head into the library and do the right thing."

"You mean suicide?"

Blanchard shrugged. "That's the proper end for a rascal, isn't it? The only way a gentleman of quality can make amends for his wrongdoings before he's carted off to the courts and prison labour and universal scorn."

"You claim to be innocent?" Holmes declared. "Of what?"

"Of all of it. I didn't forge that will. And I wasn't palming aces at the Senior Educational."[27] He slumped further. "But no-one will believe it now. No-one."

Holmes had limited sympathy at the best of times. He sat across from the intemperate young man and pursued his interview. "What were your relations like with your father?"

"Tolerable," Blanchard allowed. "Cooler after mother passed away, but he made me an allowance, saw me through university."

We knew from notes that the late Danny Hanvers had made that Andrew Blanchard had an income of about two thousand pounds, which would have increased fivefold had he inherited his father's estates. He had no need to work, but had interested himself in a number of building schemes, including investment in the booming market of necropolis companies that were blossoming to service the swollen population of our capital.[28]

"What about when there was the... difficulty at your club?" I ventured.

"Yes, father heard about that, dammit," Blanchard growled. "From that blithering old idiot Hoag, I expect. But I told father that I hadn't done it and he took my word."

"You were expelled from the Senior Educational?"

"I resigned. I won't have damned lies spread about me. I'd have challenged that Russian-bearded fumbler who claimed I'd dealt him a second ace of clubs but I can't even find him."

"Indeed?" Holmes murmured. "He was not a regular member?"

"A signed-in guest. But they wouldn't tell me whose, or his name. They were too busy showing me the door, blast them. And I... I must have drunk

---

27   Watsonian misdirection. The Senior Educational Club appears in literature only in T.S. Eliot's poem "Bustopher Jones: The Cat About Town" from *Old Possum's Book of Practical Cats* (1939), listed alongside euphemisms for many other St James's Street gentleman's establishments. Eliot later identified "The Senior Educational" as referring to the Oxford and Cambridge Club, and its rival "The Joint Superior Schools" as being the Public Schools Club.

28   The massive population increase of Victorian London placed intolerable strains on the traditional graveyards of the world's biggest city. A number of Necropolis Companies met demand for burial grounds by establishing large new cemeteries at rural boundaries, serviced by "funeral trains" that carried mourners and coffins to special stations inside the new necropolis. It was a boom investment market.

more than I thought I had, because I wasn't in my wits enough to argue it."

"This was the 19th of last month?" Holmes verified. "Four days before your father's Will was made? The first version."

Blanchard rubbed his forehead. "I suppose. I didn't even know there was a Will. Not until the curate wired a week last Wednesday to say that father had died in his sleep and that I should come home."

"This would be the Reverend Galliard, of St Swithin's, Stonehampton. The executor."

"Yes." Blanchard turned sullen again. "I'm not a forger. I'm not! I wouldn't even know where to begin."

"When did you learn of the wills, then?"

"Of the one that disinherits me, after the funeral. Galliard had a quiet word with me and warned me, so I wouldn't make a scene at the reading. But by then I'd already had a telegram from the solicitor Cleremont informing me that his firm was holding a Will too—but it was dated *after* the one Galliard held." The young man's face fell. "The one they say is forged."

"It is unmistakably a forgery," Holmes assured Blanchard. "An excellent forgery, I will attest. There are probably less than thirty men in England skilled enough for this counterfeiture—although four of those are sufficiently skilled as to be undetectable from the real thing two times out of three. But forgery it is, matching ink and penmanship with excellent precision."

"You do not believe me either," Blanchard mourned. His eyes flicked towards the library door.

"I am inclined to accept that you are not the forger," answered Holmes. "Your handwriting is rather distinctive, betraying a natural left-handedness that was of course corrected in your school days. Your scuffed cuffs and buttons betray a certain carelessness which is not often found in a superior counterfeiter. Nor do I rate you with the intellectual capacity to conceive and execute your plan. It is feasible that some accomplice might have aided you, but for now I shall reserve judgement."

"What?" the baffled, inebriated youngster responded.

"Keep your hands off the whisky bottle and the revolver whilst I conduct my investigation," Holmes instructed him. "Come, Watson. We shall visit Stonehampton and follow the footprints of Danny Hanvers!"

We caught the 13.57 express to Worcester and the branch-line to Ludlow. From there it was no more than a pleasant twenty-minute trap ride to Stonehampton, amongst those gently rolling Shropshire fields with their ancient hawthorn hedges. The village was quite small, no more than thirty dwellings at a Y-shaped junction, with a small daughter church—St Swithin's—and a middle-sized Tudor-beamed manor house that had been the former home of the late Edward Blanchard.

"You have formulated questions," Holmes observed of me as we paid our driver and made our way past a country cross. "You were contemplating them on our ride out here but withheld them for discretion's sake while our cabbie might hear us."

I suppose my attempts at wrestling with the problem at hand must have been obvious to a man of Holmes's capacities. "I don't see how Blanchard could hope to get away with it," I admitted. "If he did it, forged the supposed later will—and it's hard to see who else would—then he must have known that the earlier document would come to light. The witnesses to the genuine article would speak out."

"Young Blanchard was certainly in a position to know about Hoag's illiteracy," my colleague and friend pointed out. "For the plot to work, however, he would have to silence the curate—which he did not."

"We only have Andrew Blanchard's word that his last encounter with his father ended amiably; that Edward Blanchard believed his son's vow to not have been card-sharping. It might have been a very different meeting. That could be how young Andrew knew that a will might be drawn up to settle the Blanchard fortune on the nephew."

"There are several anomalies in the case which raise it above the obvious, Watson. But we have not yet gathered all the testimony we require."

He passed me a folded letter from his coat pocket. It was the reply from Sir Alwyn Cresset to enquiries about Hanvers's death, confirming from study of the deceased's nails, hair, and urinary tract that almost three times the accepted lethal dose of arsenic was present in his corpse.

I shook my head in dismay. "So it was murder."

"Of special interest is the raw data that Sir Alwyn includes with his report," Holmes suggested.

I looked over the numbers and the terse medicinal description of the observed symptoms. "There was no prolonged exposure," I concluded. "Hanvers ingested one large dose, sometime within twelve to thirty-six hours of his death, probably closer to the twelve." There had been little residue in nails and hair except for the most recent growth, suggesting a very recent poisoning.

"White arsenic is easy to come by," Holmes pointed out. Any corner pharmacist sold the stuff for pest control, and although records of the sales were kept in shop registers, any member of the public could purchase supplies of it under a false name and address. "It can be disguised in a number of ways, in beverages or foodstuffs. Several hours after consumption it will begin its work, provoking nausea, vomiting, and diarrhoea, then coma, and then causing death by organ failure."

"Surely any competent physician would notice such symptoms?" I objected.

"Not every general practitioner shares rooms with a murder investigator, Watson. I'll warrant there are countless undiagnosed cases of domestic homicide that are never detected. Your average medical man is untrained in suspecting death by foul play. I might fault Hanvers's attending physician and the Crown Coroner of undiligent observation, but no judicial enquiry would find them at much fault."

I did not like to hear my profession criticised for negligence, but who better than Holmes would have an overview of the problem?

"Hanvers must have been given the poison in the last two days of his life," I reasoned, pushing past my discomfit. "You investigated where he went in that time?"

"His work journal was helpful if not comprehensive," Holmes allowed. "These were the two days he was retained by Cleremont's to look into the matter of the wills. He travelled here to Stonehampton to interview Galliard and Hoag, to Ludlow to attend at the local Probate Office, and then to Oxford to see young Blanchard."

We had asked the young sprig about that, but Andrew Blanchard had claimed he had never met with Hanvers and had never even heard of him.

"Did Danny's diary specify that a meeting took place?" I asked.

"Only an intention to track the young man down at his Oxford chambers, and then to trace the London address of Blanchard's friend Cauldwell, who had been present at the club on the night of the card scandal. We cannot know from those records if they met."

"Here we are following in his footsteps," I noted. "Perhaps we should be careful where we take tea?"

Holmes snorted. We had by now found the lych-gate into the churchyard of St Swithin's. He creaked it open and we passed by the small medieval daughter-church and found the connecting gate to the vicarage.

Holmes had wired ahead. The Reverend Tobit Galliard awaited us. We were shown into a tidy study that overlooked the rear of St Swithin's. The

Blanchard manor was visible past the yew trees.

"Please come in," the curate told us. He was a well-made chap of around thirty, not long out of Cambridge. When he offered us refreshments, Holmes accepted immediately, even eagerly. Doubtless my friend has his cunning tests already in hand.

"You are investigating the extraordinary matter of the Blanchard will," Galliard recognised. "How may I be of assistance?"

"You wrote out the document that passed the estate to the deceased's nephew, cutting out his son," Holmes mentioned. "What were the circumstances of your coming to prepare and witness such a testament?"

The curate had evidently been asked this question before by investigating authorities. His answer was well-rehearsed. "I am curate under the Reverend Donald Acre for the parish of Bitterbury and Stonehampton. I am relatively new to my post, but am having to serve both settlements because of the illness of the vicar. Reverend Acre is now in his seventies and his health is declining. I spend two days a week here and the rest in Bitterbury and its outlying villages, which has the larger population.

"Reverend Acre has been here for over forty years and was well known to Mr Edward Blanchard. They were friends, if not close ones. It was Reverend Acre whom the sick man summoned after the disturbing visit of Mr Andrew Blanchard, but he was not well enough to attend."

"You had not met the late Edward Blanchard before that?" Holmes clarified.

"Oh, many times. This is a small parish and he is—was—an important figure. I called to introduce myself during the earliest days of my curacy, and weekly thereafter to visit him and render the sacraments. But for a matter of great import, that upset the invalid so much, he naturally sent for his old familiar counsellor."

"What was the nature of Blanchard senior's concern?" I wondered.

Galliard flinched. "I will answer your questions in the interests of furthering a vital investigation," the curate conceded, "but I ask that this information be held in proper confidence."

"You may rely upon our appropriate discretion," Holmes told him exactly.

The curate was satisfied. "I had never met Andrew Blanchard before the funeral," he revealed. "He had left home to live in Oxford before I received my position at Stonehampton. I gather that he moved away from the family home after his mother died, back to the place he had been content at university. There was some old dispute between father and son which kept them from meeting regularly."

"You have no inkling as to the nature of it?" I pressed.

"Suspicions, but nothing I would be comfortable speculating on given the present situation."

"Carry on," prompted Holmes.

"On the evening of Wednesday the 23rd of last month I went to see Edward, in place of my vicar. Edward was very agitated, as ill-looking as I had ever seen him but red-faced with choler. I wanted to summon the doctor, but he wouldn't have it. Hoag told me that young Andrew had been to visit. Indeed, his father had summoned him to account for his behaviour. News had come about the disgrace at some gentleman's club."

"How had the news come?" Holmes pounced.

"Via Hoag, I believe. I did not think to enquire. But evidently Andrew had been accused of cheating at cards, had been expelled from the establishment. His name was blackened, the family name. In the interview earlier that same day I was summoned, recriminations had been cast by both father and son. Eventually Andrew departed in high dudgeon, telling his father that he may go to the devil, preferably sooner rather than later."

"Given Edward Blanchard's health, that was perhaps indelicate," I owned.

"It offended the invalid very much. As I say, he was furious. He called for Reverend Acre to prepare and witness a will, disinheriting his wayward son. Of course, it was I who attended, but when I saw that the old man was in sound mind, if not body, and determined in his course, I was obliged to do as he asked." Galliard sighed. "I hoped that in a few days he might calm down and I could convince him to a reconciliation, but of course his health steadily worsened. Scarcely three weeks later he was gone."

"And the second will?" Holmes probed.

Galliard shook his head. "I have seen it. I was shown it when it was produced at Probate. If I had not known it to be false I would have believed I had written it. The script, the signature, both perfect reproductions of my own hand! But they are faked. On the 28th I was all day in Bitterbury, save for a morning brief visit on Edward wherein he was unresponsive. I was with Reverend Acre much of the time, attending to parish business that has become neglected during his debilitation. I slept over at the vicarage and did not return to the manse here until the next day."

Holmes shifted his line of inquiry. "You were visited by an investigator named Hanvers."

"The odd fellow from the London solicitors? Yes, he was here just three days ago. I got the impression that his employers were rather unhappy about the position in which they had found themselves."

"You received him here?"

"At the manor. He arranged to interview me there, after he had spoken to Hoag and the other servants. He asked much the same things you have."

"Did you take tea while you were visiting? Refreshments?"

Galliard frowned. "I suppose so. I am usually given hospitality there. Hoag is not a man to forget his duties. Is it important?"

"Have you heard that Mr Hanvers is dead?"

The curate's brows rose. "An accident?"

"Probably not," Holmes cautioned. "Card-sharping, forgery, and fraud have turned into murder."

Holmes asked a great many other questions, but I could see there were no further answers to be found in this quiet curate's study. At last Holmes rose and took his leave.

We went to find Arthur Hoag.

The manservant proved to be an inveterate gossip. Perhaps all the furore regarding the forged will had gone to his head, or else he felt that he had something to prove.

"The Family have always had somewhat difficult relations," he told us when Holmes had won his confidence. He seemed to capitalise "Family' as he spoke, and I wasn't clear whether he was talking about difficult conversations between Mr Edward Blanchard and his kin or about the eccentric members of the late General Blanchard's dispersed household in general.

To coax the old retainer's indiscretions we encouraged him to map out the Family's family tree. He obligingly described it so that I could sketch out a genealogy.

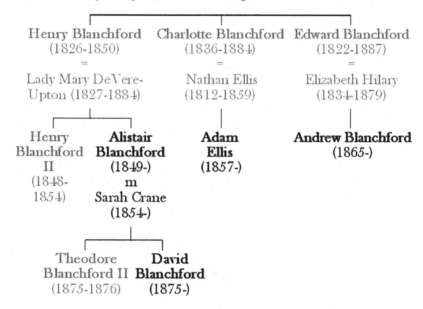

General Sir Theodore Blanchford (1782-1869)
=
Lady Mary deVere-Fitzhampton (1806-1871)

Henry Blanchford (1826-1850)	Charlotte Blanchford (1836-1884)	Edward Blanchford (1822-1887)
= Lady Mary DeVere-Upton (1827-1884)	= Nathan Ellis (1812-1859)	= Elizabeth Hilary (1834-1879)

Henry Blanchford II (1848-1854) · **Alistair Blanchford (1849-)** m Sarah Crane (1854-) | **Adam Ellis (1857-)** | **Andrew Blanchford (1865-)**

Theodore Blanchford II (1875-1876) · **David Blanchford (1875-)**

"Sir Theodore had three children as survived to adults," Hoag lectured us, as if he was a tour-guide showing us round some stately home. "Henry was the older son, and his surviving child is Master Alistair, and young Master David is *his* son. Master Edward was the other male heir, and *his* only surviving issue is Master Andrew. There's a sister was born between the Earl's sons, Lady Charlotte, and it's her son Adam as will inherit from Master Edward now."

We enquired about Lady Charlotte and her 'issue'.

"Well now, that's the thing," Hoag confided, cheered from his mourning at the chance to pass on gossip. "Lady Charlotte made an unfortunate alliance below her station, with an equerry in his grace's estates. As I understand it, her son was born prematurely seven months after the wedding." He waggled his eyebrows to underline the scandal.

"The Family were unhappy with the match," I surmised.

"His grace settled an allowance on the couple. They were encouraged to emigrate to the Colonies and ended up in the Caribbean. Lady Charlotte and her groom are both gone now."

"And their son?" Holmes chased.

"Grown up, and returning to England to deal with this inheritance mess," Hoag reported. "What to make of it I do not know."

"You knew young Andrew, of course?" I checked.

"Of course I did, young firebrand as he is! He grew up here, and was home for the holidays from boarding school and sometimes between terms at Oxford. He's been here less since his mother passed on."

"He came last month though, to attend upon his father."

Hoag nodded confirmation, then clarified censoriously, "Once, he came. No more."

"That would be on the 23rd of May, around one in the afternoon."

"Something about that, yes. It was just about when Master Edward took his luncheon—on a tray, in his bedroom, since the poor fellow couldn't rise to table no more."

"Edward was eating when his son went in to him," I noted.

"What was the nature of the conversation?" Holmes asked.

"It was private," the manservant insisted. "Behind closed doors."

I had no doubt that Hoag's ear had been against that door. "What mood were they in, before and after the conversation?"

Hoag thought. "Well, Master Edward was irate beforehand. They were quiet together behind closed doors. Afterwards, Master Andrew departed quite quickly with few farewells—just took his coat and then his leave. Master Edward seemed exhausted."

"Not angry?" I checked.

"It's sometimes hard to tell with the Master. But about an hour later he sent for Vicar, and Reverend Galliard came."

"Why did your master send for his son?" Holmes wanted to know.

The gossip looked unhappy. "I had heard something—about a problem in a gentleman's club down in the City. A bit of a... a misunderstanding. I thought I'd best... in the end I mentioned it to Master Edward."

"How did it come to your attention?"

Hoag frowned. "In the pub, as it happens, the Rose of Ludlow, as I was enjoying my half-day off. Some big bearded chap as I'd never seen before came up to me and plain asked me about it. Offered me a two-bob tip, as if I'd dish out about the Family for cash, even if I'd known something. But I didn't. All I knew about the trouble at the gentleman's club was from this bloke's questions."

"Have you seen the man again?"

"Never before, never since."

I thought of the stranger who had played cards with young Blanchard and had found himself dealt two aces.

"What happened when Galliard came to see Edward Blanchard?" Holmes pushed on.

"That same day as Master Andrew called? Curate and Master were together about half an hour. This wasn't one of the usual visits to take communion. This was a proper confab. Then Curate calls for paper and ink and they close themselves in again. Twenty minutes later I'm called back. 'Hoag' says Reverend Galliard, 'you'll need to witness the signing of this legal document, to verify that your Master was the one who put his name to it'. I thought at the time it looked like to be a Will, but I just kept quiet and placed my mark where I was told."

"You've never signed a second like it?"

"No sir. I'd have liked to know what it was all about, but it's not my place to ask. Then Curate folds it up in an envelope and puts it in his pocket. 'I'll see to it' he promised the Master. And then he went off and I thought naught more about it until Master Edward went to Glory and all the trouble began."

"Have you seen Andrew Blanchard since?" I asked.

"He was here for the funeral, of course. And after that, Curate had some kind of word with him and then there was all the fuss. Master Andrew has always had a temper. It runs in the Family."

"And an investigator named Hanvers called upon you?"

"The common enquiry agent from the City?" Hoag sniffed to indicate that he preferred a superior class of interrogator such as ourselves. "He was only interested in trying to keep his firm out of bother."

Holmes winkled out of the manservant that Hanvers had conducted interviews with all the staff, beginning with Hoag himself. "Same stuff as the Clerk of Magistrates asked and as you asked, sirs."

Had Hanvers been offered refreshments? "Pot of tea," Hoag admitted reluctantly. "I saw no reason as to feed a fellow who was only here to try and stir up trouble for Master Andrew. But Curate came round to talk to him as well, so we had to make some provision."

Did Hoag know that the detective was dead? "Why, *no!* God bless him, then. What happened?"

"I need to verify a few points," Holmes answered. "Then I will know."

The day was drawing late and I had expected us to retrace our steps back to Baker Street. Instead Holmes halted our journey at Worcester to rattle off a number of cryptic telegrams. Then we purchased tickets to break our journey at Oxford again.

"I'm puzzled, Holmes," I admitted. "Are we going to speak with young Blanchard some more?"

"That depends upon the answers to those enquiries I have sent off, Watson. I have arranged for replies to wait us *poste restante* at the telegram office at Oxford railway station. I expect responses in the two hours it will take us to travel there at this time of the evening. One good thing about a private enquiry agent's murder is that his colleagues will be swift to aid our investigation if it can solve the mystery of his demise. We have eager and willing accomplices carrying out necessary legwork even now."

"What work?" I wondered. The guard's whistle blew and our train began to pull away from the platform.

"I would like to know who signed the bearded card player in to the Senior Educational. I would like to have some background on Lady Charlotte's sole offspring. I have questions for the local doctor in Bitterbury. And I am interested in the graduating lists of Emmanuel College, Cambridge."

We left Worcester Foregate Street on the Great Western line. I checked the timetable, though I knew that Holmes would have memorised it.

"We are on the express," my friend assured me. "There are no stops between here and Oxford. It is an ideal train for our purposes."

"Our purposes?"

Holmes allowed himself a thin, predatory smile. "This is a compartment train with linking corridors. We can pass from our seats here and see into each chamber, and reach the second and third-class carriages."

"And why would we do that?" I enquired.

"To find our murderer. Come, Watson, you must have fathomed it by now."

I confessed to having failed to do so. "Whom do you expect to find aboard the train?"

"A stranger with a black beard," Holmes told me. "Young, athletic, and intending to visit Andrew Blanchard with lethal consequences."

I frowned in bafflement. "He is going to kill the young man? Why? How?"

"The *how* I can only speculate about. Blanchard has spoken of suicide, so it might be hanging, or a gun in his library as he threatened. I suspect it might be arsenic in whisky; our villain has shown a preference for that tool."

"How can you know he is here, on this train, and that such is his intent?"

"It in ineluctable logic, doctor. Think! While Hanvers's poisoning was undetected, our adversary was safe. He had quieted the one man who might have eventually fathomed the plot—although knowing Danny Hanvers I am not confident of that outcome. Now that the wrongdoer knows that his efforts are discovered he has no choice to but escalate his plans. Blanchard junior must go."

"To silence him?"

"To close down any further investigation into the matter of the forged will. Ask yourself this, Watson: how could Andrew Blanchard come to know that his father had made a Will disinheriting him, to require such an extraordinary and pointless attempt to forge a later statement? Hoag is a gossip, but he could not know that the Will passed the Blanchard estate to anyone other than Blanchard's son."

"Andrew might have guessed that his father had made other disposal of his assets."

"More likely, a sick, dying man might want to leave a few bequests to people other than his main heir; gifts to old servants, keepsakes to old friends. Unless father and son had quarrelled beyond reconciliation there was no reason for Andrew to panic and set some Byzantine forgery plot into motion."

"Then how would Andrew Blanchard know about the proper will?"

"He could not!" Holmes told me in triumph.

I began to catch up. "The *only* person who seems to benefit from the fake will is Andrew. If he is not responsible for it—not even aware of the need for it—then there is only one other possibility, isn't there?"

"And that is…?"

"That the fake will, the exposed fake will, discredits Andrew Blanchard even more thoroughly than the alleged card-cheating!" I looked around the train. "This wasn't about a stolen inheritance. It was always about ruining young Blanchard! The bearded man is his enemy."

"You are almost right, Watson. Our bearded quarry was certainly keen on Andrew's disgrace and ruin, and is now set on ending his life and making it look as if Blanchard took the gentleman's course. But there is a greater ploy too. Father Edward left substantial estates in his Will. And then if anything happens to the late Edward's elder brother Alistair Blanchard and to young Master David Blanchard, Andrew becomes heir of the entirety of the entailed fortune inherited from the General, a prize that is a magnitude greater still. Right now Andrew is heir presumptive after his

"It in ineluctable logic, doctor."

uncle and the boy, and after him…"

"The Caribbean nephew," I calculated. "The one you wired off about."

"The same," Holmes agreed. "A forgotten scion of a near-disavowed branch of the Family, who has now, by apparent fortune and Andrew Blanchard's fall, come into significant funds and is one step closer to the vast ancestral Blanchard estates."

"You think he was the bearded stranger?"

"I suspect he was. And I believe this fellow to be on this train."

Another question came to me. "How would he know, then, that we were on to him? That Hanvers's poisoning was discovered?"

Holmes snorted. "We told him, Watson! You were sat there across from him when we spoke."

I tried to chase after the great detective's reasoning. "You… you wanted to check the Emmanuel College records…"

"Did you not notice that Reverend Galliard had an Emmanuel fob on his waistcoat chain? He is a recent graduate of that institution. I have sent for a description of him, and preferably a photograph."

"You mean…?"

"I wonder whether a young curate has been replaced by a cunning and prepared villain, who substituted himself to perpetrate a dastardly long-term plan of gain and revenge. Remember that Reverend Acre fell ill when Galliard was appointed. Vomiting and diarrhoea, I wonder? Something that caused slow decline and growing disability, anyhow. Edward Blanchard sickened too, despite taking holy communion from the curate every week."

"You suspect arsenic?"

"The only person who could prepare a will changing the beneficiary without Sir Edward's knowledge was the man who wrote it out. A clever fellow may disguise his own script and signature by making subtle errors that approximate forgery. If there were two similar-looking documents prepared, one confirming Blanchard and the other naming the nephew, it might be easy to exchange one for the other to be signed by an invalid and be witnessed by an illiterate. Certainly it would be no challenge for a man who could arrange for himself to be dealt two aces of clubs."

"Then Galliard is the nephew and he is playing to win all!"

"I suspect that Adam Ellis has been back in England for some time. Enough for a proper education at one of the superior schools and at one of the senior universities. His diction and body language are incontro-vertibly those of a well-tutored well-brought-up public school man and Oxbridge scholar. His preparations betray a devious and brilliant mind and a compete lack of conscience."

"But we will find him on this train," I got to the point.

"I expect so. It is the fastest and most logical route to conclude his business with the cousin who had everything he did not, and who stood barrier between him and great fortune."

"Then we had best find him."

"That will not be necessary, Dr Watson," Adam Ellis told us. He had approached our compartment as Holmes had explained things to me, and now he stood in the doorway and levelled a pistol at Holmes's head.

"I count it bad fortune that you became involved in this matter," Ellis told Sherlock Holmes as he held us at gunpoint. "Without your investigation I could have passed the whole affair off without further casualties. My error was in disposing of Hanvers in so prosaic a manner."

"It was a lapse," Holmes agreed with him. "You suspected that he had some inkling that Tobit Galliard was not whom he seemed. You had to act quickly to thwart further enquiry."

"I should have found some other method of his demise, not relied upon the tool I had at hand to poison his cup as I poured out the tea."

"You were the one who sent the fake will to Cleremont!" I accused.

"And the one who ingratiated his way into Mr Cauldwell's good graces to be invited to the Senior Educational," Holmes surmised. "You have been smart. I congratulate you on it. But your inexperience is showing. Shooting myself and Dr Watson on a busy passenger train will hardly save your machinations now."

"I think it might," Ellis considered. "In any case, it will prevent any further interference from a meddling consulting detective." He grinned like a schoolboy. "I am, as you note, *very* smart. I am certain I will devise a way to recover the situation—once you and Blanchard are no longer alive to get in my way."

Holmes gave the murderer a disappointed look, as if Ellis had failed a crucial final examination.

"The days when the truth could be silenced by sudden assassination largely passed with the advent of the telegraph," my companion warned. "Had you struck before I could send off wires of enquiry and summaries of my concerns then you might have been able to escape, even triumph. Once I had laid down my shillings and sent off my messages,[29] you were done. You are exposed now, Mr Ellis. Your name is known. You are wanted for the murders of Daniel Hanvers and your father, and the suspected murder of the real Tobit Galliard. Other charges will follow."

I kept up the pressure, doing my part. "You doubtless hoped to eliminate those people who stood between you and the family fortune you coveted, but that is forever denied you now, sirrah. Society is closed to you. Your appearance and manner are circulated everywhere, with or without counterfeit beard. Here and now, or soon, you will face justice."

"In short, Mr Ellis," Holmes continued the assault, "you have made a fatal error, overestimating your wits."

Ellis's pride was pricked. He cocked his pistol. "The fatal mistake is yours, Mr Holmes! I am a man who intends to go far. Your journey ends here."

"You are clever," Holmes told him, "but your maths is deficient."

"True," I agreed as Ellis tried to parse the insult. "Need we explain?"

Adam Ellis snarled at us, unhappy to be baffled.

Holmes enlightened him. "There are two of us and one of you, Ellis. You might shoot me but then Watson will have you."

"If you kill Sherlock Holmes you shall not survive it," I promised the murderer.

"And if you harm Doctor Watson, you will regret it for the remainder of your short days," Holmes added chillingly.

Ellis looked from one to other of us, suddenly uncertain.

"And then there is this," Holmes went on, holding out the facsimile of the forged will that we had borrowed from Mr Cleremont. "You see what's here, do you not?"

What was there was a distraction. As Ellis's eyes flickered over the presented paper, seeking some nonexistent flaw that had betrayed him, I seized the emergency communications cord and yanked it hard.

The train's brakes jammed on full, causing the wheels to shriek and spark along the iron track. Passengers were shaken and rocked in their seats as the engineer brought the locomotive to a swift halt.

Only Holmes and I were braced for the interruption. Ellis, on his feet by the doorway, was caught off-balance by the deceleration. It thwarted his aim; a shot passed through the window behind us, shattering it.

29   The fixed price for electrical telegraphy in Great Britain from 1860 was one shilling for twenty words carried up to 100 miles, 1/6d up to 200 miles, and 2/- up to 300 miles. Local messages within large towns were 6d.

Holmes brought his walking cane down across Ellis's gun-hand, a sharp blow that forced the villain to release his weapon. I lunged in to grab the fellow.

He was young and fit, more than I had expected. I took a hard knock to the chin and was spun back to the carriage seat.

Ellis could do mathematics well enough to calculate when the game was up. He dived back out of the compartment and hared along the connecting corridor. Holmes sprinted after him.

A number of passengers milled out from their own compartments to find out why the train was halting and what the bang had been. They got in the way of Ellis's exit, causing him to stumble. He tripped amongst a knot of travellers, tangled amidst the tumbled people.

He could not bring any other weapon to bear as we closed on him. Holmes collared the murderer and clinched him in some Oriental lockhold. Travellers scrambled up and away, dismayed at the violence. I used the villain's own pistol to hold him quiet.

"The chap was travelling without a ticket," I explained to the shocked bystanders.

"The stain on your character is removed," Holmes assured young Andrew Blanchard as the Court of Probate was dismissed.

"Ellis will face the gallows for his crimes," I reassured the young sprig.

Blanchard spat. "He is my cousin—and I hope to see him hang!"

We watched the young man stalk away from the courthouse to the carriage that Hoag had waiting for him.

"Well, I am satisfied that the matter is properly settled," Mr Cleremont assured us. "The matter is resolved and justice has prevailed."

"The old vicar is in competent medical care," I reported. "He may recover from his slow poisoning."

"The diocese may wish to consider their means of verifying their curates, however," Cleremont observed. He tipped his hat to us and departed for his office.

"You were right to pursue Danny Hanvers's death, Holmes," I adjudged. "Now his family and friends may rest knowing that his murderer is caught. The remaining members of the Blanchard family are safe from poisoning.

Adam Ellis can do no more harm in this world and shall answer for it in the next."

"He was an enterprising villain, though," Holmes adjudged his vanquished adversary. "He kept me occupied for a whole day."

I do not know whether Adam Ellis would have been glad of the testimonial.

The Adventure of the Giant's Wife

"**A**LL THIS LANDSCAPE were becos' of a marital dispute," the dour guide who led Holmes and I up the steep slope beside Carr Beck informed us. Mr Slaithwaite had evidently taken Londoners on walking tours up to Burley Moor before. "At least that's what t' legends say."

The slushy remnants of a fading late winter made the ground treacherous. I was glad of my walking cane. The sharp wind off the peaks above us made me gladder of my Burberry.

"Burley Moor, y'see, and Ilkley Moor up there, are both rightly part o' Rombald's Moor," the local went on. "And Rombald, well 'e were a giant, back in t' olden days 'afore t' Romans ivver come."

I glanced to see how Holmes was taking the impromptu history lesson. His attention seemed transfixed on the local landscape, the wild ridges and sudden valleys of the Yorkshire hills.

"Well Rombald, 'e were a fierce old monster that fritted[30] everybody. When 'is temper flared there were storms. 'E tossed around lightning and 'ole mountains. So they reckon, in the stories. But… he 'ad a *wife*."

Holmes paused momentarily to examine an ancient waystone, half lost in a clump of vervain. Under frost and green mould the rock had prehistoric cup and ring carvings; there are more than four hundred such stones scattered about the area, and many more lost over the years.[31]

"Supposedly, this Rombald's missus weren't the sort t' put up wi' much. And one day, these two get into such a fight over 'is burned dinner that she starts tossing huge rocks at 'im. Old Rombald, 'e legs it off t' try and get away from 'er. And 'is wife, she runs after 'im, chucking hills at 'im." Slaithwaite gestured round the cold misty incline. "And this is what they left, 'im crashing through and splitting mountains into valleys, 'er lobbing giant boulders after 'im. We're heading to t' Great Skirtful of Rocks, what

---

30   Frightened.

31   This remarkable Mesolithic and Neolithic landscape is well-described in Prehistoric Rock Art of the West Riding: *Cup-and-ring-marked Rocks of the Valleys of the Aire, Wharfe, Washburn and Nidd* (2003) by Boughey and Vickerman, ISBN: 1 870453 32 8, but the volume is out of print so readers are advised to track down the CD version, or refer to the summary on Rombald's Moor at http://www.stone-circles.org.uk/stone/rombaldsmoor.htm

fell out of 'er pinny[32] as she chased 'er man. Over yon's the Little Skirtful of Rocks, and below us the Skirtful Spring. Up there over that ridge is't famous Cow and Calf Rocks, what Rombald broke as 'e scrambled away. There were a Bull Rock an' all until eighty year or so back, that got quarried away to build Ilkley. But point is, according to t' owd wives tales, all of this were caused by a do-mestic incident, as they calls it." Slaithwaite breathed before his punchline. "And *that's* why tha' don't go peeving a Yorkshire lass."

"We're not hunting Burley's first giant," Holmes acknowledged. It was the first indication that he had been listening to the fellow at all.

Slaithwaite became suddenly shy. "Well," he responded, a little abashed by my companion's sudden attention, "it's only a bit un a story, like."

"But we are here seeking giants," Holmes reminded us. "And one of them a murderer."

It was true. In Holmes's Inverness coat pocket was the letter that had brought us to this wild Yorkshire landscape chasing an unconventional killer:

Stephill Farm,
Burley Woodhead,
West Riding,
Yorkshire.

Mr Sherlock Holmes,
221B Baker Street,
London.

10th April, 1888

Dear Mr Holmes,

Knowing your acuity and memory from long back I have no doubt that you will remember me, Samuel Rudd, who worked in your father's service as stable boy at his estate in Mycroft[33] up to his passing. Since then I have received a groom's position at Stephill

---

32   Pinafore.

33   According to W.S. Baring-Gould's biography *Sherlock Holmes* (1962), the great detective was born on January 6th 1854 at Mycroft in the North Riding of Yorkshire. His older brother was named after the location. This same source records Holmes's parents as Siger and Violet (née Sherringford) Holmes and gives his full name as William Sherlock Scott Holmes.

Farm stables near Burley-in-Wharfdale and have worked there these dozen years.

I hope you will pardon my letter, in which I am forwarding details of a troubling and unpleasant series of events that have recently disturbed our quiet little farm, concerning the death of its owner Mr Lister.

The former proprietor of Stephill, Mr Giles Packworth, died in the summer of 1887. He had no remaining close relatives, his son having been lost in the Indian Hill Wars, so the estate was sold, farm, stables, and pastures, to Mr Hogarth Lister of York. Mr Lister had made his money in coal but now wished to retire and breed horses.

Mr Lister took up residence in September of last year, and there was, if I may be so bold as to admit it, some tension between the town staff that came to Burley Woodhead with Mr Lister and the people who had been in service at Stephill during Mr Packworth's time. Indeed, Mr Lister dismissed some of the older staff for getting into disputes with the newer folks. Not wishing to speak ill of the dead, but Mr Lister was not an easy master.

Mr Lister was not popular with the local folk. An antiquarian, he organised a dig into one of the old barrows up on the ridge, looking for burial treasures, despite the protests of the people of Burley Woodhead. Indeed he had the right, having permission from the landowner Mrs Duexbury, but it was a controversial thing and led to bad feeling in the neighbourhood and a distance with some of the gentry.

This excavation took place in early March, as soon as the frosts first passed and before the late frosts we have now, when the ground could be cut. A wedge was sliced from the tump and some old metal bits and shards of broken pot were discovered, but no treasure trove. For several nights afterwards the horses were disturbed, and since then the main house was awoken by loud thumps as of someone rattling the shutters and tossing stones onto the roof.

Mr Lister was angered by what he spoke of as 'ignorant country tricks by feeble-minded yokels'. One of the young grooms was blamed and dismissed without references, but the noises went on. There was a small fire in the hay-barn but it was discovered and doused before it could spread. A few things in the big house were tampered with, moved or disappeared, including a clock that had belonged to Mr Lister's late mother. Mr Lister complained to the bobby from Burley-in-Wharfdale and was angry when nothing was done.

Some of the more superstitious of the staff, including Mrs Ophelia our housekeeper, were convinced that the house was haunted and Mr Lister cursed because he had opened and disturbed the tumulus.

Mr Lister was a man of fixed habits. He rose early and walked his dog, leaving the stables at six sharp and returning for his breakfast at seven. He was fit for his age, which was around sixty, and in apparent good health. On Monday, 2nd April he left as usual on his constitutional but returned early, hastily, and as pale and scared as I have ever seen a man. I was walking one of our broody mares in the long pasture when he hastened down the hill.

I asked him what was wrong, worried for his heart. He replied that he had seen ghosts, giant ghosts, and that one of them had killed the other.

Now, there are stories about Ilkley and Rombald's Moor (which Stephill Farm edges onto) and of sightings of such spectres. Children here dare each other to go up onto the tops at dawn and look for the phantom. I tried to reassure Mr Lister that he had not seen aught that many others hadn't perceived over many years, but he was curt with me and threatened me with dismissal. These ghosts, he insisted, were unlike any other, and he was certain that they had acted out murder. He had seen one, a woman, creep upon the other, a man, unawares, and strike him down with a blow from behind. The attacker had then fallen upon the downed spectre and had hit him repeatedly upon the head, perhaps with a rock.

Mr Lister was convinced that he had seen some apparition, and that it was some portent of doom.

He spoke no more of it after that morning, and for eight days he did not take his morning walk. Yesterday, the day after Easter, he vanished before breakfast without word. When he was missed, Mr Slaithwaite our Head Groom organised a search. I was amongst those who took the steep track past the lower tarn towards the barrow and stone ring up there.

It was the dog's barking that led us to the place where Mr Lister had fallen. He was dead. He had tumbled down a steep slope and might have hit his head going down. That was the policemen's conclusion at first, but the police doctor has since said that the cause of death was several blows to the skull, which would be hard to take on a fall of no more than twenty feet.

Some of the local lads blame the curse and the 'moors knockers', and I admit to a bit of a tingle of fear myself when I remembered Mr

Lister's fright of the week before, and that he might have somehow seen a phantom prediction of his own passing. In the village they are saying that it was a punishment on him for disturbing the tumulus.

When I was questioned by the inspector of police who came out from Ilkley I mentioned that I had been in service to your family and had tended to your pony when we were boys. I asked for permission to write and seek your advice on the case, and Inspector Shotley was kind enough to say that he would appreciate any insight you might have on how to untangle what happened. I enclose the Inspector's address if you wish to wire him.

Wishing you the best of health and fortune, in remembrance of happy times in service at Mycroft, most sincerely yours,

Saml. Rudd esq.

This was the message that had roused my friend from his morose chagrin at his mistakes regarding the matter of Mrs Munro and Lucy Hebron,[34] and set us on the next train north in search of spectral giants in the dim watery pre-dawn light of the Yorkshire moors.

The path we had been following diverted from the Carr Beck—that fast-flowing freshet ran deep and chill with mountain-snow meltoff, tumbling down too steeply to follow up further, but it was not so wide that we couldn't stride across. We traced left along the contour of the ridge. Below us all was white haze. The scattered houses of rural Burley Woodhead were less than a half-mile behind but they were quite invisible now.

"Mr Lister was said to be a fellow of regular habits," Holmes noted.

---

34   Mr Grant Munro consulted Holmes in the first week of April 1888 to discover why his wife was requesting significant sums of money and sneaking away to secret rendezvous at a rural cottage. Holmes concluded that Mrs Munro's supposedly-deceased American first husband had returned to blackmail her. For once the great detective erred. The occupant of the Norbury cottage was actually Lucy, Mrs Munro's daughter by her first marriage to the now-deceased lawyer John Hebron. Since Hebron was a Black man and the child of mixed race, Effie Munro had been afraid to reveal Lucy's existence to her second husband. On learning the truth, Mr Munro welcomed wife and step-daughter into his care, to Watson's approval.

The account is given in "The Adventure of the Yellow Face" in *The Memoirs of Sherlock Holmes* (1893), wherein Holmes ruefully says, "Watson, if it should ever strike you that I am getting a little overconfident in my powers, or giving less pains to a case than it deserves, kindly whisper 'Norbury' in my ear, and I shall be infinitely obliged to you."

The story is notable as a rare occasion where Holmes is proved wrong and does not solve the case—events work out despite not because of him—and of a sympathetic Victorian treatment of mixed-race marriages and children.

"What route did he take for his morning walk?"

"Why, t' same path as we're on now," Slaithwaite answered. "There's a loop, along t' low ridge overlooking t' tarns as far as t' Grubstones, then back along t' 'igh ridge, coomin' past the Great Skirtful and t' broken barrow, and so back down t' way you coom up."

Holmes checked a sketch-map he had made of the local geography, that showed the moor's footpaths and streams, along with some ground contours indicating the steep inclines up from the farm. I could easily trace the anticlockwise route that Lister had walked his dog each day, a stroll of perhaps two and a half miles.

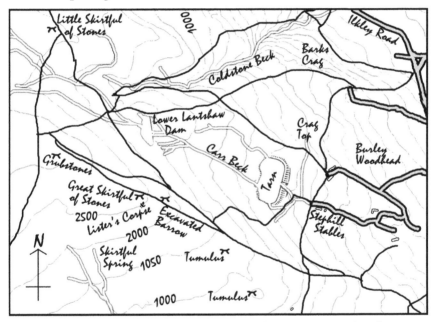

"You were one of the people who found Mr Lister up by the cairn ring," Holmes observed to Slaithwaite.

"By t' Great Skirtful, aye. Well, when they worked out e'd gone missing there was three on us went up there looking for 'im, sent out by Mrs Ophelia, 'is 'ousekeeper like. Me, an' Lister 'oo you knows, and George Sutton that's a stable-'and. Some others went off towards Menston and Burley-in-Wharfedale, and a couple went agate[35] t'Ilkley Road a few miles.

---

35   Yorkshire dialect of "off away", from the Danish *gata*, meaning 'way or street'; "Get agate!" is a brusque dismissal meaning "Be on your way."

"Wait," I interrupted. "Why search anywhere but where he took his daily walk?"

"'Cos none of us knew as 'ed gone out that day, 'till 'e were missed at breakfast. 'E'd been up in't night, chasing that moors-knocker round t'ouse and getting nowhere, so they jus' thought as 'e'd slept in. Besides, there'd been an unseasonal late snow an' it weren't fit t' go a-hikin' up on't moors, not for someone on 'is years. But old Jack Widdison, 'e says, 'Ee taks gawm, lookee up't gill where 'e were so glottened before'."

"Ah... right," I responded

Our guide saw that he had lost us at last with his local patois and deigned to translate, "That is, sirs, 'e says 'Listen to me, look up on't hill where Mr Lister 'ad his fright t'other time."

"Where he saw the giants," I supplied.

"Well aye. So's we coom on up and we 'ears 'is dog barking like a mad thing, an' there 'e is, poor feller, fallen down t'scar[36] wi' 'is ead all spretched—that is, cracked open."[37]

"How was he laid?" Holmes enquired.

"On 'is front, wi' one arm under 'im and t' other out t' 't side. And one leg bent right unnatural where it 'ad broken. And I said t' George Sutton, 'Well that's 'im gone, then,' and George Sutton says t'me, 'Well what d'y' expect when e' goes digging up that old barrow-like?' 'Cos them places was graves once, they do say, from the old days 'afore the churchyards."

Holmes ignored the commentary for now and continued his interrogation. "Was there blood? Was it dried?"

"There were plenty, all over t' glocken[38] snow—which were wet, o' course, so it 'adn't storkened.[39] 'Ee'd split 'is skull when 'e tumbled, I reckoned. But them perlice-men says no."

"There was snow. Were there tracks? Any prints but his?"

"Nobbut some sheep prints an' small game, either up on't ridge or down in t' scar, and 'is setter what 'ad morrised about all over t'place. It were t'devvil's own job getting down t' 'im where 'e'd tumbled. They 'ad t' fetch ropes to 'aul 'im out."

---

36   Yorkshire dialect for a steep rockface, from the Old Norse *skera*, meaning a cut.

37   From the Norwegian *sprekk* and Swedish *sprikka*, meaning "to crack".

38   Yorkshire dialect for "starting to thaw or clear", from the Icelandic *glöggur*.

39   Stiffened, set, or coagulated, from the Old Norse *storkna*.

This testimony and Holmes's demands for additional details took us a hundred yards up the slippery track, to the t-junction onto the loop that was Lister's regular circuit. I had expected Holmes to take the left path, which would lead us past Lister's excavated barrow and bring us more quickly to the ruined ring of stones above where the body was discovered. Instead he set off right, following the dead man's customary route.

"Tell me about the moors-knockers, Mr Slaithwaite," the great detective instructed our guide.

"Well, sirs, I don't 'old wi' boggarts and hobs," Slaithwaite insisted. "I was minded as the mischief were done by 'uman 'ands, and if I finds 'oo set a fire in the barn or let our 'orses out into the night or messed up my tack-room then 'ee'll feel the back o' my 'and! But I were on watch some nights per Mr Lister's orders and I nivver saw owt as explained them bangings an' goings on! So maybe George Sutton were right about t' mound being cursed."

"Did you suspect anyone of playing tricks?" I wondered.

"Aye, well, at first I thought it might be them Champions, young Alice's kin after she were dismissed for cheeking Mrs Ophelia on t' matter of washing vegetables proper. 'Er brothers aren't above a bit of poachin' and roguery. And George Sutton, 'e's 'er cousin some times removed. But none o' them could 'ave got inside the Big 'Ouse t' do stuff."

Ezekiel Slaithwaite was not the first resident of Stephill that Holmes had interviewed on this topic. Indeed, I knew that beside Rudd's letter in Holmes's pocket were the notes I had compiled for him based on our interviews yesterday about the people and timings of the farm haunting:

Residents in the Big House at Stephill:
Hogarth Lister, 61 (deceased)—disliked owner, since September 1887;
Punch, his setter;
Mrs Mary Ophelia, 56, housekeeper, hired in York;
Betty Coombe, 22, parlour maid, transferred from Lister's York town-house;
Sukie Murgatroyd, 17, maid of all work, local, hired in November after previous local maid Alice Champion dismissed for impertinence;
Larry Tope, 16, page, local.

Residents of outbuildings at Stephill:
Ezekiel Slaithwaite, 48, head groom and stableman, local, 23 years service at Stephill;
Samuel Rudd, 39, groom, ostler, 12 years service at Stephill;

Carl Ophelia, 32, groom, son of housekeeper, hired in York;
George Sutton, 26, stable hand, local, hired in February after dismissal
of previous local man Fred Clough after row with employer;
Jack Widdison, 67, general labourer, 38 years service at Stephill;
Lewis Wilson, 21, jockey, hired in York in December last after dismissal
of previous local man Adam Boothe for row with Carl.

Day-Labourers:
Up to fifteen local men hired as required for field and stables duties.

Principal disturbances at and around Stephill:
Monday 5ᵗʰ March—Cutting begins at the barrow; row with protesting
locals;
Tuesday 6ᵗʰ March—Landowner Mrs Duexbury refuses to revoke per-
mission for dig;
Wednesday 7ᵗʰ March—Dig concludes—spear head, palstave, and sev-
eral amber beads were found, tentatively dated to Bronze Age;
also Wednesday 7ᵗʰ March—First night-time disturbances at Stephill,
knocking on doors and shutters;
Thursday 8ᵗʰ March—Night-time knocking continues, Lister complains
to police, sets watch;
Friday 9ᵗʰ March—First sounds of stones rattling off roof slates, no mis-
siles found the following morning;
Saturday, 10ᵗʰ March—Knocks and bangs, more roof rattles; no prints
in snowfall;
Monday 12ᵗʰ March—Knocks on shutters despite watch by Slaithwaite,
Rudd, Ophelia;
Tuesday 13ᵗʰ March—Coal scuttle overturned in kitchen, more knocks;
Wednesday 14ᵗʰ March—Spoons moved to cupboard under sink (dis-
covered by Mrs Ophelia); protest from domestic staff; horses set loose in
night;
Thursday 15ᵗʰ March—Jam jars in cellar broken across floor, 'tappings
in walls';
Friday 16ᵗʰ March—Betty Coombe finds maggots in her bed; hysterics;
Saturday 17ᵗʰ March—small fire in hay-barn, discovered and doused by
Rudd;
Monday 19ᵗʰ March—'Bad night', many knocks, rattles, bangs at Big
House and in stables;
Tuesday 20ᵗʰ March—Lister's shaving kit moved from his dresser to the

pantry, smeared with unidentified grease;
Wednesday 21st March—More roof noise, spoons again moved to cupboard under sink (discovered there by Sukie); several stable stalls opened, allowing horses to escape;
Thursday, 22nd March—Saturday 24th March—Lister on business in York; no disturbances;
Monday 26th March—upper floor shutters and windows opened during snowfall; Betty accused, tearfully gives four weeks' notice;
Tuesday 27th March—Mrs Lister's clock moved to head of main staircase, along with six spoons (discovered by Lister himself);
Wednesday 28th March—Lister rages out of house at 11p.m. to 'chase the idiots throwing stones at his window'; thinks he sees someone fleeing across the pasture field;
Thursday 29th March—Saddles and equipment in stables tack-room scattered over floor, some damaged (discovered by Widdison, 3.15p.m.);
Saturday 31st March—Mrs Lister's clock disappears; Lister's antiquarian notes and finds scattered around his study (door still locked, only Lister held key);
Monday 2nd April—Lister walks dog, encounters spectral giants, returns home shocked, does not venture outside again until day of his demise;
Tuesday 3rd April—Friday 6th April—more general disturbances, knocking, thumping;
Friday 6th April—Lister writes to his man of business about quitting Stephill and returning to York;
Saturday 7th April—Volume on local history loaned by Mrs Duexbury found torn to pieces and thrown on dining room fire (discovered by Tope);
Monday 9th April, approx. 10.15a.m.—Lister discovered dead below the Great Skirtful of Rocks.

To this summary of our interviews Holmes had appended in his own cramped handwriting:

Of note:
No disturbances on Sundays or on Friday 30th March (Good Friday).
Possible romantic relationship between Carl Ophelia and Sukie Murgatroyd?
Rudd says servants suspect occasional 'irregular' relationship between Lister and his 'town maid' Betty Coombe—but Betty has now given notice.
Local estate owner Mrs Claire Duexbury is a widow of considerable

worth. She has been a frequent visitor at Stephill.

The clock.

The spoons.

I reviewed our evidence so far, trying to see the case as Holmes would, but as usual the trick eluded me.

We left the ridge's shelter and were assailed by the bitter Yorkshire cold. It seemed unfair that we should suffer both chill wind on the high ground and freezing mist in the valley below.

Holmes led the way, setting the pace with his long gangly legs. He checked his pocketwatch, and then a compass. "Nine twenty-five," he noted with satisfaction. "Almost the time that Mr Lister observed his giants. We must hurry."

"You expect to see them also?" I asked, doubtfully.

"Only if we are fortunate, Watson. But if the spectres favour us with an appearance then I guarantee that we shall encounter more of them than he did."

Slaithwaite was eager to take us up the remainder of the incline. Looming above to the left was the mist-smudged silhouette of the moor cairn where Lister had cut open the ancient tumulus and had experienced his extraordinary encounter. A short way beyond it, but not visible from our lower path, was the badly damaged Bronze Age cairn called the Great Skirtful where the deceased had been discovered.[40]

---

40   The Great Skirtful of Stones is found at OS Map Ref SE141446. (2300 B.C.—700 B.C.). All that now remains of the badly damaged Bronze Age cairn is a low ring of stones about twenty-six yards in diameter and eighteen inches high. A larger stone that might be a boundary marker or milestone stands in the middle of the site. Previous unsympathetic digging has partially destroyed the site, rubbish has been dumped into the holes, and much of the original stone had been robbed away. A smaller 'barrow' cairn to the southeast has been reduced even more—by Mr Hogarth Lister according to Dr Watson's account.

        A 1901 article in the *Shipley Express* (reprinted in *A History of Menston and Hawksworth*, Alistair Laurence, 1991, ISBN-10: 1870071751), describes "a huge cairn of small boulders, nearly a hundred tons on a heap, although for centuries loads have been taken away to mend the trackways across the moor… The centre of the cairn is now hollow, as it was explored many years ago, and from the middle human bones were taken and submitted to Canon Greenwell and other archaeologists."

        Near the centre of the giant cairn is a large once-upright stone of more recent centuries upon which is etched the words, "This is Rumbles Law." The *Shipley Express* article explains that "'law' was always used in the British sense for a hill, and Rumbles Hill, or cairn, was a conspicuous boundary mark for many centuries. [Historian Mr Turner] found in the Burley Manor Rolls, two centuries back, that on Rogation Day, when the boundaries were beaten by the inhabitants, they met on this hill, and describing their boundaries, they concluded the nominy by joining in the words, "This is Rumbles Law.""

"T' tarn, tha means? Aye."

"It's not far now, sirs," Slaithwaite assured us.

But Holmes halted and called our guide back. "I wish to remain here for the moment, Mr Slaithwaite. We are approximately half way to the fork that leads to the Grubstones or the reservoir, are we not, at an elevation of around one thousand and fifty feet?"

"T' tarn, tha means? Aye, it's ovver there. That track teks y' above it, an if y' goes far enough y' find t' Little Skirtful.[41] There's cairns and Ne-o-lithic enclosures all 'cross these moors, and nobbut 'alf mile that way's t' Twelve Apostles stone circle."[42]

Holmes was not interested in any of those features for now. His attention was focussed on the crest west of us, the ridge where Lister's high return path ran. Behind and below us I could just glimpse the tarns, still partly iced over. In no direction was there any sign of civilisation, not even a house. With fog below and a cloud-heavy slow-dawning sky above, the bleak fields and ling were almost monochrome.

I confess to a moment's nervousness. There was on that lonely moor a sense of timeless mystery, of being close to things that were forgotten but not gone. Slaithwaite shifted uneasily.

Holmes checked his watch again. "By this time in Lister's regular routine he would have reached the Great Skirtful," he judged. "It was evidently his custom to sit there on the old stones for five minutes and recover his breath. Then he would progress on towards the excavated barrow." He consulted his compass and watch again. "An understanding of the geography of the area is vital, quite vital."

Above us on the crest, something caught my eye. Something was moving in the mist by the cairn—something huge.

"Holmes!" I exclaimed, drawing the detective's attention to the thing.

"The giant," he whispered back to me, in fascinated tones.

What we saw was a mere silhouette, a darker shape in the obscuring mist, but it was unlike any outline I had ever seen. It loomed impossibly, supernaturally large. As well as a shadowy smudge in a vaguely humanoid form, the moving object was surrounded by a glowing aura. It shimmered

---

41   The Little Skirtful of Stones at OS Map Ref SE138452 is another Bronze Age round cairn, rather better preserved than the Great Skirtful though its centre has been dug out.

42   The Twelve Apostles at OS Map Ref SE126452 is a stone circle of about twelve yards diameter with twelve remaining stones up to four feet high. It has been 'modified' in the last two centuries and unofficially 'restored' in recent years, with fallen stones re-erected, making its original layout hard to determine. From this site, the rising summer solstice sun appears exactly above the turf-cut White Horse at Kilburn.

with rainbow arcs and seemed to rise up higher even as we watched it. Then a second shape shimmered in beside it, and a third.

We had found the giants of Rombald's Moor.

The spectral titans loomed over the sundered barrow, looking towards us like primitive gods.

Slaithwaite muttered an oath. "Ah've not seen t' like o' that since I were a bairn," he whispered.

The central giant raised his arm and lifted his hat to us. I turned and saw that Holmes had raised his deerstalker cap in a similar fashion, as if greeting the apparitions.

My mind raced back to my friend's conversation yesterday on the train from King's Cross:

"The *Brockengespenst* or Brocken Spectre is named for the Brocken Mountain in Saxony-Anhalt, tallest of the Harz range," Holmes had lectured me. "It was originally described in the literature from first-hand observations by Lutheran pastor Johann Silberschlag in 1780. He was climbing the Brocken's slopes one morning when he saw ahead a vast shadowy giant looming from the mist, surrounded with a rainbow aura."

"And his account was believed?" I asked.

"Silberschlag was a man of science. He carefully observed and noted that the spectre mirrored his own motions. When he raised his hand so did it. As he approached, the apparition diminished in size. In this way he concluded that he had encountered an unusual and fascinating optical phenomenon. The dawn sun behind and below him was projecting his shadow onto low cloud in the mists about him. Air-moisture refracted the light to cause the fractal glow. In short, Watson, the spectre was not spectral but of the spectrum."[43]

---

43   The Brocken Spectre was a known phenomenon in the 19th century, though its cause was perhaps not universally understood. It makes an early fictional appearance in James Hogg's 1824 novel *The Private Memoirs and Confessions of a Justified Sinner: Written by Himself: With a detail of curious traditionary facts and other evidence by the editor.* Dickens mentions it in *Little Dorrit* (1855-7) Book II Chapter 23 wherein Flora Finching says, "...ere yet Mr F appeared a misty shadow on the horizon paying attentions like the well-known spectre of some place in Germany beginning with a B..." Lewis Carroll's humorous 1869 poem "Phantasmagoria" includes a Spectre who "...tried the Brocken business first/but caught a sort of chill."

"That is a most remarkable weather condition," I owned. "You believe that this accounts for Lister's vision?"

"The so-called 'Brocken Giant' has been witnessed on other hillsides in similar conditions at dawn and dusk. I believe there are accounts of a Big Grey Man of Ben McDhui in Scotland, for example.[44] And you will note from Rudd's missive that the children of Burley brave the moors to view their local spectre often, which suggests a replicable event."

"Lister was rather affected by a mere optical illusion, Holmes!"

"By reputable accounts the vision can be somewhat disturbing, doctor. The shadow falls on water droplets at varying distances from the eye, confusing depth perception. Movements of the clouds can seem to impart the giant with independent motion. Running from the giant actually causes the shadow to swell in size and appear to be catching up. And of course, at the highest climes in thin oxygen the mind is scarcely at its most acute. In Hogarth Lister's case, however, I suspect that it was the violence he witnessed between those shadows that disturbed him the most. He was convinced that one had murdered the other."

Perhaps the most complete reference is in Coleridge's "Constancy To His Ideal Object" (*Poetical Works*, 1828), which also notes how often the phenomenon is interpreted as a supernatural encounter. The poem closes:

"And art thou nothing? Such thou art, as when
The woodman winding westward up the glen
At wintry dawn, where o'er the sheep-track's maze
The viewless snow-mist weaves a glist'ning haze,
Sees full before him, gliding without tread,
An image with a glory round its head;
The enamoured rustic worships its fair hues,
Nor knows he makes the shadow he pursues!"

44   Holmes refers to the *Am Fear Liath Mòr* that is encountered on Ben Macdui, the highest peak of the Cairngorms and second-highest mountain in the British Isles. His source for the legend is unclear, since the first published account of the Big Grey Man is commonly held to be climber J. Norman Collie's 1925 report of an 1891 encounter. Collie's report includes auditory phenomenon also, though: "I began to think I heard something else than merely the noise of my own footsteps. For every few steps I took I heard a crunch, and then another crunch as if someone was walking after me but taking steps three or four times the length of my own... [as] the eerie crunch, crunch, sounded behind me, I was seized with terror and took to my heels, staggering blindly among the boulders for four or five miles."

A Scottish Brocken Spectre at Bidean nam Bian in Glen Coe featured on the BBC news website at https://www.bbc.com/news/uk-scotland-highlands-islands-46277410 as recently as November 2018. The page includes some amazing photographs of the phenomenon.

"But Holmes… if we accept that Lister saw human silhouettes projected onto cloud or fog, then perhaps he did witness an attack! Then the mortal murderer had strong reason to go for the sole observer of his crime."

But as usual, Holmes would not be lured into theorising without sufficient data. "We must wait our time, my friend—and then we must hunt our ghosts!"

And hunt them we had. As I peered through that cold wet miasma at the swollen apparitions that filled the sky before us I felt the same prickle of superstitious awe that primitive man must have felt at such encounters in an age before scholarship or civilisation. Here on the edge of the Neolithic moor we seemed on the border between the settled realms of Britain and something from a lost and uncanny time.

As I turned to Holmes, so too one of the Spectres resorted to his companion.

"Remarkable," Holmes murmured. "All the accounts are verified. The shifting stratus clouds indeed produce an illusion of independent activity."

I thought of how carefully Holmes had positioned us. "We are almost exactly east of the barrow," I realised. "This is the only place that lines up the rising sun, the shadow-caster, and the monument."

"And the ridge-edge hides us from view from anyone further along the higher track. The drop acts like a ha-ha in a landscaped garden,[45] obscuring the persons whose shadows are projected whilst their silhouettes are shown large upon the mists."

"We coomed oop 'ere as lads," Slaithwaite reminisced, "if we durst. T' giants al'us appear in our likenesses.[46] My granny, she said that's 'ow's they shews themse'ns when they comes in judgement. Like as we're testing of ours'en."

"They surely tested Mr Lister," I admitted. "Holmes, if there were two people at this spot on the morn that Lister saw his Spectres, then surely

---

45 The ha-ha, a visual garden feature that hides a dividing trench and makes a lawn terrace appear continuous despite a boundary ditch, originated in New France from 1686 (as in Saint-Louis-du-Ha! Ha!), and appeared in the gardens of the Château de Meudon around 1700. It was described in Dezallier d'Argenville's *La théorie et la pratique du jardinage* (1709) and translated into English in 1712 by architect John James. Thereafter the feature was made fashionable by influential landscapers Charles Bridgeman, William Kent, and Capability Brown.

46 "In search of the Brocken spectre on Burley Moor," a *Guardian* picture essay by Rebecca Cole and Janise Elie in March 2019 (https://www.theguardian.com/environment/2019/mar/04/search-brocken-spectre-burley-moor) includes excellent images of the local phantom giants, which are indeed a long-known feature of the terrain and weather.

what he apprehended was an act of violence between two mortal beings. One assaulted, perhaps murdered the other." I cast around the barren ridge-track for any sign of lethal deeds.

"Too much time and too many boots have passed since Easter Monday," the detective cautioned. He replaced his cap and strode on, dismissing the apparitions now they had offered their testimony. "Come, we must proceed to the monuments."

His Brocken Spectre turned away too and rippled into insubstantial cloud. The instant of primal awe faded and I felt like myself again.

We climbed out of the wet mist, along a left fork that led us up a steep edge until we were a hundred feet higher. Eventually we reached another junction where a spur track doubled back to the Grubstones.[47] There was little to see at the ancient site save for a dozen stubby rocks in a circle in the heather and bracken. Some part of the ring may have been lost to a more recent grouse but.[48]

Another short brisk walk brought us to the Great Skirtful of Stones where the wrathful giantess had emptied her pinafore of gritstone slabs. The scatter of rocks was frost-rimed white, a low strand that appeared suddenly as the rising sun peered above it as we approached. The phantasmal mist melted away.

"Mr Lister were ovver there," our guide told us, pointing beyond the low brow of the scattered monument. He brought us to a shallow drop that might have been dug out as a hunting hide. A steep bank dropped perhaps twenty feet and there were some protruding stones that might have caused serious injury to a falling man, but it was hardly the precipice that I had been expecting.

Holmes questioned Slaithwaite again on the detail of the scene as it had been discovered, but the head groom had absorbed little additional detail. "'E were just dead in't sike,"[49] he shrugged.

We clambered down with difficulty to where Lister had lain guarded by

---

47   The site is located at OS Map Ref SE137447. It has been variously interpreted as a Bronze Age ring cairn, a robbed round cairn, or the foundation wall of an Iron Age hut. English Heritage notes it as a stone circle. Only twenty stones remain, some almost buried in the heather.

48   A trench dug as a hide for grouse shooting. There are many of these on Ilkley Moor, some of which have been lined from stones 'borrowed' from the cairns and circles nearby.

49   Yorkshire dialect for gulley or small stream, possibly from the Icelandic *siki*, meaning a rill.

his agitated setter. "Was the dog fierce?" Holmes wanted to know. "Might she have gone for a stranger who tried to harm her master?"

Slaithwaite shook his head. "Punch were a town dog," he revealed, as if he was confessing some terrible defect. "She's as timid as owt."

"Where is she now?" I wondered.

"Missus Duexbury's 'ouse at Crag Top. Poor thing were frit t' death," our guide reported, then added, "T' dog, I mean. Missus Duexbury din't seem mort[50] bothered when she 'eard about Mr Lister."

"But the staff seem to feel there was some closeness between the lady and your employer," I noted.

Slaithwaite blew out his cheeks. "Some folks 'as too much time t' gossip on stuff that's now't of their concern," he disapproved. "May'ap as Missus Duexbury did take a shine to Mr Lister. She's been a widder-woman these ten years an' more, and 'er a fine figure of a lady wi' lands and a fair income. If she saw Mr Lister as a good prospect then 'e 'ad no less a reason to court 'er. Though *I'd* look carefully if my daughter was to be walking out wi' that sour old fellow as 'er second."

"Why?" I wondered. Rudd's letter had not painted his employer in an entirely favourable light, but there was something in the head groom's tone that suggested more than a casual caution."

Slaithwaite paused, reluctant to speak ill of the dead. At last he ventured, "'E weren't alus kind t' lasses. That Betty Coombe for one."

"Miss Coombe denied any special relationship with Mr Lister," Holmes mentioned.

"Aye, well, it's not my way t' repeat stories. I didn't see now't nor 'ear now't. But I'd'uv looked askance at my lassie stepping out wi' Mr Lister. Nobbut that would be different from 'is courting a rich lady like Mrs Duexbury."

Slaithwaite could not be drawn further on the subject. We trudged on along the high ridge path to the broken ground where Lister had cut open a barrow mound to such local consternation. The heather-topped tump was little more than a swelling out of the slope, scattered with more of the same stones that formed so many prehistoric relics on these moors. A wedge of newly-turned soil showed where diggers had broken into the cairn to seek for treasure.

"Who undertook the work?" Holmes enquired.

"Them as wanted Mr Lister's brass more'n to drink quietly in any public 'ouse in these parts," our guide assured us. "Local fellers and some blokes 'ired in Ilkley and Burley-in-Middleton. You've no idea of the rows. George

50   Much.

Sutton, 'e nearly clouted a bloke in't White 'Orse. But they was only 'ere for three days, for there were now't in't 'cairn but for a few scraps."

"Why was the dig so controversial?" I wondered.

Slaithwaite screwed his face up with thought as he tried to express his feeling. "T' mound... it's on Mrs Duexbury's land alright, but... it's not 'ers. She's a newcomer, only been 'ere these twenty-five years. That mound, it's been ere for... well, since Moses were a lad. And it's... well, it shouldn't be maithered,[51] that all."

Holmes climbed atop the ruin and ascertained that the lower path was not quite visible, because of the gradients between.

"This is close to where Lister must have witnessed the Brocken spectres," I judged.

Holmes agreed absently, but I could tell his attention was occupied by the scatter of dig debris. He squatted down and examined some of the overturned stones more carefully.

"These have been shifted twice," he determined, bringing out his magnifying lens to look more closely at a small cluster of rocks. "The first time was when they were disturbed by the excavation. You can see the ancient water-marks and lichen patterns on the side that was formerly exposed. But they have been moved again since they were put back into the hole. Note these much fainter traces of exposure, and the way that the frost coats this section differently?"

Holmes carefully lifted the stones away. Buried beneath them was a burlap bag no larger than a fist, tied up with a piece of twine. He carefully pulled it out and sniffed it. "Ah. Yes."

"What is it?" I enquired inevitably.

"*Pimpinella anisum,* if I am not mistaken," my friend answered. He carefully sliced the twine, leaving the knot intact for later inspection, and opened the bag to reveal sage-coloured dried ovoid fruits the size of peanuts. "Aniseed," he verified triumphantly. "A carminative digestive and expectorant. The Romans attributed it with aphrodisiac qualities and used it regularly in cooking."[52]

"What's it doing a-buried there?" Slaithwaite puzzled. "Aniseed's not from these parts."

"From Egypt originally, Mr Slaithwaite," Holmes instructed. "As for its

---

51   Bothered, disturbed.

52   The spiced Roman aniseed cake *mustaceoe* was served as a final course at erotic feasts and is cited as the origin of the mediaeval tradition of a wedding cake.

placement and concealment, well... that was part of the plan to murder Hogarth Lister!"

Holmes interviewed the housekeeper.

"Why no," Mrs Ophelia told us, "I didn't know Mr Lister before we came to Stephill. My boy and I answered an advertisement for a cook and handyman at Mr Lister's York house after his previous housekeeper had resigned. But before we ever moved in, Mr Lister sold up and came out here to the wilds of the West Riding. The local people? Well some of 'em's alright but there's others what wouldn't give you the time of day. The disturbances? Well, first I thought it were that Alice Champion's family a-causing trouble, but now I'm convinced it was the work of spirits. How else does you account for all them knockings and rappings of a night? It's a buried prince under that barrow that was disturbed, or I'll be bound. Betty Coombe? Well I'm not one to talk but when you hears a quiet tread creeping to 'er room in the attic some nights, you 'as to wonder, don't you? And Mr Lister the only fellow in the house? Mrs Duexbury? Didn't see much of 'er except to serve up tea. She and Mr Lister spent a fair bit of time getting excited about that there cairn, but I reckon that the bloom came off the rose a bit after they found nought much. I daresay she discovered the master's bad temper, like as not. And he had one."

Holmes questioned the maid of all work.

"Oh yes, this place is 'aunted, sirs, no question of that. Why, if you only 'eard t' knockings and bangings of an evening! Such a racket as you'd scarcely believe. It's just as old Jack Widdison warned." Sukie Murgatroyd leaned in confidentially. "*No* good comes of breaking into t' moors mounds. Just look at pore Mr Lister! Yes, it was me as discovered t' spoons in the bucket under t' kitchen sink—and *'ow* they got there from their drawer with neither me nor Mrs Ophelia seeing owt I cannot say. Me, I took service 'ere after Alice Champion went last November. Service is service in these times. But she warned me, like, to steer clear of old Lister's wanderin' 'ands, though. 'Don't you end up like that Betty Coombe from town,' she told me, and I've been careful. Yes, I 'ave sometimes taken a stroll with Carl Ophelia. Can't a lass chat with a fellow without there's nasty rumours? I'm a good chapel girl. No, I don't 'ave keys to the 'ouse.

Only Mr Lister and Mrs Ophelia 'as them, and Mr Lister was the only one with keys to 'is study."

Holmes spoke with Larry the page boy.

"It was me what found Mrs Duexbury's book all tore up on't fire," he revealed proudly. "An' I was second one there when t' coal scuttle got pushed over, after Mrs O. 'erself. And I saw all t' jam jars brokken i't cellar—'ad to clean 'em up—*and* I saw Mr Lister's study when it was all tore up. We all thought 'e'd go into a mighty rage at that, but instead 'e just went all quiet-like. Aye, I've know Sukie an' Alice all me life, played together as bairns. No, I stay away from't stables if I can. That Lewis Wilson clouted me round' t'ear-oil. Aye, I know t' giant. But you 'ave t' pick your morning and be lucky wi't weather. An it's not alus safe to go t' giants, 'cos sometimes they take a misliking t' you, like they did wi' Mr Lister."

Holmes confronted the town maid.

"Like I told you before, it's nobody's business but mine if anybody tried to take liberties," Betty Coombe insisted. "Some people just 'as nasty minds. If there was any mischief then it was Mr Lister 'oo started it and what's a pore girl to do what needs to keep 'er place? But I'd 'ad enough of the old miser and 'is grousing. And then Mr Lister accuses me of opening all the upstairs shutters an' letting the snow in. No, it was the last straw. I gave my notice. I'm back to York and good riddance t' this place! Ghosties and knockers and fire-starters and giants! And what about them wriggly maggots in my bed, eh? Brrr, I shudder to remember it! I'm leaving this accursed place an' never coming back. Mrs Duexbury? Don't talk to me about Mrs Duexbury. I 'ave nothing to say about Mrs Duexbury."

"Gaw, it's not boggarts!" old Jack Widdison insisted. "Nor any other foolishness. 'Tis men as caused Mr Lister's death and men as made mischief in't stables and big 'ouse. I said as opening t' mound 'ud bring trouble, but not 'cause of t' soo-per-natural. We 'as enough troubles wi'out t' divvil getting involved. But that dig as caused so much bad feeling in't village an' came t' nowt, that were t' start on it. 'There'll be trouble,' says I, and lo, we 'as fires and rackets and things gone astray, and then we 'as bloody murther! Aye, I found t' mess i' tack room, but that were no bogie or moors-knocker. That were a bloke as needs a thrashing."

"Hardly knew Mr Lister," Carl Ophelia declared, "'cept that 'e gave me orders about the 'orses and yard. Saw and 'eard some of the strange events, and I was one of the men on guard some nights. Me mum thinks it was unquiet spirits. She's chapel but I'm not really a believer. 'Er and Sukie are both a bit gullible like that—too gullible. I've been watching to see 'oo's not about and 'oo is when trouble 'appens, not but what things 'aven't gone quiet since Mr Lister turned up dead. I'm watching Lewis Wilson, the jockey, specially 'ard. There's something about 'im. I didn't get on with the fellow afore 'im, but Wilson… well, I don't like t' turn my back on the man."

"Carl Ophelia's a cheat and a liar," Lewis Wilson countered when we saw the jockey. "'E cheats at cards and I reckon as 'e's leading young Sukie on. 'E got the fellow before me sacked, an' I reckon it was 'cause Ophelia owned 'im money. Lister? Well, 'e 'ad a nasty temper. Beat that page lad something cruel when 'is clock vanished. Dismissed one of the maids on evidence as wouldn't hang a dog. But he got 'is comeuppance with the hill-spectres. 'E were a different man after that. I didn't think 'ed ever venture onto those moors again. Why would he? But 'e did—and that were the end of 'im!"

"I dunno," the groom George Sutton told us. It seemed to be his favourite word. "It's all a mickle mystery. I was there a-watching out all t' night and I 'ears the noises but I sees nowt. I dunno but it must be bogies. I've nivver known owt like it, sirs. I've been 'ere since Fred Clough were let go, an' it's not what you'd call an 'appy place. Fred? 'E's working over Manchester way now, pore soul.[53] As to why Mr Lister went back oop t' 'ill, well… I reckon the giants must uv called 'im. No other reason, is there? Trick o' t' light? Aye, some says that, but I dunno…"

"I 'ope y' don't mind me callin' you like this, sir," Samuel Rudd repeated to Holmes as he had when we had first arrived. "It's just that it's so murky, an' I bethought, 'Well, Sam, 'oo could ivver get to t' bottom o' this? So I wrote."

"And right you were to bring me in," Sherlock Holmes assured the stableman. "The matter is hardly complex but it offers a patina of interest that diverts me from a recent failure. You brought me my telegrams from Ilkley? Splendid. Now we shall progress towards a solution."

We arrived at Mrs Duexbury's house in time for high tea. "Your recent opening of the cairn near the Great Skirtful has been rather controversial," Holmes began as he sipped his Oolong.

That was enough to set the lady into a long recitation of grievances, about who had said what in the village, about the complaints from vicar and Methodist minister, about what some grouse-hunting colonel had demanded, about letters of protest from people who had never even been to

53   Manchester is in Lancashire, the neighbouring county and great rival to Yorkshire, which is why Fred, forced to work there, had George Sutton's sympathies.

the shire. That led her to discussion of Hogarth Lister, whom she described in a manner that suggested any affection she might have felt for him had significantly cooled. "I had thought him a gentleman," Mrs Duexbury sniffed when I dared broach that topic, "but I was proved wrong."

"How did you come to this understanding?" I asked.

"I received a visit from... an individual who appraised me of some of Mr Lister's personal failings. Then I felt rather foolish for supporting him in the matter of opening the tumulus in the face of local opposition. And for... considering any suit he may have brought."

"This individual informed you of an infidelity that brought Lister's character into disrepute," Holmes observed, telling rather than asking. "Did you inform Mr Lister of what you had learned?"

"The information was confidential, but I was able to verify it. I merely told Hogarth—that is, Mr Lister—that I was not minded to receive him on the same terms as before."

"This would be on or just before Saturday the 7th," Holmes supposed. To me he explained, "The date that Mrs Duexbury's book was shredded and burned. May we assume that this particular event was not initiated by the ghost? Young Larry Tope discovered the volume in the hearth and drew an erroneous conclusion,"

"Mr Lister was not pleased at my rejection," Mrs Duexbury admitted.

"You took his dog in," I observed.

"I saw no need for Punch to suffer abandonment as well."

"Did you have any further communication with Lister after the 7th?" Holmes checked. "You sent no message?"

"I did not. I was done with him. I had not previously understood the viciousness and intensity of his temper, nor the core meanness of his personality. I consider myself fortunately warned."

Burley Woodhead not being large enough even to have its own constable, our last visit of the day was to the police house in Burley-in-Wharfdale. Inspector Shotley met us there to hear what progress Holmes had made in a case that seemed impenetrable to the rustic officer. "I'm not even sure but it's not a matter for the church rather than the constabulary," he confessed to us.

"I think we can avoid a liturgy of exorcism," Holmes assured him. "There were from the start a number of features that helped distinguish between diablerie and the merely diabolic. Any evil here comes from wholly mortal roots. I refer you to the following facts: that disturbances at Stephill took place both inside and beyond the big house, but never on a Sunday; that a bag of aniseed was buried where the barrow had been opened; that Burley Woodhead is a small insular village in a tightly-knit community; that Mrs Duexbury turned down Mr Lister on discovering something from a third party; that Mr Lister's mother's clock was moved and then vanished; and that the ghost was attracted to Mr Lister's spoons."

"How can any of that untangle this mess?" Shotley demanded in gruff frustration.

"Holmes can find sense where the rest of us founder in supposition and confusion," I warranted my friend.

The great detective responded modestly with an acknowledging bow. "There are a few more details I must confirm," he told us. "I am awaiting a message from Lister's man of business in York, and another from the County Registrar. Then I will tell you who murdered the Brocken Spectre and why, and we may bring Hogarth Lister's killers to justice."

We returned to Stephill Farm, and Holmes spoke to Sukie as she took our coats. "Let Mrs Ophelia and Mr Slaiththwaite know that all the staff must gather here at eight-thirty sharp tomorrow. I have an announcement and will be setting the ghosts of Burley Woodhead to rest." To me he added, "The information I expect from my long-range enquiries will be here by then, and I will have all the proof I require to offer you answers to this elementary little puzzle."

We retired to the parlour, where a fire had been set because of the unseasonal chill, and we watched the sun set over Rombald's Moor. "Whatever happened to old Rombald when his wife caught him?" I pondered. "Or is he still running?"

"We have seen spouses do dire things *in extremis*, Watson, and go to significant lengths to avoid being caught for it," Holmes reminded me. "Domestic disputes can raise the very devil. Ah, Betty, thank you." The parlour-maid had brought us our evening toddies.

"Are you able to tell me who and what you suspect yet, Holmes?" I ventured. "I know that you affect the showman's preference for the grand reveal, some habit from your days treading the boards,[54] but pity the poor

---

54   Baring-Gould's Holmes biography reveals Holmes's travels as part of Michael Sasanoff's theatre troupe in 1879-80, including an American tour where "Holmes's Malvolio offered the most adequate presentation of that character that America had ever seen up to

fellow who has to write an account of this. At least tell me the significance of the spoons."

Betty left us alone watching the darkening Yorkshire wilds. Holmes offered me one piece of important advice and then noted, "I am reminded of a case from 1716, recorded by none other than the founder of Methodism the Reverend John Wesley, who experienced events similar to those at Stephill as a boy growing up in his family home at Epworth, Lincolnshire. Wesley's father, the parish vicar, was unpopular in the neighbourhood because of his support of legislation that would drain the local fens, depriving many men of their lucrative smuggling side-trade. For two months the family endured a persecution of supposed knocking spirits, of petty mischiefs attributed to phantoms, and of all the trappings of a fine rural ghost story. The Wesleys' accounts are perhaps the most comprehensive study of such events ever to be committed to paper."[55]

"You draw parallels with the apparent hauntings here at Stephill?"

"Indeed. An unpopular 'outcomer' moves to a lonely pastoral setting and comes into conflict with the denizens. Attempts are made to frighten him, to drive him away. The question is why. In Samuel Wesley's case it was almost certainly because of his political views. Here the matter is more personal: the assault upon the shaving kit, for example. Then there was the vanishing of Lister's mother's clock, an object which was precious

that time." Baring-Gould attributes Holmes's predilection to quoting Shakespeare to this period of the great detective's life.

[55] Diaries and essays from several family members and visitors chronicle the poltergeist-like events witnessed by 13-year-old John Wesley in 1716.

John Wesley reported, "My father was thrice pushed by an invisible power, once against the corner of his bed, then against the door of the matted chamber, a third time against his study door. His dog always gave warning by running whining towards him, though he no longer barked at it as he did the first time."

John's mother Susannah Wesley wrote, "One night it made such a noise in the room over our heads as if several people were walking; then run up and down the stairs, and was so outrageous that we thought the children would be frightened, so your father and I rose and went down in the dark to light a candle. Just as we came to the bottom of the broad stairs, having hold of each other, on my side there seemed as if somebody had emptied a bag of money at my feet and on his as if all the bottles under the stairs (which were many) had been dashed into a thousand pieces [...] Sometimes it would make a noise like the winding up of a jack; at other times, as that night Mr. Hoole was with us, like a carpenter planning deals; but mostly commonly it knocked three and stopped and then thrice again and so many hours together."

There are several good summaries of the incidents. I.A. Watson's monograph on the topic appears in his essay book *Where Stories Dwell* (2014, Pro Se Press, ISBN 10: 1500666173).

to him; perhaps a caution that he was running out of time. The recurring tampering with the spoons is the key to the case, of course, and I have the advantage of having corresponded with Hogarth Lister's man of business regarding that matter."

"The man mentioned cutlery?"

"He was able to tell me that some thirty-three years ago Lister acrimoniously dismissed a staff member for the theft of some silver spoons. She denied the allegations but was released without references, with a stain upon her character."

"Lister was a fellow prone to jumping to conclusions and punishing his domestics with little evidence," I noted. I doubt I would have got on with the man in life.

"At Epworth Rectory I would have begun by reviewing where any perpetrator of the ghost's tricks must have been located to perform his hauntings. Since some things happened inside the house and others outside I would have begun with the hypothesis that at least two persons were involved, one with access to the family—or one of the family—and another able to approach the house in the darkness to work mischief outside."

"Here we have had events inside and others in the stables," I recognised. "And presumably someone rattling shutters and disturbing to roof. That speaks to more than one hoaxer."

"There was always likely to be more, Watson. It takes a pair to project two Brocken spectres."

"But one killed the other. Lister witnessed it."

"Did he? Think on the occasion. Lister was following his regular and fixed routine, walking his dog. He was delayed until the sun was right at the excavated barrow. Punch was fascinated by the dig and would not come away."

I puzzled as to how Holmes might deduce this, then remembered his discovery. "The aniseed bag! Dogs react to it as a cat does to catnip! She would have been hard to drag away from that spot. And that put Lister in the exact and only place where he might witness the cloud giants."

"Who is to say that the cairn was not put there those thousands of years ago to mark the precise place where such encounters occurred? But watch."

Holmes held his hands so that the lamp projected their shadows onto the parlour wall. He seemed in silhouette to stab two fingers of the right hand into the left, but I could see that his hands were six inches apart, one behind the other.

"Two actors might mime an assault, were they both lined up with the rising sun," I realised. "What Lister took for a vision of murder may have been another charade to scare him."

"Much of the pantomime here seems to have been intended as a message: 'Do the right thing at last', or 'Your sins will find you out'. Almost all the most distinctive hauntings were directed at the old man personally, right up to the ransacking of his study—though that may have had a secondary reason. Lister's will is missing."

"His will? Why would…?"

"Murder was the final resort," Holmes suggested. "When ghostly raps would not suffice to make Lister relent, the phantoms became more imaginative. At last they deployed the giants of the moor to give their warning. When that failed to move the victim they had to arrange his demise."

"But how would they lure Lister back to the moors after his previous fright?"

"There are several ways, but the most likely would be a simple ruse. Perhaps a message came, supposedly from Mrs Duexbury, seeking a reconciliation, a secret dawn meeting at the Great Skirtful? There are other possibilities; I do not insist upon that interpretation."

"You sound to have already decided who the murderer is, Holmes."

"It was always only a matter of gathering evidence to prove a theory, Watson. But now we must retire. We may expect a long and interrupted night."

I smelled smoke around five in the morning. When I rose to investigate I found the corridor and landing thick with fume.

Holmes appeared from his chamber. Like me he was full dressed, ready for adventure.

"If you are right about our bedtime drinks," I told him, "then we have just survived a murder attempt. If we had been drugged insensible then we would be smothered by smoke inhalation."

We wrapped scarves across our lower faces and plunged through the fumes to find the source of the fire. A blaze had been started in Lister's ground floor study, directly below the rooms where Holmes and I had been lodged. Some accelerant—Holmes believed it was stable paraffin—had been used to hasten and magnify the blaze.

I sounded the alarm, pounding on the dinner gong to warn the house-hold of the danger. I judged that the fire was too well set to douse now. It would claim the big house.

Holmes counted out the bleary, surprised staff. Woken by my alarum, the stable crew began to appear, clamouring to see what could be done in the way of fire-fighting.

"We are missing Betty," Holmes alerted me. "Come, Watson, we must venture back upstairs. Rudd, it's too late for a bucket chain. Evacuate everybody to the stable tack room. Send Sutton to summon Inspector Shotley and the police fire-watch."

With these words he plunged back into the smoke, making for the attic where the parlour maid slept. I surged after him, trying to hold my breath as we passed through the worst of the fire-fumes.

We used the servant's steps to reach the attic. Flames were licking at the stair treads as we chased up them. Holmes quickly found the room where Betty Coombe was quartered.

I half expected the girl not to be there. It was she who had brought us our toddies, the drink that Holmes had warned me not to consume. "Kitchen staff may add all kinds of things to their preparations," he had cautioned. "Who can now say what hallucinogen Lister had ingested on the day he encountered Brocken Spectres?"

But Betty lay there, unconscious, either from the thick vapours that now choked the upper floors of the house or for more sinister reasons. She too had drunk a bedtime cup. I checked her pulse and found it, though it was thready.

Holmes hoisted her across his shoulder in a fireman's lift. We groped our way back along the passage, escaping down the main stair which had not yet been consumed by the spreading conflagration.

It felt icy cold outside the house, away from the flames. Rudd and Slaithwaite were watching in consternation as the building went up. They hastened forward to help us carry Betty to the distant tack room.

I did a quick check of who was there. Of the staff, George Sutton and Carl Ophelia had gone for aid but the others were all present.

"What 'appened to Betty?" Rudd asked urgently.

"She has been drugged," I opined. "The same narcotic was meant to se-date Holmes and I, so that we all died in that fire. Somebody heard Holmes announce that he was ready to reveal Lister's murderer, and therefore took decisive action."

"I might have preferred a less pyrotechnic way of dispatching me," the detective added. "I am sorry to have endangered the rest of you. I had not realised how damaged Mrs Ophelia was."

The housekeeper startled as she was named. "Me? The fire never touched me."

"But Hogarth Lister did," Holmes revealed. "Thirty-three years ago, when you were in service to him under a different name. His man of business remembers it all. How you claimed he had married you, but the certificate was false, the wedding a sham. How you were with child. But then you were accused of theft and dismissed without reference, pregnant, disgraced, and forgotten."

"I don't know what you're on about," Mrs Ophelia protested.

"Come, now," Holmes chided her. "A pious woman who would not allow the haunting to happen on Sundays and holy days should not resort to falsehoods. It is time for the truth—Anna Siddle."

Mrs Ophelia blanched at the name. "You'd think a man would remember a woman 'oo's child 'e fathered, 'oo's life 'e ruined," she spat. "But I suppose I've changed a lot over thirty 'ard desperate years, doing as I 'ad to t' bring up a son."

Sukie's eyes went wide. "You can't tell 'un...!" she blurted.

"She need not. It is evident," Holmes declared. "When appeals for support and attempts at blackmail failed, Mrs Ophelia and her lad took service in Lister's own household,. The previous housekeeper had resigned in protest at Lister's treatment of Betty, and Lister sought to escape the growing rumours of his behaviour by rusticating to the country."

I realised what had happened. "And Lister brought the Ophelias along! With the mother in the kitchen, preparing all food, and with access to keys, and the son in the stables able to roam freely at night, they were well set to go into the haunting business."

Holmes crooked a long finger at the housekeeper. "'God has given you one face, and you make yourself another,'[56] Mrs Ophelia."

"It were you?" Slaithwaite demanded, pointing an accusing finger at the snarling woman.

"Not her and Carl alone. More agents make for better alibis and a far better ghost story. That's why Carl had to suborn Sukie, so that a young and inexperienced maid in her first service would add her efforts to the spookery. And why Alice Champion's aggrieved family were probably

---

56   Holmes quotes *Hamlet, Prince of Denmark*, Act 1 Scene III, where Hamlet rages at Ophelia, accusing her of corruption. The maiden in the play has cause to feel betrayed and abandoned by the prince who had formerly courted her, and at his rejection she runs mad and eventually kills herself.

" 'God has given you one face, and you make yourself another.' "

engaged to avenge their kinwoman's dismissal. The Champions and the Murgatroyds are allied by marriage several times, I believe."

Sukie trembled, her eyes flicking from Mrs Ophelia to Holmes. "I nivver thowt t' kill no-one!" she promised. "It were just t' skeer t' nasty owd man so's 'e'd do right by Carl. Nivver a penny's inheritance! Nivver an acknowledgement of 'is own lad! But—" She cast an anguished, betrayed look at the housekeeper.

"Lister seems to have done a dirty trick on you long ago," I told Mrs Ophelia. "But you have committed murder."

"Her and Carl, miming on the hill," Holmes agreed, "and then when even the Brocken Spectres did not move Lister to honesty, the message luring him onto the moors again, to make the prophetic vision come true."

Mrs Ophelia was defiant, even venomous. "Saying it's one thing. Proving it's another!"

"The only other victims of your campaign were those whom you saw as rivals," Holmes went on. "The maggots in Betty's bed, were they to drive her away from an abusive employer or to punish her for succumbing to the same pressures as you once did? Did she suspect too much, living and working beside you these months, that she had to be disposed of as Watson and I were to have been? Did she know that you had sneaked a copy of Lister's study key so you might find, perhaps substitute, his last will and testament? And of course it was you, not Betty, who revealed the truth of Lister's character to Mrs Duexbury."

"All supposition," Mrs Ophelia crowed.

She was no match for Sherlock Holmes. "Your true identity can be verified. Watson and I have samples of the drinks you prepared for us. When she wakes, Betty can testify as to who prepared the toddies. And I doubt that Sukie here will withhold much once she is interviewed by Inspector Shotley."

"Carl Ophelia!" I cried. "He went to fetch the police!"

"Sutton went for't bobbies," Slaithwaite corrected me. "Ophelia went t' get 'elp from t' other farms."

"Or t' flee away ovver t' moors," Rudd added wrathfully.

"I hope he does," Mrs Ophelia snarled. "I 'ope you never catch 'im."

There was more leg-work to be done, detail to verify, but that was routine that Inspector Shotley's investigation could pursue. Mrs Ophelia—Anna Siddle as she had been when she was a young, naïve girl who had believed herself lawfully and fortunately wed to coal tycoon Hogarth Lister—had lived a difficult and disreputable life, as any woman cast out without reputation or family and with a child swelling her belly might suffer. Sukie Murgatroyd, her head turned by the glamour of an older city suitor, would quickly confess her misdeeds. The surly Champions would confess too; they had intended mischief, not murder.

But Carl Ophelia was gone. The man who had met Lister alone at the Skirtful of Stones and battered him to death for his mother's sake was fled over the moors.

"Ah doubt it," old Jack Widdison told us. "Not 'afore dawn coomes oop. It's not easy ta flit o'a t' moors by neet. It's not safe, all scars and sikes, an' t' boggarts dooan't like it!"

"It's not easy," I agreed. "Not when one is being pursued by Sherlock Holmes."

We set off at first light, when Shotley had brought men to douse the big house blaze and to begin the manhunt for Ophelia. Holmes led Rudd and one group up past the tarn to the low ridge track, while I took Shotley, Slaithwaite and others by the high ridge. We climbed through the mist, aware that the damp clinging fog might obscure a fugitive only yards away from us.

As the sun rose before us, I saw for the second time that strange, eerie phenomenon of the Brocken Spectre surrounded by its rainbow glory. Holmes had achieved the same spot as we had occupied before, and it was the great detective's distinctive giant silhouette that loomed huge on the grey westward clouds. He rose vast and implacable, a titan of justice, and I felt a pang of pity for Carl Ophelia or any wrongdoer who saw him approaching.

I often wonder if that Spectre was the last thing that the hunted man ever saw. It was my search party who found him, fallen into one of the grouse buts not far from the Little Skirtful. His neck was broken.

To Slaithwaite, Widdison, and Sutton, the ancient giants of Rombald's Moor had claimed their vengeance.

The Woman Who Collected Sherlock Holmes

From the Diary of Miss Alexandra Doré, Tuesday February 25th, 1894:

I travelled up to London to lunch with John, it being the second anniversary of Mary's death. I know well how he broods on such memorials—how clearly I remember his stoic misery on the 4th of May last year[57]—and insisted that he meet me at Simpson's on the Strand for a proper meal. He assumed that I had come again to pester him with questions about Sherlock Holmes, and I did not disabuse him of his belief; he finds some comfort in reminiscences of his old friend, as attested by his obsessive writings, and it is no hardship to hear about the cases they shared together.

I ventured to suggest that we might rendezvous on some occasion when we were not commemorating such losses—John has so many of them it breaks my heart—and was not rebuffed. Perhaps I shall find excuse to visit the capital on business again in a few weeks time and see if I can coax the good doctor into some gayer mood?

From the Notes of John H. Watson M.D.:

I was joined for lunch again by Miss Alexandra Doré, whom Holmes and I had encountered after her apparent murder some years before, and who still called upon me occasionally when business compelled her up to the city. We met as we were accustomed to at Simpson's, where they keep an excellent grill, to catch up on each other's news.

"I suppose you are still collecting Holmes," I guyed her. Miss Doré was formerly a notable collector of Victoriana, with a small museum in her front parlour dedicated to sculptures, pamphlets, Toby jugs, and knick-knacks with the image of Her Majesty upon them. The lady had moved on from that passion, though, and now she retained an assembly of items

---

57   That is, the second anniversary of Sherlock Holmes's final encounter with James Moriarty at the Falls of Reichenbach, at which Holmes was presumed to have died; described in "The Final Problem", *The Memoirs of Sherlock Holmes* (1893 but dated 1894).

connected to the cases of Sherlock Holmes.[58]

"I did bring along a few items for your consideration," she admitted. "I did not like to pester you at our last meeting, but if you are able to presently review the things in my carpet-bag I would be gratified." She hesitated then added, "I have taken the great liberty of engaging a private lounge for us to use after our luncheon, so that you can see what I have acquired."

Miss Doré had a charming smile, and knew it. No gentleman could deny such an invitation. Besides, the alternative was a dreary afternoon of medical casework, sorting through files for my moribund Kensington practice.[59]

We had a pleasant meal discussing matters of the day: the resignation of Lord Gladstone,[60] the Dark Blues' fifth consecutive victory in the Boat Race,[61] Waterhouse's painting of 'The Lady of Shalott', now acquired for the National Gallery,[62] and the forthcoming World's Fair to be demon-

58   The episode to which Dr Watson refers was included in *Sherlock Holmes Consulting Detective* volume 13, in I.A. Watson's "The Woman Who Collected Queen Victoria".

59   Most Holmes chronologies list that Dr Watson purchased a small medical practice in Kensington, London in late 1886, probably shortly into his first marriage, and sold it again around a year later following the death of the first Mrs Watson, whereafter he returned to Baker Street. During his second marriage (to Mary Morstan from *The Sign of Four*) from May 1889 he "bought a connection in the Paddington district"—that is, purchased a share in a group general medical practice. In June 1891, shortly after Holmes's apparent death and possibly with Mary's health declining, he sold this share and repurchased his former, smaller, Kensington practice, so as to spend more time on his writing. He retained this surgery until May 1894, whereupon he sold the practice to young Dr Verner for his first asking price, not knowing at the time that the purchaser was a relative of Holmes's and being funded by the detective so that Watson could afford to comfortably retire back to Baker Street.

60   The venerable Conservative politician took the post of Prime Minister for the fourth time in 1892, aged 82, and resigned two years later, ostensibly on health grounds, after failing to pass key reform legislation, prevent the introduction of new taxes, or oppose military expansion. He was succeeded by Archibald Primrose, 5th Earl of Rosebery who formed a minority Liberal Party government.

61   The annual Thames Boat Race is a traditional fixture between the teams from the Universities of Oxford ('the Dark Blues') and Cambridge ('the Light Blues'). The 51st match, held on 22nd March 1894, was accounted an easy victory for Oxford, who won by 3½ lengths in 21 minutes 39 seconds.

62   In 1894, John William Waterhouse's first painting (of three) of the character from Tennyson's Arthurian poem was acquired by philanthropist Sir Henry Tate for display in the National Gallery of British Art (nowadays called the Tate Gallery).

strated in Chicago, which Miss Doré would have liked to have visited had she known of a suitable travelling companion.

When we retired to Miss Doré's salon she opened her capacious travelling case and produced a portion of her collection for my examination. First out were copies of *Harper's Weekly* and *The Strand Magazine* for September and October 1893, containing "The Adventure of the Greek Interpreter" and "The Adventure of the Naval Treaty". Miss Doré, a woman of delicacy and insight, had kindly omitted the December *Strand* that contained my account of "The Final Problem", Holmes's last case.[63]

"You will sign these editions, even if you will not set your name to the work in print," she commanded me.

I explained that I preferred to leave the hard work of authorship to my literary agent Doyle, but the lady would have none of it. "But you have published nothing this year," she noted. "You meant it when you said you were finished writing your Holmes accounts."[64]

"It was beginning to feel morbid," I owned. "I should not have written of Holmes's death at all, except that the libellous and disingenuous accounts of Colonel Moriarty regarding his sinister brother had to be countered. But once I had written that case up, I felt I was done."

Miss Doré looked stricken. "I did not think to raise unhappy memories, John. I would not thinkingly cause you pain! Shall I put these silly things away and—?"

I hastened to assure her that there was a world of difference between a reading public complaining for want of more of Holmes's exploits (and complaining publishers haranguing my poor editor) and a much-welcomed visit from a lady who wished to review her more recent acquisitions of Holmes memorabilia.

"Then I shall show what I have collected, like a schoolgirl in class," she told me.

"You remain fixed, then, in your passion to 'collect' Sherlock Holmes?"

"I find the hobby much more satisfying than arguing with obscure experts over the provenance of Dresden figurines. And so far nobody has threatened my death for it—unless I try your patience too hard?"

I assured her that she would never inconvenience me with conversation about my dear friend. "We are both alike admirers of that great man."

---

63   This story was also published at the same time in *McClure's Magazine*.

64   In "The Final Problem," Watson had begun, "It is with a heavy heart that I take up my pen to write these the last words in which I shall ever record the singular gifts by which my friend Mr. Sherlock Holmes was distinguished."

"Then see here: a bond certificate prepared by the forger Stamford,"[65] she told me proudly, proffering a fine elaborately-printed sheet announcing it to be issued by the Bayern und Bamberg Königliche Bank with a redemption value of 500 marks. "It's a beautiful piece, don't you think?"

"As a work of art it has merit," I admitted. "As an instrument of finance it is not worth the paper on which it is printed."

"It is worth something to me," Miss Doré promised, "and shall be framed upon the wall of my collection. Now this item is somewhat more sinister…"

I recognised a medical drug-case but had to be told that it was formerly property of the poisoner Morgan.[66]

"And this thing?" she quizzed me, demonstrating the battered old smoking pipe.

"I confess that one pipe is much like another to me," I admitted. I am no Holmes.

"You have seen this one before. It was left by mistake at your Baker Street lodgings by Mr Grant Munro, from which Holmes deduced so much, at the beginning of 'The Adventure of the Yellow Face'.[67] It was donated for my collection by Mrs Monroe, with whom I have corresponded."

"I am alarmed that you were able to identify the lady and contact her. I went to pains in my account to conceal her identity."

"And I shall maintain that confidentiality. Piercing your façade of obfuscation is all part of the Great Game, you know! But you offer anonymity where it is best, and I would never wish to thwart that, John, never."

"I also recall Holmes deducing that the misplaced pipe was much-loved, having been mended rather than replaced."

Miss Doré shrugged, apologetically, charmingly. "Effie Monroe has convinced her husband to give up tobacco. I am only doing my part in assisting his resolution."

---

65   This case was publicly mentioned in "The Adventure of the Solitary Cyclist", first published in *The Strand Magazine* and *Collier's* in December of 1903 and collected in *The Return of Sherlock Holmes* (1905) , so Miss Doré must have heard of the forger from some other source, either newspaper accounts, collected testimonies, or in conversation with Dr Watson himself.

66   Morgan was only mentioned in Canon in "The Adventure of the Empty House", *The Return of Sherlock Holmes* (1905), collected from *The Strand Magazine* and *Colliers'* editions of September 1903, but the story in which he is name-checked, which describes the return of Holmes after his seeming-death at Reichenbach Falls is set in 1894.

67   "The Adventure of the Yellow Face" was collected in *The Memoirs of Sherlock Holmes* (1893).

I recalled comments made to me on a previous occasion by another lady who did not appreciate my smoking, and became sober for a moment.

Miss Doré evidently read it. She pushed quickly on, digging deeper into her carpet-bag. "Here is a door-plaque for The Red-Headed League. Here a business card for the devious Mr Arthur Pinner—I have one of his brother's cards at home.[68] Here the very bible used by the confidence trickster 'Reverend' Terrace Crouch.[69] As you see, I have been quite busy expanding my collection." She smiled prettily. "Your own little contribution, the traced sides of the Jhansi treasure manuscript, has a pride of place, of course."[70]

"I was pleased to pander to your obsession," I assured her.

"Here is a melancholy artefact," Miss Doré warned me sadly. "It is a certificate of death by suicide. You might recognise the name."

I looked at the document, written in French, but could easily discern the person for whom it had been issued some three years before in March 1891. "Miss Mary Holder. The niece of financier Alexander Holder of Holder & Stevenson, Threadneedle Street."

"You wrote of her in The Strand Magazine in May of 1892, using a pseudonym to preserve her anonymity. As well you might, given her part in "The Adventure of the Beryl Coronet." She was traduced by a blaggard who convinced her to aid him in stealing the valuable treasure, and with whom she eloped. Sherlock Holmes predicted that she would soon receive more than sufficient punishment for her sins—and she did!"

"You traced her, then? I *must* disguise my characters a little more carefully."

"You cannot be faulted on this occasion, John. Miss Holder revealed her identity and whereabouts to me three years back, shortly after her disap-

68   A confidence trickster using the names of supposed brothers Arthur and Harry Pinner took advantage of the clerk Hall Pycroft in "The Adventure of the Stockbroker's Clerk" in *The Memoirs of Sherlock Holmes* (1893)

69   "The Red-Headed League" is discovered in *The Adventures of Sherlock Holmes* (1891). The sinister Culverton-Smith crossed Holmes's path in "The Adventure of the Dying Detective" published in *The Strand Magazine* and *Colliers'* in November 1913 and collected in *His Last Bow* (1917), but the events of that story are generally placed in November 1887, less than a months after the affair of the Red-Headed League. Holmes's brief brush with 'the Reverend' remained unpublished until I.A. Watson recovered it for "The Problem of the Western Mail" in *Sherlock Holmes Consulting Detective* volume 2 (2011), compiled in *Sherlock Holmes Mysteries* volume 1 (2015).

70   Holmes awarded this souvenir to Watson on completion of the investigation chronicled by I.A. Watson in "Dead Man's Manuscript" in *Sherlock Holmes Consulting Detective* volume 1 (2010), compiled in *Sherlock Holmes Mysteries* volume 1 (2015).

pearance. A letter that came from Marseilles, France, from the unfortunate young woman herself. She had eloped with her lover two months before. They had evidently fled England ahead of arresting policemen and travelled through France together, sometimes under assumed names. Her account was a sorry litany of abuses and degradations under the control of the vile Sir George Burnwell; at last the wicked villain abandoned her altogether, having determined that there was no more value or virtue he might wring from her."

"There are some bounders who need thrashing before they are hanged," I noted.

"Her letter contained a number of unpleasant details of the ways that Sir George expected to finance their travels, and of the methods he used to convince Miss Holder to compliance. I need not repeat them here. Suffice that by the end of February of 1891, scarcely two months after their absconding, the couple had parted ways, Sir George leaving his mistress in a foreign town to bear responsibility for their considerable debts, having apparently contracted her services to an unpleasant *maison de tolérance*[71] from which she found it impossible to depart."

"The girl made a very poor choice to select the cad over her cousin who doted on her. She never thought to contact her family and plead for forgiveness and return?"

"If she tried then she made no mention of it in her correspondence. She wrote to me at the beginning of March, having somehow learned of my interest in Holmesiana, thinking I might purchase her account of her theft of the beryl coronet on behalf of her lover, and of what subsequently became of her. She seemed to feel as if I would wish to hear the terrible litany of things that she endured at the hands of that awful man—and might pay to know them!"

"You are not one to revel in the sordid or distasteful, Alexandra," I consoled the collector.

"Certainly not in the confession she sent to me three years ago. I consider myself a woman of the world, having travelled and read extensively and, as you know, having survived an adventure through means of my wits. What Miss Holder wrote shocked and appalled me; there is a grimy underbelly to society that I am pleased to have never encountered. She supposed that I would send her 'what her story was worth' for a testimony that was 'more explicit and detailed' than what she had included in her letter—as if that were possible—when actually her ordeals left me sick to the stomach."

---

71   Legal French brothel.

I assured Miss Doré that I would expect nothing else with a lady of her quality and virtues. She was a good-looking unmarried woman of considerable fortune who had been wise in avoiding charming fortune-hunters, thought it was not appropriate for me to comment on it to her.

"I would not purchase any such account from lost Mary Holder," she went on, "but in charity I wired back the sum of £100[72] to Marseilles, to support a lost soul back to humanity.

"That was kindness. How did you determine that she was not simply playing a confidence trick on you, bilking you for a handout?"

"I could not know for certain, of course. But the catalogue of horrors that wayward girl had endured seemed very authentic to me, and I was unwilling to turn aside completely from such a wounded creature. I made clear in my return letter that I would offer no other support afterwards, however." Miss Doré looked down at the certificate I held. "But I delayed making my reply while I wrestled with my feelings on her. I regret that now."

"You could not know that she would take her life."

"I understand why she might. From the date on that document, I see that she must have given up on that same day that I posted my careful response to her with the banker's certification note. She need have only collected my bequest at a local bank, but of course the money was never claimed. At the time I did not trouble to check if the bequest had been used—I assumed it would be. It was only later that I realised the order had never been cashed. She was dead before it arrived."

"And that was the last you heard about the poor woman?"

"Until I saw her obituary in one of the bundles of clippings that I pay an agent a small sum to collate for me, and I recognised her name. But it proved remarkably difficult to acquire this copy of Mary Holder's death certificate. The French do love their bureaucracy, and of course I could not claim to be a relative. It has taken me the better part of three years to acquire this piece of penance."

"Penance?"

Miss Doré sighed. "I would not usually add so morbid an item as a death certificate to my museum, but I sought this copy to serve as a reminder to me; had I taken a more active interest in the fate and future of

---

72   In 1891 terms this was equivalent to the average annual wage of a working-class man or around seven months' wages for a middle-class clerk. A lady or gentleman of the upper class might spend ten or twelve times that amount each year in living expenses, so Miss Doré was effectively donating a month's-worth of her income to Miss Holder.

the unfortunate Miss Holder, had I replied to her plea even one day sooner, might she have avoided the dark path that led her to self-destruction?"

I shook my head. "Your conscience does you credit, Alexandra, but you need not hold yourself to account. Miss Holder was a foolish child destroyed by an experienced seducer who set his sights on her as a means of stealing an object of great value from her uncle's household. The blame lies squarely on Sir George Burnwell, a black knight if ever there was one. I would like to find him and pay back something of the misery he has caused!"

My lunch companion blinked in surprise, and looked away.

"What is it?" I asked.

"Nothing," Miss Doré answered. "Only, I had supposed…"

"Supposed what?" I prompted.

She clasped her hands to her forehead. "I am a great fool, John. I would not for the world upset your memories and affections of Sherlock Holmes. May we let the subject pass?"

"I would rather understand what distresses you, and what it was you erroneously supposed, which has so affected you. However might you upset my affections for Holmes?"

The lady sipped her tea but her hand trembled on the cup. She forced herself to calm and looked me in the eye. "I can tell I am making a hash of this. I apologise. I had not intended our pleasant reminiscence to take this turn. Are you sure I should speak?"

"I would prefer it."

"Then you should know—I thought you *must* know—that Sir George Burnwell is dead."

"Dead?" It was the first I had heard of it. "How? When?"

"I have seen his obituary also. He was murdered, in Narbonne on 12th March 1891, four days after Mary Holder hanged herself."

"I can't say I'll mourn the fellow. But…" I thought back to three years since, to that quiet time when I had enjoyed married life but saw little of Holmes. He had spent most of the first months of his last year alive overseas and all I had from him were letters from his travels: Copenhagen, Stockholm, Paris, and then a pause until notes came to me from Narbonne and Nimes.[73]

Narbonne… "Holmes was in Narbonne," I recalled.

---

73   In "The Final Problem" Holmes returns from overseas sometime before 24th April 1891, having been "of assistance to the royal family of Scandinavia, and to the French republic".

"Yes. Some affair for the French Government, for which he was awarded a posthumous honour—for services they failed to specify. Did he not describe it to you?"

"Holmes was sworn to secrecy on the matter. I suspect it may have been some other aspect of his campaign against James Moriarty. The battle between them was fought on many fronts, for all of that evil old man's empire had to be rolled up entirely and simultaneously. Certainly the Professor's reach extended across much of Europe, and not least to the Republic of France."

"I made some checks," Miss Doré told me. "Mr Holmes was in Narbonne on March the 11th and 12th."

"He was in the town when Burnwell died."

"When Burnwell was murdered. I have the French papers' report of Sir George's inquest. He was beaten most severely before he died of two 'expert shots' through the centre of the forehead. It was reported that there were no clues to indicate who had killed him. The coroner remarked on it."

"You believe that Holmes dispensed rough justice on the man who had driven Miss Holder to death? And you assumed that I knew of it."

"I see now that you did not. I am sorry that I ever let it slip."

I shook my head. "I doubt that Holmes would resort to such an act. Besides, he had given Burnwell his word that there would be no prosecution if he revealed where he had sold on the stones he had Mary steal for him. The bounder confessed and Holmes allowed him to flee."

"Two shots though the head are not prosecution. Nor did Mr Holmes offer an immunity for the uses to which the man had put Miss Holder."

"There are many other ways that a blighter like Burnwell could come to a bad end without Sherlock Holmes's involvement. Holmes's presence nearby might be mere coincidence."

Miss Doré allowed that it might, but the conversation hung a shadow over our meeting. She showed me the rest of her finds and made her departure, perhaps unhappy to have betrayed a secret she felt might harm me though I had assured her otherwise.

The question stayed with me, though. *Were* there circumstances under which Holmes might have taken the law into his own hands? I had seen him allow the guilty to go free on occasion, when he felt that they were deserving of another chance.[74] Might the reverse be true, and Holmes be willing to act unilaterally against some malefic offender? He had made a death-oath once, after the Adventure of the Orange Pips,[75] and had accomplished it too, on Professor Moriarty, at the cost of his own life.

If Sherlock Holmes chose to kill a man then he would never be caught, never suspected. There would be no detective clever enough to follow his trail.

These troubling thoughts returned to me over the following day, though I knew them to be morbid fantasy. I received a penitent telegram from Miss Doré, apologising for her abrupt departure from Simpson's and her 'unconscionable indiscretion in the matter of Narbonne'.

When my surgery was over I surrendered to the knowledge that I would not rest until I fathomed the truth of things. I sent a wire to Cox's Bank on Charing Cross Road, informing them that on the morrow I would require access to those document cases and steamer trunks that I had deposited with them. These were the residue of Holmes's files from Baker Street that I had not passed to Scotland Yard or to Holmes's brother; I had moved them to a secure location since the information in them would be of immense use to a man of criminal intent.[76]

The following day being a Thursday, when I was accustomed to close my practice in the afternoon, I had liberty to stroll down to Cox and Company and satisfy my itch.

In a private room I opened up the case in which I had packed Holmes's bulging scrap-books, wherein he had been wont to keep clippings and

---

74   For example, James Ryder in "The Adventure of the Blue Carbuncle", *The Adventures of Sherlock Holmes* (1892)

75   In the published version of "The Five Orange Pips", *The Adventures of Sherlock Holmes* (1892), it is to the murderous captain of the barque *Lone Star* that Holmes sends the five pips in sign of his intended vengeance; but this story saw print before Watson revealed the name Moriarty to the world. Holmesian scholars have long speculated that the actual recipient of those tokens was the hidden mastermind behind the destruction of John Openshaw, and that Holmes's message was a declaration of war upon 'the Napoleon of Crime'.

76   Such an attempt to access the 'late' Holmes's files for such reasons was made in "The Affair of the Norwegian Sigerson", recorded by I.A. Watson in *Sherlock Holmes Consulting Detective* volume 10 and *Mysteries of Sherlock Holmes* volume 2. We may infer that Dr Watson chose to take more serious precautions to protect the records thereafter, and chose the bank at which, according to "The Problem of Thor Bridge", *The Case-Book of Sherlock Holmes* (1927), he would later deposit the famous tin dispatch box containing his own notes and writings.

notes of any character worthy of his attention. In the 'B' section I located the entry for Burnwell, Sir George Everett Langham, *b.* January 14th 1849, *d.* March 12th 1891.

From these notes I learned that Burnwell had briefly held a commission in the Royal _____, had twice been threatened with bankruptcy, had been sued for breach of promise by the family of one Miss Amanda Skeritt, and had allegedly fought a duel in Larne, Scotland, where he was rumoured to have killed his opponent. It was not one of the longer entries in Holmes's compendium—the Baskerville entry a few pages before it bulged with material[77]—but it carried enough detail to portray Sir George as a man to whom one should not wish to introduce to one's wife or female relatives.

Regarding the Affair of the Stolen Beryl Coronet, Holmes had sketched out in a single line a chain of causality from a gossiping housemaid in the owner's household who had first told Sir George of its intended use as collateral for a short-term loan, to the mutual female acquaintance who had put the foul knight in touch with the loan banker's son so he might strike up a supposed-friendship and gain access to his household, to innocent orphaned Mary Holder who had been taken in there as her uncle's ward. The villain's depredations were not opportunistic but planned.

I had already conceived a dislike of Sir George Burnwell for his vicious philandering, a dislike only exceeded later by my contempt for the even crueller and more despicable Baron Adelbert Gruner.[78]

A detail caught my attention. I felt almost like Sherlock Holmes as I noticed that the script on Burnwell's recorded date of death was added in a different blend of ink to the rest of the record. Holmes had updated it in those final days before Reichenbach—which meant that he had known of Sir George's murder almost at once.

Or at the exact moment of the blaggard's end?

I imagined Holmes in those last feverish, frantic months. As his grand

---

77   It is probably redundant to footnote that Holmes encountered the last heir of the old Devon family in *The Hound of the Baskervilles* (1902), which recounted events usually placed in 1888. However, it is interesting the speculate whether Watson remarking the existence of those notes in Holmes's dossiers was part of the process which eventually led him to elect to reveal the events of the Baskerville case to the world.

78   Watson outlined Holmes's clash with the despicable and hypnotic seducer Gruner in "The Adventure of the Illustrious Client", *The Case-Book of Sherlock Holmes* (1927), which took place in 1902 and was "in many ways the supreme moment of my friend's career".

chess match with Professor Moriarty progressed towards its lethal end-game, Holmes was pressed harder than ever before to match the dark genius of his implacable adversary. I had witnessed some of the early clashes without ever recognising them. Events that seemed entirely unconnected, continents apart, coalesced into international conspiracies, underworld empires, political plots to change the fortune of nations.

From the early days of January 1891, Holmes had fought a shadow war against his great enemy. It cost Holmes much in courage and vitality, a fight to the finish where neither side could afford a moment's inattention or the smallest error. The rest of London, Holmes's friends and supporters, even the detectives to whom Holmes trusted fragments of his plans, remained unaware of the vast schemes laid about them, the good and the ill of it.

By mid March, Holmes had covered a good part of Europe. We may never know all the places he visited in those frenetic times. The last word I had was from Nimes on the 17th of March, shortly before the arrest coup by French detective François Le Villard of the ruthless thieves who sought to plunder the historic preserved Roman temple of Maison Carrée. Le Villard had corresponded often with Holmes in the past, had translated many of his monographs into French, but my singular reason for gratitude to the rising star of French criminology was that he had referred to Holmes the case of Miss Mary Morstan and the Sign of Four; for from that encounter Mary became my wife.[79] It did not seem unreasonable to suppose that the French agent had collaborated again with his old teacher and had taken the credit to keep Holmes anonymous.

But by then Sir George Burnwell was five days dead, ninety miles away in Narbonne.

I stared at the meagre notes for quite some time. There was nothing there to prove Holmes's complicity in the death of the squalid seducer. There was no evidence at all. That was what troubled me.

Who was so clever as to commit a crime and leave no traces whatsoever?

Alongside Holmes's journals and research notes was a card index of Holmes's capacious contacts list. I sorted through the annotated hand-

---

79   In *The Sign of Four* (1890), Holmes described Le Villard as having "all the Celtic power of quick intuition, but he is deficient in the wide range of exact knowledge which is essential to the higher developments of his art... He has considerable gifts himself. He possesses two out of the three qualities necessary for the ideal detective. He has the power of observation and that of deduction. He is only wanting in knowledge; and that may come in time."

written cards until I found the address of Alfonse Le Brun, a private enquiry agent whom Holmes had occasionally employed for 'leg-work' in
some Continental investigation.[80] I determined to send to him for whatever local data might be gleaned about Sir George's unlamented passing.

I spent an interrupted Friday waiting for a reply. By the first post on
Saturday I received from Le Brun a parcel containing a bundle of newspaper clippings, a coroner's inquest report, a copy of several witness statements, and—most helpfully—English transcriptions of the key documents.

The coroner's report was the most helpful to me. I scanned the medical
details, grateful to have them translated where they were not using Latin
nomenclature.

Sir George had been in a fight before he died. He had suffered mul-
tiple contusions, three broken ribs, a fractured tibia, the loss of four inci-
sors, upper and lower left cuspids, and two molars, a cracked right orbital,
and severe abrasions consistent with taking a beating. He had likely been
scarcely-conscious when he was shot in the frontal plate exactly one inch
above the nasofrontal suture—that is, dead in the centre of the forehead,
twice, on the same spot. No bullets were recovered from the scene, but the
pathologist estimated from the wound that the shots were .445s or .45s,
fired from a distance of six feet or more.

Holmes's preferred weapon in the field was an easily-concealed Webley
'Metropolitan Police' revolver, which utilises the Webley Mark II .445 am-
munition.[81]

That there had been a fight was evident by the graze on Burnwell's left
knuckles where he had missed a blow and hit the wall. There was no indication that the deceased had ever landed a fist on his opponent.

Local police had been called to the expensive hotel where the bounder
had been staying, after a page-boy had found him dead in his bedroom.
There were no evident signs of the struggle that must surely have been

80   Le Brun's freelance work came to an abrupt halt in 1902 when he dared enquire
into the affairs of Baron Gruner, was set upon in Paris by 'Apaches' (ruffians), and was left
disabled for life [c.f. "The Adventure of the Illustrious Client"].

81   Holmes appears to have possessed the special version of the 1867 Royal
Irish Constabulary Webley revolver that was custom-made from 1883 by the London
Metropolitan Police service. Weighing in at just 27 ounces with a 2½-inch barrel and
solid-frame double action, it could easily be secreted in a pocket or waistband but retained
considerable stopping power. These models had the manacled-hands Metropolitan Police
logo engraved on the frame, and Holmes's weapon was numbered '1222'. Gun-enthusiast
Sherlockians have often debated which of the Criminal Investigation Division detectives
who consulted with Holmes might have procured him the weapon.

brutal. The whole chamber had been thoroughly set back into order. If the dead man's possessions had been searched or any of them removed there was nothing to show it. His wallet was in his jacket on the coat door, untouched, though it contained less than thirty francs, raising the question of how Sir George intended to cover his *pension* bill.

From the condition of the body when it was found on the morning of March 13th it had lain there since the evening before, and the death certificate was marked accordingly.

I turned aside from Le Brun's compilation to examine a note I had commissioned from another quarter. Our former Baker Street page-boy[82] was now grown to a man's estate and seemed to make a living carrying out odd and unspecified tasks.[83] I had asked Billy to check upon Mr Arthur Holder, the son of the bereft banker who had lost the beryl coronet, a young man who had been willing to be held responsible for its theft to protect his cousin Mary. Had he left the country in March? Alas he had not, and nor had his father. Indeed, Billy reported that a notice might soon be circulated of young Holder's engagement to an industrialist's daughter from Stratham.

But there might be other vengeful kinsmen of wronged ladies in Burnwell's past. There almost certainly were.

Indeed, I convinced myself, given the kind of activities that Miss Doré had intimated had been perpetrated on Miss Holder, I would have been pleased to drub Sir George myself, and courts be d____d! I might even, at the extreme, on hearing of the suicide of that poor, misguided, misused girl, have been tempted to level my service revolver and squeeze the trigger.

I realised that I would never know what had happened that evening at the Hôtel Merlin in the commune of Narbonne. I found that I did not much care if Holmes, in extremis, struggling against all the power of Moriarty's evil organisation, had taken a moment to avenge an abused young woman.

There the matter might have rested, for where else could it go? Except

---

82   The unnamed Baker Street page-boy from "A Case of Identity" was included in William Gillette's wildly-successful 1899 stage play *Sherlock Holmes—A Drama in Four Acts*, wherein he appeared as Billy the Buttons. Billy's inclusion in the play and in three subsequent Sherlock Holmes stage productions raised public perception of the character's significance. Doyle transported Billy back into three of his written works; the page plays a prominent part in catching the malefactor in "The Mazarin Stone".

On the London stage, the part of Billy was the debut performance of a juvenile actor called Charlie Chaplin.

83   One such task was to assist Watson and Lestrade in "The Affair of the Norwegian Sigerson" in the days after Holmes's erroneous funeral in May 1891.

I did not care if Holmes had taken a moment to avenge an abused woman.

that the following Monday I received an urgent and disturbing letter from Miss Alexandra Doré.

The Letter of Miss Alexandrina Doré to John Watson, M.D., Sunday, 19th March, 1893

Dear John,

A strange and alarming thing has happened, which I feel you should be made aware of, since it somewhat pertains to Sherlock Holmes and a recent conversation.

A little after luncheon today, around 2.20pm, I received an unannounced caller. Sparling brought in his card, pronouncing him to be Mr P. F. Dover of the banking firm of Shennig, Cole & Ratner. He portrayed himself as having travelled a long distance on urgent business and begged my pardon for disturbing my Sunday peace. I sent back word to the front door that Mr Dover might return at an appointed time in business hours, and that he might find me at home the following afternoon at the same time.

Mr Dover was evidently dissatisfied with his appointment. Whilst Sparling was occupied at the main door dealing with our uninvited caller, another man overcame the lock on the kitchen door and gained access to the servants' cellar. He was accompanied by a third fellow whom I assume was selected for his bulk rather than his brains or countenance.

These three were an organised and co-ordinated team, producing firearms to bundle us all inside my house—guns at Sydney Place, Bath! The servants were all gathered together and locked into the scullery, though how my dear cook Mrs Brace avoided being shot during the tirade of scolding that she loosed on our assailants I do not know.

Sherlock Holmes required details, and I imagine you have inherited his preference. Here then are descriptions of the three men. The first, who had sought entry as Mr Dover, was perhaps thirty-five, brown-haired and clean shaven, well dressed and in every sign the banking agent he had portrayed himself to be. His nails were well-trimmed and clean and his clothes were new, perhaps even bought for the occasion.

Of his two colleagues, one was clearly in charge of the other. The senior was a bulky man of around forty with oiled black hair slicked straight

back. He customarily wore a signet ring on his right hand but had removed it for his present activity. He spoke good English but I thought I
caught an echo of French inflections when he was speaking unguardedly.
His subordinate was the largest and youngest of the trio, standing well
over six feet and broad-shouldered. He did not speak at all, but undertook
tasks as instructed by the other two. I took him to be 'the muscle', as the
Western American adventure stories like to call it.

It was apparent that these intruders had a reserve plan in case their
Dover ruse faltered. I wonder whether, had they chosen some other time
and day to attempt their call, they might have succeeded in gaining their
interview? It seems a strange ignorance of English domestic custom.

In any case, I was conveyed to my front parlour, which you will recall is
where I keep my collection of memorabilia. Mr Dover spoke to me in a civilised way, apologising for his intrusion. 'We have no intention of harm-
ing you, Miss Doré, if you will but assist us with a matter of delicacy and
discretion. There is an item that has come into your possession, into your
collection, which is rather more significant that you may realise. Lives de-
pend upon its safe retrieval for its proper owner. If you would be so good
as to render the item then we can leave you to your pleasant afternoon.'

I suggested that delicacy and discretion did not go hand-in-hand with
armed invasion, and such a breach of courtesy did little to encourage my
co-operation.

The second man spoke. 'Do not imagine that we will hesitate to offer
whatever encouragement is required, woman. There is no resort at which
we will baulk to retrieve the document that we seek. You have staff here
whom you value. Nor would we be deterred to cause you harm to induce
you to yield.'

'There is no need for that,' argued Dover; I thought them equal partners
in their endeavour, and not working quite as one. 'Miss Doré must see
reason. And we have plenty of time to search.'

I suggested that we might get on more swiftly if they revealed to me
what item it was that they so rudely sought.

'The letter!' Slicked-Hair snarled. 'The letter you received from Mary
Holder!"

I explained that I had not retained the sad confession of Sir George's
abandoned mistress. That document had been burned. I had hoped it was
the last closure on her miserable life.

'Not the letter that Mary Holder wrote to you," Dover clarified, 'the
letter that she enclosed in the envelope with it. The other document.' He

emphasised the word 'other', signifying that there was an important second enclosure in the packet I had received from Marseilles.

Except there was not. I explained as much to the intruders and received only threats in return.

'You will produce the Holder letter—the one she stole for Sir George Burnwell—or you will suffer for it,' Slick-Hair threatened me. I know I should have been frightened, John, but honestly it was more exciting than terrifying. Perhaps you, Holmes's trusted companion in adventure, know the sensation?

'There is no need for menaces,' Dover told his compatriots again. 'What we seek is in this very room, and I can tell you where.'

My eyes flicked across the chamber to the mantelpiece, where lay a black and white ivory box, donated to my collection by none other than Mr Sherlock Holmes himself.

'In the box,' Dover deduced from following my glance. 'An untrained eye seeking to conceal one object in a cluttered room will naturally be drawn for the briefest check on the one place from which the viewer wishes to draw attention. A trained observer can thus discern the item's actual location.'

Slick-Hair snorted and reached for the box. Dover cried for him to wait, but it was too late. Slick-Hair had opened the container and had discovered the sharp spring inside it, set to strike at any who opened the lid unwary, and to draw blood.

You will remember this box, John, as that same weapon that the reprehensible Dr Culverton-Smith sent to Mr Holmes as a trap, having laced the needle with some slow, painful, and fatal Coolie disease to end the detective's life. Holmes had been too clever to fall for the trick, but Slick-Hair was not.

'Did you think yourself the only one to read about Sherlock Holmes's methods?' I challenged Dover. 'I am his collector. If you know aught of his cases then you will also recognise the ivory box which delivers a fatal dose into an unwary thumb. It is not a Sumatran plague this time, I'm pleased to tell you. This poison will be quicker but far less painful.'

Slick-Hair called me a reprehensible name. Dover chided him for trying to suck his pierced thumb and so ingest any poison on there.

'Where is the antidote?' Dover demanded of me. 'You are a logical and organised lady. You would not employ a poison without keeping a cure nearby in case of accidents. I caution you that if you do not produce the counter-toxin at once then I must resort to unpleasant measures.'

I am sure that you will have already guessed, knowing me, that there was no venom at all on Holmes's keepsake. Culverton-Smith's cunning mechanism still bites but is now a mere curiosity. Still, in their sudden misapprehension, the intruders were willing to believe that there was danger.

Dover's demand gave me excuse to open my desk drawer, purportedly to find the antidote there. In actual fact it is where I keep my Smith & Wesson .38 Safety Hammerless Revolver. You may remember that there was another time I feared for my life and required precautions to protect myself; hence the loaded firearm in my desk.

In the brief moment of inattention when all three weapon-toting men were occupied with potentially-lethal puzzle-boxes I drew my snub-nosed revolver and levelled it at them.

'Sirs', I told them, 'I am aware that I cannot prevail in a gunfight against three armed marauders. However, I have you all in my sights. I am confident that I could finish one or maybe two of you before you got me. The exchange of shots would certainly occasion significant attention in this, the most exclusive part of Bath, where even royalty owns property. It would hardly offer you the discretion and anonymity you seem to value. It will not get you the document you seek.'

'There is no antidote,' Dover understood. 'No poison. She has played us, and played us well.'

'There is no letter, either,' I informed the intruders. 'I give my word on it. There was no enclosure in Mary Holder's begging letter to me. Nor does her correspondence exist any more.'

'But you sent her money,' Slick-Hair insisted. 'One hundred pounds!'

'In charity. I was not purchasing whatever document you believe she acquired for Sir George Burnwell from your client.'

'That's consistent with the reply you sent to Miss Holder on March 8th 1891,' Dover admitted with some reluctance. 'Could it be...' He bit off his speculation in my presence.

I also had in my desk drawer a police rattle, with which I might summon assistance. There is usually a constable walking the Sydney Place beat.

'I suggest you withdraw,' I said. 'I acknowledge that I could not restrain all three of you from leaving without an exchange of gunfire. But nor can you compel me any further to assist in your intrusion. It is a stand-off, an armed stand-off—unless you elect to depart.'

Dover evidently made a sensible calculation. 'I am inclined to take your word, Miss Doré,' he told me, before the interlopers made their exit.

In all, the importunate intrusions of three sinister enquiry agents took less than half an hour of my afternoon, though as you can imagine it caused considerable disturbance in our household. The Bath constabulary is most perturbed and the local Member of Parliament intends to raise the outrage in the House.

I am writing to assure you of my general wellbeing. I have survived and my staff are unharmed. All that remains is a mystery that I might only wish we still had Mr Holmes to solve. What was the document that Miss Holder procured for her wicked master, and what became of it at the last? What connects a stolen letter, a sad suicide, and a murdered lecher? What, if any, part did I play in this?

I feel I must know, John.

Consequently, this is also my notice to you of my intention to make a voyage to Narbonne and Marseilles in the tracks of Sir George Burnwell and Mary Holder (the frivolities of a lady of means—how the anti-liberationists would choke!).[84] I wish to get the bottom of things, and I confess that includes the role that Mr Holmes played in the events of 12th May '91. The best and possibly only way of doing so is to go and see for myself.

I own that the voyage may be somewhat challenging for a single lady to make without support, but I will overcome difficulties and hardship to resolve this matter, alone if no friend is willing to offer companionship.

Subscribed with my warmest affection,
Alexandra

From the Notes of John H. Watson M.D.:

It was impossible to ignore an appeal from a lady in need. Attempts to deter Miss Alexandra Doré from her proposed expedition proved futile;

---

84   In 19th century Britain and in most of the rest of the world, the legal doctrine of *coverture* distinguished between a *feme sole*, an unmarried woman who might own property and manage business in her own right and a *feme covert*, a married woman whose entire goods and lands were in the control and at the disposal of her husband, and who ceased to exist as a legal entity by herself. A woman wed could not even make a will without her husband's ratification. Successive *Married Womens Property Acts* in 1870, 1882, 1884, and 1893 granted female spouses ever more rights and protections in the face of strong lobbying for and against women's rights. 'Anti-liberationists' were quick to write outraged letters to newspapers over the latest 'madness' of women seeking to control their own assets, liberty, and bodies, predicting economic, political, and moral disaster.

she is a woman of fixed goals and singular stubbornness.

I had to object to the details of her travel plans, however. Miss Doré countered my concerns.

"The men who called upon me were organised, competent. They had good information, including evidently access to my reply to Miss Holder's original correspondence. They had resources. We may imagine that their sponsor who lost some valuable document to Miss Holder is a man of wealth and influence—probably in France. It therefore behoves us to travel incognito so as not to further announce our interest in this matter."

"I can see that, but Miss Doré... we cannot travel pretending to be man and wife!"

"On the contrary, John, we must. The ruse works on two levels. If our travel documents are taken at face value then we are Mr and Mrs Ormond Sacker,[85] taking the air on the French Riviera. If our guise is penetrated then we are identified as Dr John Watson and Miss Alexandra Doré, an adventurous couple enjoying an amorous encounter away from straight-laced English society—it is what the Continent is for!"

"Your reputation...!"

"I am already an eccentric spinster of odd habits, John. If a little more gossip must accrue to me then so be it. I am not dependent upon a good name for my fortune. Indeed, a little scandal might deter some of those ambitious gentlemen who seek to annex me." Miss Doré smiled. "Sir George Burnwell eloped with Mary Holder and treated her most heinous-ly. I trust that you will be kinder to me as we travel in their wake."

I argued for some time that the lady must see sense, and made many valid points. However, my experience of women in three separate conti-nents has taught me that after a certain point all logic is futile.

For some modicum of propriety, as well as utility, Miss Doré consented to take a young companion maid, Flora, who eyed me with constant suspi-cion throughout our travels as if I were Gilles de Rais reborn.[86] I prevailed

---

85   Ormond Sacker was the draft name by which Doyle first wrote about Holmes's friend and confidante, amending it to John Watson before publication. Clearly Miss Doré was aware of the initial pseudonym under which Dr Watson's case accounts were credited.

86   Gilles de Rais, Baron de Rais (1405 -1440) was the soldier, companion-in-arms of Joan of Arc, and later a confessed serial child-killer on whom the legend of wife-murdering Bluebeard was probably based.

upon our old buttons[87] Billy to accompany me as valet and factotum; his French is sadly deficient but his ingenuity is bottomless. It became quickly evident that Billy and Flora's frequent collie-shangles[88] would keep us entertained on our journey.

Miss Doré proved an apt travel agent. We took the night-boat from Portsmouth for a choppy crossing to Le Havre. By the time we emerged from the sleeping car, the ferry was docking and we could step off it onto the express train to Paris. We breakfasted in the dining car and some two hours after passing into France we emerged from Saint-Lazare station into the 8th arrondissement. My companion pointed out the locations from which Edouard Manet had painted "The Railway" and Gustave Caillebotte had painted "Le Ponte d'Europe".

Despite our intention to travel under *noms-de-voyage* I had sent one telegram ahead in my own name, for it was only as a friend and associate of Sherlock Holmes that I was able to secure us an interview with M. Dubugue of the Paris Prefecture of Police. Dubugue was one of those confidantes upon whom Holmes had called during his final spectacular round-up of Moriarty's international operations.

"I recall perfectly the scandal about which you enquire," the dapper officer of the law assured me as we met for croissants at a street café on Place de la Bastille. "I had received a wire from M. Holmes to caution me that Sir George Burnwell was in France and likely looking for opportunity. The fellow had sold three gems from an English lord's crown and had got away with it. He would indubitably seek to perform a similar coup again."

"You know the details of his passing through Paris, then?" Miss Doré enquired. "You know what he and Miss Holder were up to?"

Dubuque angled his croissant in an ironic manner as only a Frenchman could. "Sir George's knighthood opened certain doors to him in high society. It has ever been his best advantage, along with his looks and manner. Once known to the moneyed class he would seek to ingratiate himself for advantage. Only this time he had his mistress in tow also."

Miss Doré had learned from Miss Holder's missive that it was in Paris that her swain's gambling debts required payment, and that the poor girl

87   A 'buttons' was slang for a liveried house page, who traditionally sported two or more rows of bright brass buttons on the chest of his uniform tunic.

88   That is, spats or minor arguments; the term comes from the quarrelling of collie puppies and is recorded by none other than Queen Victoria herself in her *More leaves from the journal of life in the Highlands*, from 1862 to 1883 (1884, available online at https://archive.org/details/cihm_25356)

herself was to become the coin by which such dues were settled. From the information that Miss Doré passed on, the next two weeks involved a series of introductions wherein Miss Holder was 'loaned' by Sir George to a series of rich suitors.

Dubuque confirmed this. He was able to name several of the wealthy gentlemen who had enjoyed liaisons with her.

"Can you tell us who the most significant of these was?" I pressed the Parisian inspector. "Was there any report of a robbery?"

"Ah," sighed Dubuque regretfully, "there I am bound by professional discretion. When a powerful figure from an ancient family suffers from a personal theft that might bring a noble name into disrepute, all wise policemen had best curb their tongues."

"But surely..." I began.

Miss Doré, with a subtler mind and a better ear for nuance, laid a restraining hand on my sleeve. "The noble gentleman was evidently much distressed," she noted. "Without ever betraying his name, might we understand some of the details of the crime?"

Dubuque sipped his Turkish coffee and lit a cigarette. "We may suppose that there are gentleman of good breeding and high destinies who are still subject to the desires of all flesh," he ventured.

"It may be so," the lady assented.

Dubuque paused a moment to admire Miss Doré's aesthetics and then continued. "We might speculate that such gentlemen would not be averse to meeting with *une jolie brunette Anglais*. We might consider that the gentleman would be generous with his pocket-book to a fellow gentleman who facilitated the meeting; it is a not-uncommon arrangement."

I stifled a remark about men who might do such things; they are not gentlemen in any proper sense of the term.

"An engaging young woman under the control of a ruthless master might be put to many uses," Dubuque considered. "She might, for example, be instructed to leave the bed of a sleeping gentleman she had satiated and force open the drawer of his bedroom desk. Perhaps in there is some item of value, some token presented to him by a grateful nation for services well-rendered? Perhaps it is encrusted with gems? If that *jolie brunette Anglais* were to drop the item from the window to her puppeteer then it would be hard to recover, embarrassing and expensive; especially since there would be no proof of who carried the treasure away."

"And any prosecution would have to reveal the method by which the young woman had access to the bedroom desk," Miss Doré surmised.

"*Précisément.*"

"Was such an item stolen and ransomed?" I demanded. I have little time for oblique hypotheticals.

M. Dubuque shrugged. "If it was then the thief was a fool. He might simply have ransomed it back for a handsome sum. But alas, the bereft owner overreacted. He 'set the dogs' on the robbers, as you English say. The thieves fled Paris and disappeared."

"The jewels were not recovered?"

"Later, from a third party to whom they had been sold."

As with the beryls from the cornet, I thought. Burnwell had a method and was reluctant to deviate from it.

"From where was the item retrieved?" Miss Doré asked.

"Narbonne," Dubuque revealed. "The day after the demise of Sir George Burnwell."

The inspector of the Paris Prefecture would not name the prestigious person from whom some valuable object had been distrained. He finished his pastry, wiped his chin with his napkin, and bade us a *bonne après-midi*.

"Well," I said to Miss Doré as we paid the tab, "that seems to confirm some suspicions. Your unwelcome visitors might have been working for the amorous gentleman who lost a treasure."

"They were not seeking jewels, though. That object had been recovered. They sought a document." The lady paused in thought. "Suppose that the gift of a grateful nation was not all that Miss Holder took from that desk? That was the theft that her suitor reported, but what if there was more? Some document of significance, perhaps for blackmail?"

"Then he would certainly wish it recovered without fuss. He might not mention it to the *gendarmerie.*"

"And he is still looking for it now."

I frowned at that. I was troubled by the uncouth interruption in Miss Doré domestic situation a mere days after I had initiated a search into Burnwell's affairs. I was no longer certain of the confidence I had placed in the investigator Le Brun.

We rendezvoused with Billy and Flora at Gare Austerlitz and climbed aboard the provincial train for Limoges-Bénédictins.

Billy had spent his time in the City of Lights productively. He had traced the *pension* where Burnwell and Miss Holder had stayed in Paris, and had picked up some lurid tales of what had happened there that further coloured in the history that had been confessed to Miss Doré.

The owner had been very willing to talk, to complain even, since Sir

George had decamped without remembering to cover his bill. He remembered his guest obsessively quizzing him on aspects of the then-current political topics of the creation of French Guinea, negotiated through exchange of territories with Britain and the other European powers in Africa,[89] and the knotty question of assimilating Algeria into the administration of France.[90] In particular he had wanted to know about one of the politicians involved in setting up the deal with other nations, an agreement that had literally drawn lines upon a map of the African continent, and who might now become part of the Commission on Algeria; but the hotelier was unable to recall the luminary's name no matter how much he was bribed.

I wondered that Billy, with his very limited French, might get so much out of the man. It turned out that my valet had persuaded Miss Doré's companion to accompany him as translator.

We pulled out through the grimy southern suburbs of Paris at 15.22 and settled in for a taxing seven-hour journey, changing at Dijon then steaming through Lyon and Avignon to Nimes, where Holmes had solved some puzzle in his European campaign against Moriarty. A third train took us southwest along the curve of the Mediterranean bay, passing through Montpellier and Béziers, until we finally drew in at Narbonne at 22.17, six minutes delayed.

On the whole I found the French railway to be efficient but fussy; it cannot compare to the British railways system.

During the journey, Miss Doré and I compared notes on Sherlock Holmes.

"You have the much more intimate view, of course," she said. "You were

89   The West African Colony of French Guinea was established in 1891 from informal holdings that the French had seized and administered as Rivières du Sud in the decade previously. Its creation was part of a formalisation of territories conquered by European colonists during "the rush for Africa" and was controversial in France at the time, though the soldiers and diplomats involved in the campaign and subsequent treaties were lauded and rewarded for their efforts.

90   The French were brutal in the 19th century capture and subjugation of Algeria. The indigenous population declined by one-third. As the 20th century approached, the French debated "the Algerian question" about the best way to "civilise" the Magrab territories.

his great friend and companion for eleven years, and his self-appointed chronicler. I can only claim to an outsider's perspective, as one who views things after the fact at a detached distance."

"That kind of study can sometimes bring out new insights. What conclusions have you drawn?"

"Well, on the face of it, Sherlock Holmes was a difficult man to be friend to. He was moody, sullen, secretive, obsessive, manipulative, ruthless, and dangerous to know. But for all his vices he had redeeming virtues that you saw when few others did. Your great gift to him was unpacking the man, showing the rest of us of what stuff he was truly made."

"Holmes was a great man; a formidable opponent of wrongdoing, a fearless truth-seeker, one of the pre-eminent minds of our age or any other, and a loyal and steadfast friend."

"We see that now, the world, because you have shown it to us, John. There is no Sherlock Holmes without Doctor Watson; the equation does not sum."

"And no Watson without Holmes?" I wondered. I missed him.

"Genius needs support," Miss Doré supposed. "The rest of us get on by ourselves, do we not?"

We engaged a cab from the station to Hôtel Merlin, where Burnwell had died, but we need not have. The place was on Rue de Capitole, close to the glorious Cathédrale Saint-Just et Saint-Pasteur, only a short distance from our point of arrival. The three-storey edifice had been impressive once, with grand balconies and those tall French window-doors, but the place had a slightly seedy aspect now. I could understand why a man who gave himself noble airs might select it while on a budget.

Miss Doré had engaged rooms for us there as Mr and Mrs Sacker, and had even purchased a ring to complete her impersonation. "This way, Ormond," she told me as she took my arm and pushed into the foyer. I remembered that the lady had previously evinced a supreme talent for impersonation; she was unlikely to neglect any detail.

The reserved room did not suit Madame Sacker, however. Money changed hands and the helpful desk clerk found us a different suite one floor up with a good view of the park and of the Canal de la Robine in the distance. Usefully, these were the very chambers where Sir George had been discovered murdered, although the hotel manager did not bring that up.

We had no hope of finding clues there. Even Sherlock Holmes would have struggled with forensic examination after the room had endured three more years of constant use.

But we had come with a plan. Billy was to seek out what information could be gleaned from hotel staff and locals about the Burnwell murder. He claimed Flora as his companion, arguing that her linguistic skills were needed, but I suspected he knew that her sweet innocent face would loosen French tongues also. Miss Doré and I would pursue a more official route and track down those police and medical men who had been involved in the case.

We set forth next day after a Continental breakfast that left me yearning for Mrs Hudson's kidneys and kedgeree and sought the truth behind the mysteries that had brought us so far on such a mad voyage. Each of us had an instructional time.

Billy and Flora made short work of the hotel staff. The events of three years previous had left strong impressions on the maids and footmen. There were still those present who remembered having to be wary of Sir George Burnwell and who recalled the police investigation into his slaughter. Officers had been sent all the way from Paris to investigate, but had been thwarted by an absolute absence of useful evidence. It had been re-marked upon. Several of the staff had received heavy tips for intelligence about Sir George's business dealings in Narbonne, but none had known of any packet of documents he carried, so none could collect a reward.

Of special interest was word amongst the *demi-monde* of gamblers, fix-ers, and escorts that always dwell on the fringes of hotel enterprise that they had been questioned three years earlier about the same things that Billy sought now. The querent then had been a limping old man with fraz-zled grey sideburns, asking at just about the time that the *chevalier Anglais* had been found *mort*.

The enquiries that Miss Doré and I made were met with a front of of-ficial bureaucratic indifference until the lady indicated her willingness to resort to her pocketbook. Then we were informed 'unofficially' that pres-sure had been brought to bear from 'the highest level' to close the murder swiftly and without demur. An agent acting 'on behalf of the government' had demanded that a verdict of 'murder by person or persons unknown' be found by the coroner's inquest, and that the police investigation con-clude that the Englishman's gambling or womanising had finally caught up with him. Given lack of a clear lead and a steer from above, the local *gendarmes* had done little more to pursue the matter.

We did somewhat catch Holmes's trail from March '91. He had ap-peared briefly at the Gendarmerie Nationale there—that is, the military police service that is part of France's armed forces and covers matters of regional or national interest including political crimes, as opposed to the civilian Sûreté that covers the cities and larger towns and is more like traditional British constabularies. There had been a raid on warehouses along the River Aude and the arrests of three prominent businessmen on charges of smuggling, peculation, and espionage. Two of the men had killed themselves in police custody and the third had been fatally injured in a jail-yard brawl before his case came to court.

After a hectic day we reassembled that evening in the very chamber where Sir George had perished. Miss Doré assisted me in assembling a listing of the relevant dates that we knew:

Friday, 19th December 1890—Mr Holder appeals to Holmes regarding the theft of the Beryl Coronet

Saturday, 20th December—Holmes tracks down Sir George Burnwell and recovers the jewels; Sir George and Miss Holder flee together

Monday, 26th December—Holmes leaves for Scandinavia

Wednesday, 28th December—Holmes writes from Copenhagen

Friday, 30th December—Holmes writes from Stockholm

Early January 1891—Sir George and Miss Holder active in Paris

Wednesday, 25th January—Sir George and Miss Holder flee Paris

Monday, 30th January—Sir George and Miss Holder active in Marseilles

Friday, 3rd February—Holmes wires from Paris

Sunday, 26th February—Sir George abandons Miss Holder in Marseilles

Wednesday, 1st March—Sir George present in Narbonne

Thursday, 2nd March—Miss Holder in Marseilles writes letter to Miss Doré in Bath

Saturday, 4th March—Miss Doré receives Miss Holder's letter

Wednesday, 8th March—Miss Doré writes back to Miss Holder; in Marseilles Mary Holder ends her life

Saturday, 11th March—Holmes writes from Narbonne

Sunday, 12th March—Sir George Burnwell beaten and murdered in Narbonne

Friday, 17th March—Holmes writes from Nimes

Sunday, 19th March—M. Le Villard closes a serious crime case in Nimes, to great acclaim

Friday, April 24th (or before)—Holmes reappears in England

Saturday, 25th April—Holmes and Watson flee England, pursued by Moriarty and Moran

To which I reluctantly had to add:

Thursday 4th May—Reichenbach

"What have we learned so far?" Miss Doré asked as we had completed our time-line. "It seems to me that there are three interconnected questions that we must answer."

I listed them: "Who killed Burnwell and why? What became of the stolen document? And what was Sherlock Holmes doing in Narbonne, and does it play a part in the rest of it?"

"Why, Mr 'Olmes must 'ave been chasing down Perfessor Moriarty's plots," Billy insisted. Holmes had no more loyal worshipper. "It makes sense, as 'e were setting up his grand slam against the wicked old spider! And it weren't enough to jest knock the old man down in Blighty, in London. 'E had to be denied every one uv 'is hidey-holes, and all his followers 'ad to be rooted up and all. I reckons Mr 'Olmes was 'ere plugging up rat-'oles—and he did!"

"But did he also 'plug' Sir George?" Miss Doré wondered.

"There was the old man with the whiskers," Flora ventured, still unsure in this strange company on this strange investigation. "William mentioned that Mr Holmes was accustomed to seeking out information in many odd guises."

"William?" I asked, and saw Billy wince. "Um, yes. Well, I admit it unlikely that Holmes would fail to apprehend that Sir George was here. He may have checked up on him."

"How might the document that Mary Holder abstracted from Paris play into the larger conflict, though?" Miss Doré puzzled. "Or does it? Need everything link with everything else?"

"We found no record of the police discovering or returning any item stolen along with the supposed document, whatever that treasure is," I noted. "Yet Dubuque seemed certain that something had been recovered."

Billy considered that. "That Sir George, 'e was a bad cove but 'e wer'nt that good at fencing 'is goods—that is, 'e didn't seem that smart about it. 'E sold them bits of beryl coronet for less than 'e might 'ave got, and 'e weren't savvy enough to go to someone 'oo wouldn't peach on 'im. And *that* were in London, which was 'is home pitch, so to speak. In France 'e were on the run from 'ooever he'd pinched from's bully-boys, 'e were getting short of cash—'e evidently cashed in Miss 'Older –and 'e wouldn't know where to go to make a good sale. If what 'e'd got to sell was special and distinctive-like, a one-off piece of kit, it was bound to give 'im away when 'e tried to shift it."

"And the thing was retrieved quietly, with no police involved?" I wondered.

"Before or after the elimination of the loathsome Sir George?" Miss Doré mused. "Or during."

"That nasty oily fellow who locked us in the scullery, he was the sort who'd do that," Flora agreed with a shudder.

"But if they found Burnwell and got the jewels back off him then why didn't they also recover the document?" I puzzled.

"Perhaps he wouldn't tell them where it was?" Miss Doré suggested. "He was beaten before he died. Perhaps he wouldn't talk."

I didn't account Sir George the kind of man to hold out by courage against a proper drubbing. He was a cad and a coward, a lion terrorising helpless women, but I doubt he'd have stood long against a fellow who could match him. Bullies fold.

Miss Doré kept on chewing the problem. "Perhaps he had already lost the document when his pursuers caught him? Perhaps Mr Holmes had found him first and extracted it? Sir George would be telling the truth when he swore he no longer had it, but they beat him anyway and then finally gave up and executed him."

I liked that theory better than Holmes as the executioner.

We passed the night in Narbonne and caught the midday train to Montpellier, for our investigation now led to the place where Sir George had been just before his demise, the place where he had betrayed and abandoned the young woman he had seduced from home and loved ones and brought to ruin in a foreign land.

The route had us retracing our previous travel, returning along the coastal line as far back as Nimes and then taking the branch at Tarascon-sur-Rhône and following the Toulon line as far as Montpellier. It was a journey of marvellous vistas, the rugged Occitanean landscape to our left, the shimmering Middle Sea on our right.

Billy was entranced. "Well, Dr Watson," he told me, "I'm not saying as it's as good as old London Town, but there's maybe something to be said for a bit of French seaside!"

"London!" Flora objected. "Dirty grimy old place as it is, turning out dirty grimy young fellows with no appreciation for art or beauty. Don't you talk to me about London, my boy!"

"You don't know naught about London!" Billy defended his home. "You come from some middling-posh resort as the toffs like to go to paddle their toes and you think you can look down on the greatest city in the world? I means it. There's places an' secrets in our capital that would strike even you dumb, unlikely as that may sound, Flora Gibson, and things so beautiful as to make you weep! You jest look at the dome of St Paul's, or the carvings on Westminster, or Tower Bridge, or St James' Palace. Or go up and watch the sun rise over the roofs and all the masts of the boats at harbour, or... well, you just go see before you sniffs at it!"

"And I suppose you know all the places and, and rooftops?"

"'Course I do. Why I could show you..." Billy fell abruptly silent. "Anyways, it's not bad here," he allowed at last. He stuck his hands in his pockets and intently gazed from the carriage window.

"Travel is always stimulating," Miss Doré observed to me.

The great trading port of Marseilles is ninety miles round the bay from Narbonne, but the journey took us half a day on local trains and we were glad to disembark at Gare de Marseille-Saint-Charles.[91] Still, fatigued as we were, the beauty of the ancient city lifted our spirits.

"See, William?" Flora hissed to Billy.

The late afternoon sun painted the Vieux Port. We explored the tightly-packed winding pastel-coloured streets of Le Panier that sloped up to the public hospital of Vieille Charité on the Place des Moulins. We admired the Romanesque and Byzantine domes of the Cathédrale de la Major and stared up at the new and opulent Basilique Notre-Dame de la Garde on its prominent hilltop.[92]

We still had no lead as to where Sir George Burnwell had stayed during his stop-off in the city. Since the bounder had then been fleeing whichever rich and powerful man he had offended with his Paris robbery he was unlikely to have used his real identity; yet he had reclaimed his name and title in Narbonne, as soon as he felt himself safe from pursuit.

Since we could not again acquire rooms that Sir George had chartered,

---

91   Watson's experience of arrival would have been rather different from the traveller today. The grand staircase envisioned by Eugène Senès to connect station with city was not yet accomplished, and remained unfinished until after the First World War. The site expanded extensively after World War II and since linking to the TGV (France's intercity high-speed train service) is one of the busiest terminals in France today.

Marseille-Saint-Charles station was in the news in 1983 when a bomb was detonated there by Ilich Ramírez Sánchez, "Carlos the Jackal", and again in 2017 when a jihadist knife attacker killed two women.

92   The Basilique Notre-Dame de la Garde, built between 1853 and 1864, might have been new from Watson's perspective but it is now an historical monument.

We stared up at the new and opulent Basilique Notre-Dame de la Garde.

Miss Doré indulged us with a stay at the splendid Hôtel Maison Saint Louis in the Old Quarter, where an enthusiastic staff misunderstood our circumstances and had to be dissuaded from offering M. and Mme. Sacker the honeymoon suite.

Miss Doré and I enjoyed a light supper at one of the many excellent dining places along Rue Pavilion and then returned to plan the continuation of our campaign.

"If it's all right with you, Dr Watson, I'd like to 'ave a chat with some of the cabbies an' bellboys hereabouts," Billy requested. "See if I can pick up any whiff of wicked Sir George while 'e were 'ere. Cove like that was bound to 'ave run up debts. I might check the tailors and tobacconists and all, and maybe the bookmakers." He paused before casually adding, "I'd, um, I'd probably need to take Flora with me."

Miss Doré's maid sighed theatrically.

"It's better that you do go with William tomorrow," her mistress assured her. "After all, tomorrow Ormond is taking me to visit a brothel."

"What?" I objected.

"We have an itinerary," the lady pointed out. "Tomorrow we chase up details of poor Mary's fate in the place she died."

"The coroner's office, the Sûreté precinct…"

"The site of her suicide. No, John, it must be done. Tomorrow you shall escort me to a *maison de tolérance.*

So reluctant was I to inflict a visit on a house of ill repute upon Alexandra Doré that we were still debating it the next day. "We have checked the hall of records and spoken to the officers of the law who were called to the scene," I argued. "Here is the autopsy report, with all the unpleasant details of a death by asphyxiation of a young woman who locked her door, knotted her sheets to a rafter, and kicked away a chair. There is nothing to indicate foul play, nothing to require a visit to the site three years after the tragedy."

"But what would Sherlock Holmes do?" Miss Doré challenged me. "The Houses of Tolerance here are rather different to the establishments in London. Since the time of Napoleon, they are licensed, official, regulated. They must be run by a woman. They must be discreet, with modest exteriors in a designated part of the city. When in operation they must light a red lamp over their door. The employees there must be registered and may only leave the site on certain days and times. There are medical standards, inspections—taxes!"

"They are still no place for a decent woman. I can go alone and take a look at the scene if you allow it."

My companion's eyes flashed mischievously. "This is France, John, and we are Englishmen abroad. The rules of etiquette are quite different on the Continent; or else why visit?[93] It is not uncommon for a liberal gentleman here to bring his spouse or mistress with him to a better class of establishment, to observe, participate, or even for instruction. Monsieur and Madame Sacker will be *à la mode.*"

"I doubt I like Ormond Sacker much, that he would treat his wife in such a manner."

"But let us use the Sackers for their purpose, John, and have them solve our mystery." The lady sobered. "Please, John? I must go there, to that terrible place, to settle the ghost of Mary Holder, to quieten my conscience. Will you not support me in my need?"

I agreed to the request. How could I not?

The Lantern Rouge lay in a quiet sidestreet in Bon-Secours in the 3rd arrondissimont, just behind the main Chemin de Gibbes. I was relieved to see it was some distance from the rough dock-fronts with their brutal *maisons d'abattage*; whatever regulations the French might have imposed upon their prostitution, those 'abattoir houses' were foul dens of desolate women and fouler men [94]

The required red lamp was not lit at noon, when Miss Doré and I applied to speak with the proprietess.

"Madame will be with you shortly," the trim girl who admitted us promised. "Please be so good as to wait a moment."

---

93   For example, during the 1880s and 90s, Edward, Prince of Wales (later King Edward VII of the United Kingdom, sometimes referred to as "Dirty Bertie") reserved at permanent suite at La Chabonais, Paris's most exclusive brothel. His chambers had his coat of arms over his bed and included a mirrored ceiling, champagne bath, and a "love seat" designed for the bulky crown prince to entertain several participations at once without crushing them. Behaviour that would have caused a scandal had it been seen in Britain was tolerated because it was "on the Continent".

94   Maisons d'abattage (slaughterhouses) were cheap French brothels catering for the common masses, often with queues of men waiting their turns on the prostitutes. An additional charge was made for a towel. These sex workers were paid 'by the client' and might serve seventy or a hundred customers per night.

The interior of the *maison* was reminiscent of a gentleman's club of the more lush but seedy sort. There was a lounge with comfortable 'waiting chairs' and potted palms, a small bar at one corner, and a brass-bannistered stairway to upper floors. A series of relatively tasteful nude prints adorned the walls.

Miss Doré engaged the concierge in conversation. We learned that the house was under new management since two years previously. Madame Charlotta had retired and Madame Seraphina now ran the establishment. There were almost no girls still working there who might remember unpleasant incidents from so long ago as three years since.

"This is a good house," the concierge insisted. "Clean and well-run." She pointed out the newly-renewed décor and well-stocked wine racks. "Gentlemen come here. They expect quality." She eyed Miss Doré. "Gentlemen and ladies."

My companion repeated that we were not here for that kind of business. "We are looking for news of a lost relative who previously stayed here," she explained. "We were hoping to find someone who might remember her and what happened to her."

"Then please address your queries to me." The request was in good English, and it came from the elegant woman descending the staircase. She wore a long exotic dress of Oriental fashion, somewhat like the robes of an Indian princess, and her bare arms were adorned with bracelets and armlets. The ensemble was completed with a Turkish veil and a high feathered diadem. "I am Madame Seraphina."

I thanked her for her time and explained the nature of our investigation.

"Mary Holder? It is a long time since I have heard that name. Yes, I remember poor frightened Mary. She was cruelly betrayed, abandoned here with nowhere else to go. It was a grim and nasty business, all too common in our profession."

"She was a prisoner of the house?"

"In a sense. She was sold here, in exchange for remission of the debts of her lover. She did not understand the nature of the contract, *naïf* that she was, but it was as good as slavery. There are certain clients of certain *maisons closes* who pay well for girls who are… inexperienced and less willing. I assure you that no such thing happens at La Lanterne Rouge now. But then it did, and poor Mary was abandoned to such a life by a man whom she had believed cared for her—loved her."

"When she arrived, did she speak about her past?" Miss Doré wondered.

"Did she talk about her journey through France, for example?"

"She was very tight-lipped. She would not have even given her name, except that her lover had told it. I think she wanted to spare her lost family from disgrace and pain. I think she wanted that to the last."

"What became of her?" I asked, already knowing the answer.

"She did not last here long. One night, one desperate night, she was visited by a new client and he said some things to her. Who can now say what happened between them? But he left, and she wept, and the following morning her body was found in her room, hanging from the ceiling." Madame Seraphina's lips pursed. "Madame Charlotta had a good relationship with the police. The matter was handled swiftly and discreetly."

"Miss Holder did not make any mention of a gentleman she had known in Paris?" probed Miss Doré.

"She was not given to speak of the things she had been made to do. Some of the girls in our work choose their profession. Others are dragged into it, criminally and cruelly. So it was with Mary."

"Is there anyone now here except yourself who remembers the time she died?" I asked.

"Some friend to whom she might confide? Some comfort in her bleak indenture? She had none. And so she ended."

Miss Doré glanced at me. I could read the disappointment in her face. "This was our last chance to discover what happened three years ago. The trail ends here."

"It does," I agreed. But an idea had come to me, a thrilling, enthralling idea. A revelation. Was this how Holmes felt when he made some connection? Was this how Sherlock Holmes felt *all the time*?

My euphoria was interrupted by a hammering on the front door. The concierge moved to answer it, peering through a small observation hatch.

She shied back and hastily unfastened the bolt. "What is it, Cecile?" Madame Seraphina demanded.

To my surprise, Billy and Flora entered. Behind them came a burly brute with one hand in at his pocket, clearly pointing a concealed gun at the two of them. And after him came another armed fellow with slicked-back oily hair and a ruthless expression, who had forced the concierge to allow admittance.

"It is he!" Miss Doré breathed. "The man at Sydney Court!"

"Sorry, sir," Billy apologised to me. "They caught us at this flower shop in that Le Panier, just as we was chatting with some rum coves what knew a little bit about... the stuff we was after." He glared at the men who had dragged him and Flora away and had manhandled them after us. "'E reck-ons as 'e's a Peeler.[95]"

"If so then his government has a good deal of explaining to do regarding his actions in England," I growled, placing myself between the armed men and Miss Doré.

"Keep quiet," Slick-Hair warned me. "You're in deep to things you know nothing about."

"Wouldn't be the first time. If you're a policeman then show your warrant card. Then we shall contact the British Embassy and lodge our formal complaint."

Slick-Hair sneered at me. "I'm not that sort of policeman, M. Sacker."

His companion bundled Billy and Flora into a corner with the concierge. I gave Billy a covert shake of the head; this was not a time for his enthusiastic and madcap attempts at adventure. I did not want him shot.

"Search the house," Slick-Hair ordered his henchman. "Bring anyone else who's about down here."

"That will not be necessary," Madame Seraphina declared. "At this time of day all the girls are resting, asleep in their rooms. Here is the key to the door on the balcony. If you lock it then they cannot come out here, even if they did awake. There is no need to disturb them or concern them in this."

Slick-Hair calculated the odds of controlling a dozen hysterical doxies and decided to accept their Madam's suggestion. He nodded for his thug to take the key and secure the connecting door.

"Will you now explain your extraordinary actions?" Miss Doré challenged him. "If you are an official, why did you make such an irregular, illegal entrance at my house? What is this document you so fervently seek? Why are you now holding us at gunpoint, in contravention of any civilised law?"

"I'm not here to answer your questions, Mam'selle Doré," Slick-Hair warned. "You will answer mine."

"Miss Doré?" Madame Seraphina repeated, hearing Madame Sacker's actual name for the first time.

Slick-Hair levelled his gun at me. "You will now confess the whereabouts of the message stolen in Paris on the night of the January 22nd 1891."

"I most certainly shall not," I replied. "For one thing, I don't know where it is. For another, I'm not in the habit of assisting cads who break into women's houses and threaten them."

"And if I threaten them now?"

---

95   A policeman; the slang derives from Sir Robert Peel being the first commander of the London Metropolitan Police.

Holmes would have had a clever answer. All I could manage was, "Then you must go through me."

Miss Doré intervened. "You are likely to further your cause better by explaining what you need," she told Slick-Hair and his thug. "It must have occurred to you that since we have been seeking the document ourselves, to understand what went on before and what is happening now, we do not have the item you seek. Indeed, you have interrupted our efforts to locate it. Your best course now is to say what you know and pool it with our own researches."

Slick-Hair lacked that level of reasoning. Fortunately, the third of Miss Doré's intruders appeared at the doorway then. He bolted the outer door fast to confine us and said, "A meeting of minds would be best for us all, now."

"Mr Dover, I presume?" I challenged. "What are your real name and purpose?"

The fellow ignored the question. He rubbed a weary hand over his brow. "I am very sorry to see you tangled in all of this, Dr Watson. I especially regret your involvement."

It occurred to me that Slick-Hair had named my companion but had not known me. He had recognised Miss Doré from Bath. How could Dover know the real identity of Ormond Sacker?

"Whatever is happening here," Madame Seraphina interjected, "it is no business of this house. Please take your encounter elsewhere so it does not disturb the reputation of this establishment."

"But it *is* the business of this house," Dover proclaimed. "I see it clearly now. The signs are obvious once one deploys the whole art of detection. I dare say that even the late Sherlock Holmes would not fault the observations that I make here today."

"What is 'e jawing about?" Billy asked angrily. "You're no Mr 'Olmes, matey, I'll tell you that much for free!"

"I understand what became of the Réquin letter," Dover proclaimed. "Yes, Saville, I have named our principal. Due to your bungling you have forced us to a crude conclusion of this mission. It is true that we will retrieve the sought document, but we may now allow no witnesses. All must vanish. Hence the need for anonymity is gone."

"Charles Réquin?" Miss Doré recognised the name. She had been reading the French newspapers. "The diplomat who came to fame with the Guinea treaty and received awards and acclaim from his grateful government? *That* was whom Sir George Burnwell was asking about in Paris! The same lauded politician whose name is now bruited for the Commission on Algeria; a man who could settle that mess would be positioned for the highest offices of French politics thereafter." She frowned. "He could not afford a scandal."

"This is not England," Dover scorned. "A brief fling with a mistress would not preclude him from greatness."

"And the jewelled trophy awarded by his nation and stolen for Burnwell was eventually returned," I added. "But the document... that was rather more sensitive, was it not? That had something on it that *must* be recovered. Something that would end this Réquin."

"That's a classified matter," Slick-Hair—Saville—snarled.

"You hunted for Mary Holder," Miss Doré surmised. "That chase led you to Sir George Burnwell. He fled here, to Marseilles, and you lost him for a while. But when he tried to sell the treasure he had taken, you found him again."

"It was a simple matter," Dover boasted. "Dr Watson would appreciate my methods if I described them."

"You were the 'limping old man with frazzled grey sideburns'," I guessed.

"But, yes. Once Burnwell was exposed it was simplicity itself to find him and question him, and to quietly retrieve the jewelled knife presented to our principal."

"And to beat Burnwell and kill him," I completed the sentence. "The local police were not encouraged to look too hard for a killer. The evidence was lacking."

"There *was* no evidence. And if anybody went looking for it, why, Mr Sherlock Holmes himself was nearby. Who except he might so carefully commit a crime that nobody could trace it? Who else but I?"

I could venture to name 'Dover' now: "François Le Villard, Holmes's French pupil, with whom he solved the Nantes business only a few days after Sir George was eliminated. Holmes's student and imitator, so proud of the methods he has learned."

Le Villard allowed himself a small bow. "The same. That is why I am so sorry to see you caught in this sad affair. It grieves me that Mr Holmes's great friend and chronicler must disappear in the clean-up."

"Holmes would be ashamed of you."

"Holmes was a man able to set aside emotion in pursuit of an important goal."

"If that is the only lesson you have learned then you do not know Sherlock Holmes."

"Holmes felt that you had some of the qualities of a good detective but lacked experience, M. Le Villard," Miss Doré remembered. "You proved that when you let me fool you with Culverton-Smith's ivory box."

"I owe you for that," Saville growled.

I kept on at Le Villard. "So to honour your mentor's legacy, you commit murder, using what he has taught you to cover your deed. Now you graduate to greater abominations by killing his friends."

Le Villard looked uncomfortable. Saville did not. "It is necessary," Slick-Hair declared. "For France."

"But this will still not recover you your document," Miss Doré protested.

"But it will," Le Villard revealed triumphantly. "Hope was lost until Dr Watson used the enquiry agent Le Brun to examine the correspondence between the dead *putain* and the rich *femme Anglais*. I picked up on the new thread his researches revealed and traced it despite all difficulties until I found the solution."

"What solution?" Saville demanded impatiently.

"I perceive that Dr Watson has discerned the same truth as I. Will you be so good as to reveal it, doctor?"

"Very well," I consented. "Miss Doré, you may ease your conscience. Miss Holder did not take her life before you were able to aid her. She pretended her death and escaped her situation."

"I do not understand?" the lady admitted.

I turned to Madame Seraphina. "I recognised your eyes," I told her. I had met her before, in Alexander Holder's drawing room, as she pleaded with him not to blame his son for the theft of the beryl coronet.

The madame unhooked the veil that obscured her face. "I was certain I was too changed to be recognised, Dr Watson," she confessed. To Miss Doré she added, "I was Mary Holder. Thank you for your attempt to assist me. By the time it arrived I had already made my getaway."

"The whore faked her suicide?" Saville understood at last. "This is why you had us meet here, Le Villard. You believe that *she* has the letter!"

The French detective enjoyed his moment. "I suspect that Sir George never even knew that she had taken it. She dropped the jewelled dagger to her master, but a single sheet of paper may be concealed easily about one's person. She presumably hoped it might offer her some vantage to vacate her miserable circumstance. And of course it did; once Mary Holder was thought dead she could begin her campaign of blackmail against M. Réquin."

"She put the screws on 'im and used the cash to set 'erself up!" Billy guessed.

"I survived," Madame Seraphina insisted. "It was impossible for me to go home, to return to genteel society after my misadventures and degradations. But with hush payments from the politician I was able to purchase the Lantern Rouge and put it under new management. If I was to be a woman of ill repute than I would manage the trade properly. I daresay that I have proved a talent for the business."

"On monies distrained from our principal!" objected Saville.

"Quite so," Le Villard agreed. "Unfortunately that source of income will cease. You will return the document. If so, I promise that you will all have clean and civilised ends."

"And if not, then it will be otherwise," Saville threatened.

Madame Seraphina laughed ruefully. "You are certainly not as clever as Sherlock Holmes, Monsieur Le Villard. Having encountered him, I am certain that *he* would have worked out the truth about the contents of the letter I stole. Indeed, he did."

"What truths?" the French detective was unable to resist asking.

"Why, that it was a draft letter with many useful pieces of information on it, set aside overnight to be translated into code and then sent on enciphered. But this rough note was in plain French, unencrypted, before it could be transmitted."

"And what did it contain?" Miss Doré enquired breathlessly.

"Diplomatic secrets. A summary of bribes given and taken. Compromising details of international treaties. Orders for criminal activity in furtherance of criminal goals. One sheet to damn a man to the guillotine and cripple an empire. All written out plainly, including the name of the man to whom the letter would be addressed and sent."

"And who might that be?" I prompted Seraphina. I had already guessed.

"The name of the recipient was one Professor J. Moriarty."

Le Villard blanched. His hand trembled on his pistol. "Moriarty? Réquin was working for *him*?"

"It was during the final war between the great detective and the Napoleon of Crime," I recalled. "Holmes was pushing hard. Moriarty's network was ever more exposed. Any error on either side might make the difference. Amidst it all, one careless loss of one paper might tilt the balance. And now, one letter that proves Charles Réquin a traitor, hiding behind French security services to disguise his treachery."

"That's not so," Slick-Hair insisted.

"But Saville, if it is…" Le Villard breathed.

"M. Saville?" Seraphina echoed. "His name was amongst those agents whom M. Réquin listed as paid."

"That's a lie!" Slick-Hair shouted.

Le Villard looked uncertain, desperately unhappy, suddenly unsure about the deeds he had done in service of his nation—apparently in service of his nation.

I had one more blow to strike. "You have missed a point," I told Holmes's would-be acolyte. "One important circumstance."

Miss Doré gasped as she came to it too. "Oh, John! Of course! It *must* me!"

"Must be what?" Le Villard demanded.

My companion turned to Madame Seraphina. "You escaped your misery and captivity. You were thought dead. Doubtless the perceptive M. Le Villard checked that you were really gone, using all his vaunted methods. But you evaded him, all this time, convinced him and *everyone* that you were deceased, until our investigation led him back to your door—for which I apologise. You managed to fake your suicide so well as to convince the police, Madame Charlotta, even the specialist from Paris. How? There is only one possible way."

"Sherlock Holmes," Le Villard concluded. "*Mais oui!* I used his methods to disguise the questioning and death of Sir George Burnwell so that none would ever penetrate the mystery. How much better might the Master extricate Mary Holder from her circumstances and create her a new identity for a new life? It was Sherlock Holmes who rescued you, Madame Seraphina."

I knew Holmes. "And it was to Sherlock Holmes that you gave the paper, was it not? Holmes told me when he returned to England, those final days before he closed the trap on Moriarty, that it took only the slightest slip to tip the balance between them. Was the Réquin note that slip? Whether it was or not, you gave Holmes the stolen document. He had it."

If so, then the paper was probably even now safe in my deposit box at Cox's, along with my friend's other documents.

"But the blackmail…!" objected Saville.

Seraphina sniffed. "A girl may remember enough details of a document she stole to convincingly squeeze a villain of a politician who once misused her. Mr Holmes got me clear and away from this life and place, but eventually I came back to it, not as a victim but as a businesswoman. I needed capital and Réquin was my source. But as for your note, sirs, you may whistle for it. To get it back you must defeat Sherlock Holmes himself!"

I smiled grimly. "And that you shall never do."

"No!" Saville cried. "The letter must be found, must be returned...!"

François Le Villard turned his gun on Saville. "You are under arrest, Monsieur, on suspicion of conspiracy to commit treason."

"What? Are you gone insane? Have you forgotten our mission? Our strict orders?"

"I think I am now wakening from insanity, Saville. When one is faced with significant new evidence then one must review all previous conclusions. If a new hypothesis better fits the facts then it must be pursued. Even from the grave, Sherlock Holmes continues to instruct us in the art of detection. You are under arrest."

"This will break your career!"

"It will certainly break someone's, Monsieur. I look forward to discovering whose."

We had all forgotten about the third agent, the thug who was working for Slick-Hair; all of us except for Billy, who chose that moment to leap on the fellow and batter him to the ground, using methods that were unsporting but efficient. If he made more of a show of it than necessary we could not object; Flora was watching him.

"Try not to break the furniture," Madame Seraphina requested the young man.

I assisted Billy in securing the brute he had subdued, and then had the satisfaction of closing Saville's own hand-cuffs on his wrists.

"Am I to take it that our lives are to be spared?" Miss Doré asked Le Villard.

"As Holmes noted to Doctor Watson, I have much experience still to gain," the French detective conceded.

"You shall have to gain it behind bars," I suggested, "paying for the murder of Sir George Burnwell."

Miss Doré was more perceptive than me. "There is no evidence that would convict M. Le Villard. He has seen to that. And he was serving the murky darker authorities of his state. Now he has exposed a treasonous plot against France. I doubt any court in his nation would dare to try a conviction."

Le Villard made another small bow. "Mam'selle Doré is correct, of course. Nor do I regret cleansing the world of Sir George, though I was misled as to his guilt in the matter of the missing document."

"The French authorities will paper over the whole affair?" I objected.

"No, Dr Watson. Not anymore. This matter must be untangled, not suppressed. If Mam'selle Holder, Madame Seraphina, will consent to turn

State's Evidence and testify against Charles Réquin, if she recalls enough of the note's content to allow facts to be verified, then all might yet turn out well for her. I shall face what consequences I must… but it may end well for me also." He looked over to the pinioned Saville being guarded by Billy under Flora's watchful gaze. "M. Holmes's great work must be respected, completed. I shall do my part."

I realised that I must be satisfied with that.

Miss Doré took my arm again. "Doctor Watson and I will be willing to remain in Marseille a few days whilst matters are cleared up," she promised.

"But we need not maintain our charade as the Sackers," I added.

To which Miss Alexandra Doré made no reply.

Researcher's Note:

Dr Watson and Miss Doré appear to have returned to England on or about the 25th of March 1894. On 30th March the Honourable Ronald Adair, son of the Earl of Maynooth, was discovered shot dead in a locked room on Park Lane; he had previously been playing cards with Colonel Sebastian Moran. On 5th April, Dr Watson became involved in the murder investigation and encountered an irritable and deformed bookseller. This strange character later called upon Watson and revealed himself to be Sherlock Holmes, survived from his Reichenbach Falls finale with Professor Moriarty and now returned from long travels eliminating the last vestiges of his enemy's organisation. Only one major player remained, "the second-deadliest man in London" after Moriarty himself—Moran. Watson's account of the events appears in "The Adventure of the Empty House", *The Strand Magazine* and *Collier's*, September 1903, compiled in *The Return of Sherlock Holmes* (1905).

Research has yet to uncover a detailed timeline of Miss Doré and Dr Watson's travel and activities in the unaccounted-for days between the conclusion of the Burnwell investigation and their disembarking at Portsmouth. Alexandra Doré's diary is silent on the matter and John Watson presumably had nothing to record during that period.

THE CASE
OF
THE FOURPENNY COFFIN

HE GALLERY WAS filled with row upon row of wooden boxes, each five feet seven inches long by two-feet six inches wide and deep, lined in rows with narrow walkways between them. Every one contained a sleeping man, cramped into the uncomfortable confines, laid on a straw-stuffed mattress, covered by a thin oilcloth sheet and whatever clothing they had added atop it. I immediately understood the slang term for the overnight accommodation, the "fourpenny coffin".

The Superintendent who held aside a flap of the access door gestured me inside. "This way, Doctor Watson," he requested in a hushed voice.

I followed him along the central aisle, past tattered derelicts, ruined old men and emaciated boys who lay on their backs like corpses. Only the slow rise of their chests and the occasional snore or cough betrayed that they yet lived.

The destitute of London lay about us, confined in parade formation in their hideous cribs. The air was pungent with unwashed sweat and dirty laundry. I shuddered because I knew that for many of the sleepers this was luxury accommodation.[96]

We reached the end of the balcony, where we could overlook the hall below. There were seventy-two homeless sleepers behind us, but thrice that number on the floor below. A few wall-lamps remained lit to show the way down the connecting stairway and to reveal the extent of the long, crowded hostel.

96   One description of such a venue appears in *The Quiver: An Illustrated Magazine for Sunday and General Reading* (1872), pg 554. "I entered a long, narrow room, upon the floor of which were rows of what at first sight appeared to be coffins. On closer inspection, however, I found they were simply wooden bunks, in which the homeless people slept. These bunks were about forty in number, and were placed endways against the walls, leaving a free passage down the centre of the room. They contained neither mattress nor covers — a necessary arrangement … both on the score of cleanliness and economy."

Gruesome as the accommodation may sound, at the time it was actually appreciated by some of its patrons, as attested by homeless food vendor John Fosh, interviewed in *Northern Whig*, 'The Sorrows of a Sandwich Man' (January 23rd, 1891), pg 7: "Fourpence for a doss. Salvation Army, Horseferry Road, a coffin bed and a leather blanket; but it's warm enough; the room is with steam pipes. At seven at night you goes in and gets some coffee and a bit of bread. When you goes out at seven in the morning you gets some more coffee and a bit more bread. Them and the doss is fourpence—and very good for the money."

These and other useful period sources are assembled in an online article by Geri Walton, 'Victorian Four Penny Coffins or Penny Beds, Homelessness, and More' at https://www.geriwalton.com/victorian-four-penny-coffins-penny-beds-homelessness/

"The Examination Room is at the back," the Superintendent whispered. He wore a peaked cap and a uniform jacket with brass buttons, sign of his authority. There was also a pair of male orderlies on duty and two dour matrons patrolling the roped-off women's section on the lower level.

"Is it always this full?" I asked, trying not to allow my horror to show. London is a crowded place and it can be brutal on the poor.

"It's worse when the cold snap comes," I was told. "Year before last, when the great cold came,[97] we ran out of places. Even the rope-lines and the sitting rooms were overfull."

My visit had included peeks into the other mission rooms where even less fortunate souls were housed. Fourpence won the homeless a coffin-box where they could lay relatively straight under covers, with bread and tea for supper and breakfast. Those who only had tuppence suffered on plain hard benches where they must sit upright, supported only by a rope strung for them to hook their arms over to prop them up; a line that was cut each morning at 6am as an unwelcome alarm call.[98] Those with but a single penny were allowed to sit but not slumber, bereft even of sleeping on a rope.

Yet even those men, women, and children were fortunate, for they had shelter from weather in a clean, vermin-free sanctuary, enjoyed what warmth hot water pipes running the perimeter of the room might offer, and safety from the violence that might befall a rough-sleeper at the hands of yet more desperate human predators. London is the richest city in the world, but there were poor souls for whom it might as well have been Tartarus.[99]

---

97   The winter of 1894/5 was the coldest in London since 1881/2 and was unmatched again until 1940/41. January 1885 was also notable for the appearance of thundersnow over Britain, a rare form of lightning storm in which snow or sleet, not rain, pelts from the sky.

98   Charles Dickens references such an establishment in *The Pickwick Papers*, as follows: "'And pray Sam, what is the twopenny rope?' inquired Mr. Pickwick. 'The Twopenny rope, sir,' replied Mr. Weller, 'is just a cheap lodgin' house where the beds is twopence a night!' 'What do they call a bed a rope for?' said Mr. Pickwick. 'Well the advantage o' the plan's obvious. At six o'clock every mornin', they lets go the ropes at one end, and down falls all the lodgers. Consequence is that, being thoroughly waked, they get up very quickly, and walk away.'"

99   A London census taken in January and February 1904 discovered 1,797 people without any accommodation, "of these 168 were sleeping on staircases, in doorways, or under arches, and the rest were walking the streets," but also noted "inmates of casual wards in London numbered 1,139. In addition, there were the vagrants in common, lodging-houses, including shelters; on the night in question there were 23,381 inmates of these houses..." (*Committee Report for the Departmental Committee on Vagrancy*, 1906).
It is troubling that the London Assembly and the Mayor of London's office estimate there to be around three times this number of homeless in modern London, with less shelter

At the end of the lower floor were three doors. The largest double door led down a short corridor to the commissary where guests would be sent on their way tomorrow morning with a hot drink and a third of a loaf. The other rooms were labelled 'Chapel' and 'Examination Room', and the latter was our destination.

The small tiled clinic was unremarkable, containing a padded metal inspection couch, a doctor's desk, a quartet of cheap wooden chairs, a preparation table, and locked cabinets of pharmaceuticals and bandages. The only atypical contents were an umbrella stand filled with second-hand crutches and a plumbed shower-bath with hosepipe in one corner for sluicing off patients.

The resident physician rose quickly from his seat, closing a ledger he had been studying and hastening to meet us. "Doctor Watson," he identi-fied me. "You need not have come."

"The Trustee Board thinks differently, Dr Manfred," Superintendent Hoker answered the worried-looking medical man. "They are concerned about our recent... problems. They are concerned about scandal, about the broadsheets, about..."

"I have already told the Trustees that further investigation can be con-ducted internally, discreetly," Manfred interrupted. "The parish coroner has indicated that he does not expect there to be any fuss."

Manfred was a somewhat seedy-looking fellow of middle years, with a growing paunch that stressed his waistcoat buttons and the dark bags under his eyes that suggested too little sleep or too much dissolution. I did not approve of his appearance—a doctor should maintain certain stan-dards of character and dress—or of his attitude.

"Three deaths, sir!" I barked to halt the fellow's bleating. "Three men found deceased over four nights. If the local coroner does not consider that remarkable then he is a duffer who should be replaced. And if you do not consider three such events costing three human lives to be worthy of every attention then you are also worthy of dismissal!"

The doctor stepped back as if I had struck him. I admit to temptation. "There was no need to bring in people whose notoriety is... notable," he tried to rally.

"Your Board of Trustees believes differently. And a good thing too, if this is the standard of your professional behaviour. No, don't bother chelp-ing your excuses, sir! My colleague will be joining us shortly, and I prom-ise that he will have less tolerance for your misplaced priorities than I."

---

accommodation.

The Superintendent looked nervous. He was a man of humble class whose authority over even an inferior physician was severely lacking. "Mr Holmes will be along soon?" he ventured hopefully.

The Examination Room door opened and a shabby chap slouched in without invitation.

"You cannot come in here," Superintendent Hoker told him brusquely. "Return to your bed or you'll be put outside!"

The intruder was a gaunt, crooked-shouldered chap with scraggly greying sideburns and a bulbous drink-reddened nose. I sighed.

"Let him through, Superintendent," I instructed. "Sherlock Holmes has arrived."

The interloper stood upright then, casting off the odd spinal twist that had so effectively conveyed his deformity and reduced his apparent height. He snorted in amusement and pulled away the spirit-gum glued whiskers, false nose, and yellowed dentures. "There was a time when I could surprise you with such transformations, Watson."

"I have studied you as you have studied me, Holmes. After your twentieth surprise appearance even I begin to suspect. Besides, you asked me to meet you here at this hour. Who else would burst in on our conference so punctually at exactly the scheduled moment?"

Hoker and Manfred were less sanguine about their sudden guest's arrival and mutation. "This is Mr Holmes?" the Superintendent frowned.

Holmes waved him a small greeting, still holding one peeled-off whisker like a giant hairy caterpillar. The world's greatest detective can sometimes betray a very boyish enthusiasm for deception and disguise. "Forgive the concealed appearance," he tried to salvage something of his reputation and credibility. "Given the recent occurrences at the Bell Lane Mission, I decided that a first-hand experience of residency might prove of consequence."

"You came in disguise to see what happens here for yourself," I understood.

"I did, Watson. I idled in with the crowd who came for their seven o-clock supper, rendered my fourpence to the steward at the door, sang 'All Things Bright and Beautiful',[100] and 'All People That On Earth Do Dwell'

---

100   This famous 1848 hymn by Cecil Frances Alexander would still include the now-omitted third verse:
'The rich man in his castle,
The poor man at his gate,
God made them, high and lowly,
And order'd their estate.'

to the tune of Old 100th, crammed down my bread and mashed tea, and found my assigned place in the common hall. Except of course I slipped the fellow who was due to sleep in Box 133 a wallet of shag to swap places with me so I could have his coffin."

"Box 133?" Dr Manfred frowned. "Why that particular place?"

Now it was Superintendent Hoker who looked somewhat disconcerted.

"That 'coffin' was the place where three men died on successive nights, Watson," Holmes instructed me.

"Not so," Manfred denied. "The first itinerant died in bed 89, the second in 54, and the third in 116."

"Actually…" Hoker ventured, "Well, that is technically true."

"The boxes are identified by the little metal numberplate screwed on to their ends," Holmes explained. "The plates have all been in place for a long time, enough to have become slightly corroded, fixed in place. Only four plates have shining screws denoting that they were recently exchanged— swapped over, in fact, to disguise the fact that one box has been site to three consecutive deaths."

Hoker glared at the ground, pale and unhappy. "Our visitors are su- perstitious and ignorant folk. If word got about of a 'death cot' then they would shy away, would go back to the ruin and violence of the gutters rather than take Godly refuge here," he argued. "If one of our visitors passes away, we customarily take the box for cleaning and then place it back in a different position, swapping it out with the one that formerly occupied that place. I switch the identification numbers to keep the rows in consecutive order."

This detail of procedure was evidently new to Manfred. "You mean to say that all three incidents took place in the same bed?" He glanced at me. "If I had known that then I would have looked more carefully at the events."

I suggested that the Trustees had been right to call upon Holmes to review the 'incidents'.

My friend was more interested in uncovering additional data for his implacable mind to process. "Since the present Box 133 is currently va- cated by it's rightful occupant—me—I suggest you send your orderlies to haul it in here," he told Hoker. "It requires an inspection that is best con- ducted in better light without the need for circumspection."

Hoker assented and dispatched the two male attendants about the work.

"What information have you on the dead men?" I demanded of him. "All the Trustees relayed to us were their names."

"Those would be from the ledger," Dr Manfred said.

"The signing-in book where every visitor writes their name or leaves

"...to disguise the fact that one box has been site to three consecutive deaths."

their mark," Holmes supplied. He must have scribed some pseudonym in that way himself earlier in the evening. "The clerk appends the name given by those men and women who are not literate."

"And not all our guests offer their real names," Hoker admitted. "But I can speak for the first man to die, Will Hosketh. He was a regular, here every night when he could afford it. A very kind old man. I was saddened to find he had passed in his sleep."

"You discovered him?" I checked.

The Superintendent nodded. "We wake the guests at seven. At this time of year we light the lamps because it is still dark out. They vacate their beds, fold their sheets, and make their way to the chapel for a brief prayer before breakfast. They are usually on their way by half past seven. One of my duties is to check the vacated boxes; you understand that occasionally our visitors are incontinent or otherwise unclean, and in that case we would need to change the mattress. And there are slow risers who need chivvying out of their beds."

"You took Hosketh for such a recalcitrant?"

"He could be a heavy sleeper, and an occasional drinker. We do not allow guests to come in if they are inebriated, but sometimes they will sneak a flask in and imbibe in the night. I thought Will might have been deeply asleep to ignore the bell, or else perhaps a little unwell. He was a man of advanced years, probably as old as seventy."

"But he was dead," Holmes prompted.

"Yessir. Even as I shook him I could tell. His lips were pale and there was a stiffness about him. I knew at once that he was gone."

"What is the procedure then?" I wondered.

"I inform Dr Manfred," Hoker explained, and glanced at Manfred to take up the explanation.

"We bring the man and his bed in here to the examination room," the resident physician answered curtly. "I confirm the death and summon a colleague to countersign the death certificate. A notice is sent to the local coroner and a judicial decision is made whether to convene an inquest. The body is removed to St Bart's hospital morgue pending funeral arrangements.[101] If there is no known next of kin then a pauper's burial is arranged in a common plot."

Holmes turned back to Hoker. "When you discovered the man, did you

---

101   St Bartholomew's Hospital, Smithfield, London, was founded in 1123. It is Watson's alma mater and the venue for his initial meeting with Sherlock Holmes in *A Study in Scarlet*. Threatened with closure in 1993, the institution was rescued by a 'Save Bart's Campaign' which included activities and a donation from the Tokyo Sherlock Holmes Appreciation Society.

observe any details that might actually be of aid? Any sign of struggle, of convulsion?" He appealed to Manfred. "Any effusion of fluids? The condition of the sclera?"

Neither man had much useful information about the condition of the late Will Hosketh. Hoker must have read Holmes's disappointment and disdain because he added, "The old fellow had no family left. His son died out on the British Gold Coast with Wolseley back in '74.[102] After that he took to the bottle and into destitution. He made what living he could as a pavement artist, with chalks and charcoal. He was quite good. He once did me a drawing of my littlest girl, Effie. I still have it today."

"The other deceased?"

"Signed in as Benjamin Crewe, Labourer, and Hosiah Swinnart, Porter. I didn't know either of them. I took Crewe to be a tramping man. We get a lot of them passing through, looking for work or avoiding the law. Swinnart had a twisted leg that he said was from an accident. He was a Londoner by his accent. I checked the books and he'd been here four times before in the last eight weeks, but I'd not noted him."

Manfred evidently felt the need to keep up with the Superintendent. "Crewe was a crude, fit fellow, with labourer's hands. I took his death to be heart-failure. These big types can go suddenly, you know. Swinnart was in his fifties, and he showed some signs of dropsy, so that may have killed him."

I dislike a doctor who does not clearly determine a cause of death. "What sort of examination did you give these dead men in your Examination Room?" I demanded.

"Enough to determine that they were beyond revival," Manfred argued. "I do not have the time or the facilities here for autopsies It is not my job. Determination of final cause is the coroner's province."

"Informed by your findings, sir! Did you do anything more than check for a pulse and make some likely guess?"

Holmes intervened before I lost my temper. It is not often that he must calm me down. "These corpses, what became of their possessions?"

Hoker answered quickly. "We have them here, sir, pending determination of ownership." He gestured towards a wall cupboard. "None of them had very much."

Under Holmes's imperious eye he produced three parcelled bundles and untied the string that held the brown paper in place.

---

102   The Third Anglo-Ashanti War took place in 1873-74, in what is now Ghana, where 2,500 British troops and several thousand West Indian and African troops under General Garnet Wolseley repelled an Ashanti invasion. British casualties were light, with more dying from disease than enemy action.

The first package to hand was the effects of Hosiah Swinnart. Holmes's long fingers raked through the humble pile, halting a moment to sniff and correctly identify the tobacco in the fellow's pouch, but otherwise finding little of value and less of interest in the crippled porter's property.

Benjamin Crewe's parcel included a browned, crumpled daguerreotype of some young woman, with the name 'Amy' inscribed upon the reverse in faded ink; any frame had long since been sold off. His possessions included a second shirt, the front half of a New Testament, and a used handkerchief of particular grubbiness.

Will Hosketh's assemblage included a tin of chalks, the tools of his trade, and a scrip of leads and charcoals. He also carried three dozen scraps of paper, clearly hoarded for sketching purposes. Most of them bore vignette images. I thought his work rather good, with an eye for faces and expressions, and said so.

"He had a bit of a talent, old Will," Hoker agreed. "When he could afford it, he bought a bit of decent paper and would do sketches of the ladies and gents promenading along Mayfair or the Mall maybe, then try and sell them pictures of themselves. Sometimes it paid off. He'd get ninepence or a shilling for a quick portrait he did right then and there. But he'd always drink his fee away by the next day, poor fellow."

The Superintendent's rueful remembrance was interrupted by the bustle of his orderlies arriving with the dead men's box. They heaved it onto Manfred's examination table and left it for our inspection.

There didn't seem much to see. The wood was cheap plain varnished ash, jointed with tenon and mortice into that coffin-like bed. A thin canvas mattress roll about two inches deep was stuffed with straw. Buttons sealed in the stuffing, which could be replaced after the cover was washed. The stamped numberplate betrayed the evidence of exchange that had alerted Holmes to the case's oddest feature.

"I don't see what agency could kill three men in this same box, Holmes," I confessed. "I have checked it carefully for poison needles and hidden traps. The fellows who died ate the common fare served from a common pot. From the little we know of them, they had no acquaintance with each other or any other circumstance in common except for their reduced positions in society."

Manfred tried to object when Holmes eviscerated the mattress in his Examination Room, but his complaints were in vain. The canvass sheath was unbuttoned and the entire contents laid out across the surgery floor. "When each man died, was the mattress exchanged? Cleaned?" Holmes pressed the Superintendent.

"There was no need," Hoker answered defensively. "None of the dead men soiled himself or left any other mess. We swapped the beds but no more was required."

Holmes raked through the pale brittle hay that he had liberated from the bedding. He dropped to the floor to conduct a closer inspection through his magnifying lens, halting to examine each jack of straw before passing on. Manfred and Hoker exchanged uncomfortable looks, surely wondering what the eccentric detective was searching for—or finding?

"Look here," Holmes called, gesturing me down to where he now held a little clump of matted straw, seven or eight strands stuck together. He parted the stalks that were adhered with a brown sticky substance.

"What is it?" I asked, not entirely sure I wished to know.

Holmes smelled the evidence but did not answer. He carefully folded the clumped wad into a paper, frowning.

He turned back to the parcels. "That was the entirety of the men's possessions?"

"Apart from the clothes they were wearing when they went to the morgue," Manfred insisted. "Even their boots are here."

"Their pockets were checked?"

"Yes," Hoker promised. "There was some loose coin, not much for two of them but old Will had the best part of five bob in change. What cash there was is in the vestry safe."

"Five shillings?" I echoed. That was a lot for a destitute beggar to carry. After all, a common dock labourer expects only two shillings a day wages.[103] "Pavement drawing is more lucrative than I had supposed."

"He could have bought a proper bed for the night if he'd wanted. I expect this was what he knew, had become used to."

---

103   Victorian incomes changed over the period of Holmes and Watson's adventures, but *Down East and Up West* by Montague Williams (1894) gives an example of a sandwich-board advertising man receiving 1/- to 1/8 per day, for a full time annual income of £12—£20. On the other hand, a young middle-class civil service clerk might earn £80 per year, rising to £200 over time ('Tempted London—Young Men', a series of anonymous articles in the *British Weekly*, 1887-8), a butler could expect between £40 and £100 per annum (*Dickens's Dictionary of London*, 1879), and a general practitioner doctor such as John H. Watson might expect to enjoy around £1,300 per year on average ('The wealth of distinguished doctors: retrospective survey', I C McManus, *British Medical Journal*, December 2005). Arthur Sherwell's *Life in West London* (1897) offers an actual weekly budget for a poor family that shows them failing to meet all their debts on £1 13s. 7½d weekly. A. L. Bowley in *Wages in the United Kingdom in the 19th Century* (Cambridge: University Press, 1900) estimated the cost of living for an unmarried professional man, including rent, taxes, and maintaining two servants as £487 per year, allowing £10 for wine.

Holmes counted Hosketh's treasury. "Four shillings and eightpence," he observed, "That and fourpence for his coffin would come to exactly a crown. Did he by any chance pay for his final accommodation with a five shilling coin?"

"I'd have to ask the clerk," Hoker admitted. "If he did then it would have been noticed. Nobody here ever produces an Oxford."[104]

"Someone did, the night of the first death," Dr Manfred broke in. "It was almost as soon as the doors opened, before there was much in the cash box. Fairbody had to come through here to me for change to break a crown. I remarked it at the time."

"Do you still have the coin?" Holmes asked urgently.

The doctor shrugged. "Probably not. I don't keep track of loose change. Do you? I do recall it was new-minted, though, still shiny. One of the modern ones with the altered picture of Her Majesty, and St George on the tail."[105]

"What of the other two men?" Holmes went back to the Superintendent. "Did you note anything about them when you discovered their bodies?"

"I was surprised to find Crewe like that," Hoker conceded. "And two men in two nights, we've not had that before. I was worried that we'd have the press and the courts, like that business with Annie Knight. But as it was, the coroner took a sensible view and we were spared. Until this third one, I suppose and..." He broke off before he finished by saying, "you."

The Knight case loomed over our entire investigation. In January 1895, a sixty-five year old woman named Anne Clifford, alias Knight, was discovered dead in her 'bunk' at a shelter on Hanbury Street, Spitalfields. An investigation and case went to court against the Salvation Army, who operated the hostel, but a jury ruled that Knight died from natural causes brought on by old age and debility.[106]

104   Oxford' was a colloquial name for a crown or five shilling piece. 'Oxford scholar', shortened to 'Oxford', was Cockney rhyming slang for 'dollar', since Victorian exchange rates were roughly four U.S. dollars to one pound sterling, the dollar therefore being valued at around five shillings.

105   Three different portraits of Queen Victoria appeared on British coinage during her long reign. Her 'Young Head' image was imprinted from 1838-1887, then changed at her Golden Jubilee for the 'Jubilee Head' picture that she so disliked, and then again in 1893-1901 for the 'Widow Head' or 'Old Head' portrait, with St George slaying his dragon on the obverse. All the five-shilling coins were of Sterling silver.

106   The *Sheffield Evening Telegraph*'s January 2nd 1895 article, "Death in a Salvation Army Shelter," offers the following account of court proceedings:

"Agnes Braid, night officer in charge of the shelter, stated [that the] ... witness did not see the deceased on Saturday night, but on going to wake her on Sunday morning found her dead. — The Corner: Are they in beds or bunks? — Witness: Bunks, sir. — The Coroner: I supposed there is something for warmth?—Witness: They put their own clothes

The Bell Lane Trustees were very shy of the notoriety and difficulties another such action might bring down upon their mission. They evidently hoped that Sherlock Holmes might resolve matters before the coroner instructed the police.

"And Swinnart's discovery?"

"I'm not sure, sir," Superintendent Hoker explained apologetically. "That being Tuesday night, which is one of my times off, that and Sunday. It was Chaffinch, my deputy, who had the duty on Wednesday morning. By the time I arrived at eight o'clock sharp, the incident was dealt with. Swinnart was already carried into this Examination Room, awaiting Dr Manfred's attention."

"You were not here?" I asked the medical man. I had understood the fellow to be present on-call during the hours that the hostel was in use.

"I had stepped out for a brief time," he told me defensively. He must have known that he had erred by his delinquency. Hoker's expression betrayed some satisfaction that the doctor's error was noted by someone of a station to comment on it. I suppose that a humble mission like Bell Lane, sequestered in a back-street between Spitalfields and Petticoat Lane Markets, would not be able to afford the best of physicians.

Holmes sorted through Hosketh's sketches, picking out the largest of them, on the best paper. It had clearly been intended as a portrait to sell, but was only half completed. It depicted a gay young lady in fashionable dress and hat, looking over her shoulder, laughing. So vivid was the charcoal etching that I could almost hear her merry voice; a most engaging woman, she seemed to me. But splatters of mud, probably thrown up by carriage wheels or horses' hooves besmirched the sheet, rendering it unsaleable. "Do either of you know what lady this image portrays?" he asked Hoker and Manfred.

Neither man could say. Holmes lost interest in the doctor and the Superintendent.

"We must make further enquiries, Watson," my friend insisted. "Would you oblige me by speaking with the parish coroner whose inattention has so far been notable, and procuring for me whatever case files he may have

---

over them [later this was amended to oil cloths being used for warmth]. The place is heated by hot water. — The Coroner: Kept at an even temperature?—Witness: No. ... The Coroner: How many come in every night? — Witness: From 200 to 300. ... A Juror: A more important question is that such a number of persons should be allowed to sleep in one room. The Coroner: A certain cubic measure is required or it would not be allowed ... In the meantime, hundreds willingly go there; otherwise they would be sitting about on doorsteps."

assembled? If there have not been proper autopsies then have them set in hand. You know the methods."

"Is that necessary?" Manfred interrupted. "After all, these are men of no consequence, who likely…"

"I shall be rendering to the Trustees my account of events so far," Holmes continued implacably, "and expressing my poor opinion of the medical attention so far brought to bear." As the resident physician blanched then reddened, Holmes continued speaking to me. "I would also appreciate you tracking down our associate Langdale Pike. You know where to find him. If anyone can identify at sight a young society beauty then it is he."

I scowled but assented; Pike is not my favourite companion, but I will own that the fellow knows his seedy business.[107]

Holmes reached for his discarded whiskers. "I must one again don my guise of out-of-luck teamster and blend in with the breakfast crowd. I shall be asking about the rumours of deaths, and by name about the three deceased. A humble itinerant may learn more in that mission hall than might a consulting detective."

Hoker and Manfred may have had more questions, but my friend resumed the slouch, demeanour, and character of the tramp whom he portrayed, and nothing could then budge him from it.

I did not approach St James's Street in the best of moods. London was damp, foggy, and cold. Since tonight would be Bonfire Night, the streets were filled with portuning children requesting "a Farthing for the Guy."[108]

---

107   The celebrated gossipmonger makes the briefest of appearances to assist Holmes in identifying a suspect in "The Adventure of the Three Gables" from *The Case-Book of Sherlock Holmes*. Secondary sources have fleshed out his background significantly but never authoritatively. Watson writes of him:

"This strange, languid creature spent his waking hours in the bow window of a St. James's Street club and was the receiving station as well as the transmitter for all the gossip of the metropolis. He made, it was said, a four-figure income by the paragraphs which he contributed every week to the garbage papers which cater to an inquisitive public. If ever, far down in the turbid depths of London life, there was some strange swirl or eddy, it was marked with automatic exactness by this human dial upon the surface."

It is generally accepted that Langdale Pike is a literary pseudonym; Langdale Pike is actually a prominent geological feature in the Cumbrian Lake District.

108   The custom of fashioning a rag mannequin to burn on Guy Fawkes Night or

My visit to the coroner had been difficult and lengthy. The fellow was one of the old-style appointees, a solicitor rather than a physician, with more interest in administrative process than in the discharge of professional medical duties. I now understood how three deaths over four nights in the same hostel might go unremarked and uninvestigated. By the end of it I had delivered a piece of my mind that shocked the fellow out of his complacency and triggered orders for some competent pathologist to examine the three corpses; Hosketh would need to be exhumed from his pauper's plot.

I had such notes as existed for the cursory examinations that had been conducted on Hosketh, Crewe, and Swinnart. Manfred had fallen back on the old standby cause of death as 'heart-failure', which is not so much a determination as a description of lack of life. Every death results in heart failure. I also mentioned that to the coroner, somewhat forcefully.

It did seem from what paltry post-mortem check had been made that Crewe at least was in good health. I was sufficiently disturbed by my reception at the coroner's office to make a side-trip to take a brief first-hand look at the two bodies still held at Bart's morgue.

I don't pretend to have Holmes's almost supernatural ability to read the people he encounters as if they had their professions and circumstances inked upon their foreheads. However, in a long lifetime of medical and military service and as Holmes's companion on innumerable investigations, I have picked up some small capacity for noting relevant detail. I observed that Crewe had the sort of calluses any hard-working manual labourer might have, and that his back bore signs of a military flogging at some time in his past. Swinnart's leg had been broken and badly reset, perhaps six or nine months ago, which had presumably led to his difficulty in retaining employment and lodgings. The man did present some symptoms of oedema as Manfred has indicated, and that can cause sudden heart or liver failure, but without cutting the chap open I could not discover more.

Hence to Clubland, and the louche Langdale Pike's St James's hideout. I found him sprawled along his customary bow window, watching the carriages pass outside. A box of Turkish delight lay on his lap and he offered me a piece of the gooey confectionary. I declined.

"Is this about the tragic Mrs Ronder?" he asked me, anticipating, or at

---

Bonfire Night, November 5th, is still observed by the youth of Great Britain, in remembrance of the thwarted Catholic 'Gunpowder Plot' to blow up the Houses of Parliament on that day in 1605. Prior to immolation, this 'guy' is displayed in a public place by children hoping to collect money for treats or fireworks.

least hoping for some scandal or gossip regarding Mrs Merrilow's mysterious veiled lodger, whom Holmes had but lately investigated.[109] I have no idea how Pike might have come to hear of the matter.

"It is not," I replied brusquely. "Holmes asks if you can supply the name and any detail about the young lady in this portrait." I handed across the mud-smeared image.

"And I don't suppose you will reveal to me what you and your great friend were doing this last year, when all was silence?" Pike probed.

"Those matters are none of your concern."[110]

"Mrs Cawdore-Farrington was not involved?"

"Who?"

Pike swept the back of is hand towards the sketch. "The Honourable Alicia Sophie Victoria Cawdore-Farrington, of *those* Hampshire Farringtons, spouse of Major Sir Albert Cawdore DSO DL.[111] She looks uncharacteristically happy."

"You can identify her, then," I recognised. "Why is her merriment not typical?"

"Why because she has the most miserable marriage in London, old spot," Pike answered me. "Everyone knows it. Nothing else is talked of. The beauteous Alicia was bought-in by the Cawdores for their stud book—the noble Farringtons are stony broke these days, they say, and desperate to fix their wagon to some name and fortune that can keep them solvent and respectable."

"The alliance between Major and Mrs Cawdore-Farrington was primarily a marriage of negotiation," I understood.

Pike smirked. "What else? She is beautiful, talented, bright, and popular. He is a craggy Highlander thirty-two years her senior, dour, mean-

---

109   Watson includes an account as 'The Adventure of the Veiled Lodger' in *The Case-Book of Sherlock Holmes*. The events therein are customarily dated to October 1896, which places Watson's meeting with Pike on Thursday, 5th November of that year and the three deaths on the 31st ult. and the 1st and 3rd inst.

110   Holmesian debate is never more speculative than in accounting for the 'missing year' in Dr Watson's reports between the conclusion of 'The Adventure of the Bruce-Partington Plans' on 23rd November 1895 (recorded in *His Last Bow*, 1908) and 'The Adventure of the Veiled Lodger' around eleven months later. No definitive story of Holmes's exploits in that time has yet been unearthed.

111   That is, Distinguished Service Order, then quite a new award for "meritorious or distinguished service by officers of the armed forces during wartime, typically in actual combat," and Deputy Lieutenant, a Crown appointment as one of several deputies to the Lord Lieutenant of a ceremonial county.

spirited, and jealous. It could hardly be a match made in heaven. One almost expects to hear of the notice of divorce as soon as the lawyers have finished drafting their causes."

"Divorce?" That was a serious matter, requiring significant evidence and substantial scandal. I had no idea what the judicial outcome of such a case might be, especially if there was no evidence of infidelity or spousal neglect or cruelty to convince a jury.

"Divorce." Langdale Pike sounded as if he might relish the long-drawn-out, gory business. I suppose it was fodder for his newspaper columns. "But not soon, I deem. If sweet Alicia tears herself from her dear lawful husband in an inuxorial display of independence then she will forfeit all the allowance made by her husband's clan, and doubtless incur severe, even ruinous penalties for breaking her marriage contract. Only with clear evidence of the Major's wrongdoing would she ever stand a chance in court of extricating herself to anywhere but the poorhouse."

"But this is certainly she?" I checked, indicating Hosketh's half-done picture.

"Unmistakably. And a rather nice sketch, I must say. I wonder to whom she was turning to speak? A shame the artist never filled in the second character."

Now that Pike had drawn my attention, it was clear that there was intended to be a second figure sketched in beside the first. The placement on the paper allowed for it, to depict the companion at whom she smiled so engagingly. Holmes had undoubtedly noted it, but I saw it only now. "Have you any idea who that person might be?"

"Speculation only, alas," the gossipmonger mourned. "A pity. Had this drawing been completed then it might have been dynamite. If it was a man with Mrs Cawdore-Farrington, a man other than the husband at whom she would never smile like that, then the Major might take any action he pleased to discipline her and to ruin her lover. It would not be incontrovertible evidence of infidelity, but it would probably sway a courtroom—juries love pictures, you know. It would certainly be enough to chain her to old Cawdore for life, or for such long miserable years as his remaining tenure on Earth can spawn."

Pike wanted to know more about the portraitist and the circumstances of the image being made. I had to admit something of the old pavement artist and his possibly-untimely passing.

The scandal columnist was unexpectedly helpful. "This was sketched very recently on Rotten Row," he opined. "Alicia is wearing the very latest fashion, and she is dressed for public riding, which means she was in Hyde Park.[112] Sketch-artists often go there and pencil hasty portraits of fashionable couples in hopes of selling them as souvenirs."

"How much might such a sketch earn them?" I wondered, thinking of the crown in Hosketh's pocket.

"Oh, sixpence or a bob, perhaps, if it takes the lady's fancy. Or a clip on the ear for cheek if her swain is feeling irritable."

"Not five shillings, then?"

"For a charcoal outline on cheap linen paper? Not likely. Besides, this picture is marred with mud. If the artist wanted to sell something to Alicia and her beau, assuming there *was* a beau not a female friend, then he would need to start again on a fresh leaf."

"Perhaps he did?" I wondered. Theories began to assemble in my head.

I retrieved the sketch though Pike was reluctant to part with it, eschewed another proffered lump of mawkish Turkish delight, and headed back to the mission to discover how Holmes's breakfast had suited him.

The sleeping hall and gallery of the Bell Lane hostel seemed as eerie empty as they had filled with shadowed, sleeping bodies. Now the long rows of stark wooden boxes were lit by watery rays of daylight through the high leaded windows. The sleeping crates did indeed resemble coffins, prepared for the influx of an army of exhausted and hopeless half-dead.

The halls smelled strongly of bleach, carbolic, and boiled cabbage. Three volunteers were sanitising the mission after its nightly hosting while others clattered in the kitchen preparing soup and rolls for a lunch-time charity run to the tramps under the railway arches. Despite the strong odours, I was still able to locate Sherlock Holmes from the chemical smells

---

112   Rotten Row is a wide track running almost a mile along the southern edge of Hyde Park. Originally established by King William III as a safe route between Kensington Palace and St James's Palace through the then-robber haunted park, in 1690 it became the first artificially-lit highway in Britain. By the 18th century, the Route de Roi was known by its corrupted name, Rotten Row, and it and the adjacent South Carriage Drive had become the fashionable place for noble and wealthy Londoners and handsome military officers to ride, to see and be seen. To facilitate Rotten Row's popular use, the road was converted into a 'modern' bridleway in 1876 with a brick base covered in sand. Its popularity as an elite social venue continued well into the 20th century, and Rotten Row remains open to the public to ride their horses along even today.

permeating from the Examination Room.

Holmes had eschewed his disguise once more, and now stood in waist-coat and shirt-sleeves at Dr Manfred's workbench. The resident physician, though he had technically discharged his shift, hovered anxiously and watched the detective at work.

I regarded the row of glass tubes and dishes on display, and the bottles of nitric acid and ammonia. "You are testing for poison," I recognised. "Atropa Belladonna?"

"Very good, doctor," my friend greeted me. "You will excuse us, Manfred, while my colleague and I catch up on our respective investigations."

Manfred, singularly unhappy at being thrown out of his own surgery, slouched away to make whatever complaint he could to the Trustees who had imposed us upon his fiefdom. Holmes added a measure of silver nitrate to the sample in his test tube and watched in satisfaction as a yellowish-white precipitate formed.

"If this proves soluble in dilute ammonia but insoluble in *aqua fortis* then deadly nightshade was present in my test sample," he told me. Then, after a glance at me, he noted, "You stepped into a puddle outside the coroner's office, and from the splatter pattern upon your left trouser leg you were stamping at the time. Did your visit anger you so much? I presume that you have now set the legal representative upon a proper course?"

"I wonder whether I need ever speak to you at all to detail my researches," I admitted, slightly grumpily and unfairly; it had been a long night for both of us, but Holmes had got less sleep than I.

"It is my incurable habit to read the people whom I encounter, and you are an open book, Watson. That is a compliment. There is no deception, malice, or dishonourable intent about you. Now come, tell me what Pike had to offer and what you observed of the corpses at Bart's."

I surrendered and recounted my expedition. Holmes asked a few pertinent questions about the conditions of the cadavers but was most interested in the identity of Mrs Cawdore-Farrington. He followed my own line of reasoning but extended it further.

"I am beginning to understand what happened here," he admitted. "There is one thing missing, but… No, let us begin with what we have. The talented but destitute Will Hosketh decided to venture his luck in drawing portraits on Rotten Row or Horseguards Parade. It is a little late in the year for such enterprise, but he had evidently had a sufficient windfall to invest in new charcoals and some few sheets of bonded paper. He sketched a likely candidate, the beautiful and fashionable Alicia Cawdore-

Farrington, in her happy expedition with a companion. He never got to complete his vignette with that companion's image because some mishap befell his drawing paper, which was besmirched with splashed mud."

"Do you agree that he likely persisted and drew a second picture?" I ventured.

"I suspect so. But he did not complete it in time to sell it to the Hyde Park revellers." Holmes indicated the patched, holed workboots that had once belonged to the down-and-out pavement artist. "That granular orange soil testifies to a recent trip to Bedford Park, well west of Hosketh's usual stamping ground. Let us suppose that Old Will, having completed his second work too late, enquires of some other person present the identity and address of either Mrs Cawdore-Farrington or her companion, and then trudges out to call upon his subject at home. He still hopes to sell the picture of such a happy meeting. And so he did."

"His shiny new crown. Pike said it was far too much to pay for any street-sketch, but if it secured ownership of evidence that might be used against the lady..."

"Then the payment might be cheaper than opening the way to blackmail," Holmes agreed. "I do not suggest that Hosketh had any such intent. Nothing I heard of him when I talked with the other guests at breakfast suggested about him any ingenuity of that kind. But I did speak with one acquaintance of his who offered a useful nugget of information."

It was time to hear Holmes's account of his undercover exploits. "My witness identified himself only as 'Snuffy'. He was on speaking terms with Hosketh and was stood in line behind him when Hosketh proffered his five-shilling coin for his night's lodgings. It was a matter of comment, when the clerk Fairbody had to go find sufficient change. Hosketh told Snuffy that he had sold a picture for the most money his work had ever bought, and had been 'sweetly rewarded and all'. Those particular words, Watson, which prove to be most relevant."

"How so?"

Holmes held up a delaying finger. "We shall get to that. First... ah, yes, the test is positive. Our sample contains not one but two dangerous concentrations of toxins, Watson. This test demonstrates the presence of belladonna. My previous experiment confirmed the inclusion of laudanum."

I frowned. "Nightshade vitiates the effects of tincture of opium," I objected.

"Not in the concentrations present in our sticky residue. The effects of ingestion of any substantial sample would have been to induce first catalepsy from the opiate and then tachycardia leading to heart-failure from the belladonna."[113]

He set the dishes aside for now and returned to his account. "Nobody who I was able to interview at the common table this morning knew aught of Benjamin Crewe. He was a true itinerant, a rough man whose demeanour suggested a violent disposition. The other visitors shunned him. Hosiah Swinnart was somewhat known and his death was a common topic. Of particular interest was the account of one of his close neighbours in a nearby bed the night that he died, who claims he heard Swinnart giggle, just once, as if pleased with himself. It may have been the last sound that Swinnart made. You see how helpful that is?"

"Not immediately," I responded. "Can you explain how three men were poisoned in their 'coffins', in different parts of the hostel hall, over four nights, under the watch of the Superintendent and his orderlies? Or even why?"

"I think I am ready to assay a possibility, Watson. Let us have Dr Manfred and Superintendent Hoker back in here, and I will put it to them."

It was easy to find the men, since Manfred was in the hall berating the Superintendent for Holmes's interference. They fell silent when I appeared, and followed me back into the Examination Room with guarded expressions.

"The key was identifying the sticky substance that matted the straw from the coffin's bedding," Holmes told them without preamble. "The compound was of molasses, brown sugar, butter, and baking soda. And a strong dose of tranquilliser to mask the working of an equal dose of lethal poison."

Hoker did not follow. "Are you saying that the mattress was poisoned?"

"No," Holmes snorted at the suggestion. "Here is my hypothesis, based upon the data so far: Will Hosketh drew, then delivered and sold, a picture that depicted two people together who should not have met. He was paid well for his work by one or both of the subjects and sent on his way, but one or other of them determined to discourage the artist from attempting any other such portrait, or from speaking of his sale.

"In addition to his fee, one new crown, Hosketh was given a special treat, a luxury to be relished by a man in such impecunious circumstance as he suffered. He was given a confection made of the elements I identified.

---

113   This is the combination of drugs that medical historians suspect was used to poison Solomon Northup, the free Black man who was kidnapped and sold into slavery in 1841 and whose story is told in *Twelve Years a Slave* by Solomon Northup, Sue L Eakin, and Joseph Logsdon (Baton Rouge: Louisiana State University Press, 1975).

A seasonal confection, in fact."

I thought of the time of year, and of the hard sweetmeat baked to celebrate Guy Fawkes Night. "Bonfire toffee!" I cried. "Treacle toffee! Surely those are the ingredients?"[114]

"They are," Holmes confirmed. "Furthermore, the strong taste of black treacle is ideal for masking the bitterness of belladonna. The hardness of the confectionary—such toughness as to require a baked sheet of bonfire toffee to be shattered with a hammer before consumption—means that the sweet must be slowly sucked; it is too tough to chew. It is the ideal delivery mechanism for a slow-acting poison."

"Hosketh was given a bag of toffee to silence him," I understood. "But the others? Crewe and Swinnart?"

"Elementary. Remember, this is a rough lodging, for all the mission's precautions. I am informed that it is customary for guests to secure whatever valuables they have in the mattress on which they sleep, to prevent pilfering in the night. The buttoned covers offer easy access to conceal humble treasures in the straw, items that can be retrieved come wake-up."

"Unless one does not wake up," I recognised.

"Indeed. And if the mattress is not changed, as the Superintendent has indicated it was not in this case, then the next occupant might find that same paper bag of treats and claim them for himself. The third box occupant clearly missed finding it, but the fourth, Swinnart, again availed himself of a discovery he doubtless thought providential."

"You searched the mattress," Manfred objected. "You scattered its contents all over my floor. There was no... bonfire toffee."

"Not then," Holmes agreed. "Only the seepage from its earlier presence, the sticky residue that allowed me to identify it had been there. After the third death, the bag itself was discovered and removed."

"By who?" Hoker demanded.

"By your substitute, of course. You said it was your deputy, Chaffinch, who had the duty that morning? Let's have him in and hear how he disposed of his find."

"Chaffinch? He's not in today. He has the day off, to spend with his wife and children and to celebrate... Bonfire Night."

---

114   Variously called bonfire toffee, treacle toffee, plot toffee, or Tom Trot in England, claggum or clack in Scotland, or loshin du or taffi triog in Wales, the molasses-based confection is a hard, brittle toffee associated with Hallowe'en and Guy Fawkes Night in the same way that mince pies go with Christmas. Its flavour is similar to that of butterscotch. It was a home-made or commercially-branded staple treat in Victorian homes, an affordable but luxury item for the poorest classes.

I followed the horrified Superintendent's thinking. "Your deputy came across the toffee in the dead man's mattress. He reasoned that Swinnart had no more use for it, but Chaffinch's children…" I stared in dismay at Holmes.

"Yes, Watson," he agreed. "We must go! At once!"

Four urgent men tumbled out of a Growler in the cobbled terrace back-road of Tenter Street, between Tower Bridge and Aldgate. A long monotonous row of London brick terraces presented one door and three windows each to the narrow thoroughfare. Holmes led us not to the seldom-used front door of Jerome Chaffinch's address,[115] but rather through the arched passageway to the rears of the properties, where small vegetable plots backed on to waste ground belonging to the Catholic School Board.

I do not know whether the Roman Church would have approved of the use of its land to host a neighbourhood bonfire to celebrate the capture and execution of Catholic protestors, but I doubt anyone had enquired. A horde of excited children and a few indulgent parents were building a nine-foot high cone of rotten wood and stuffed newspapers ready for the event to come.

"There he is!" Superintendent Hoker pointed, identifying his deputy. Chaffinch was by the growing unlit pyre, supervising the addition of some broken packing crates. The fellow looked up in surprise that turned to alarm as he saw his superior and the mission's medical man closing upon him.

"Sir?" he managed. "Sirs?"

"The treacle toffee," Holmes required urgently. "Where is it?"

"The… the what, sir?"

"It's poisoned, man," I told him shortly. "It's what killed those three guests of yours."

---

115   In many humble terraced homes, the front door that led to the 'sitting parlour' was reserved for important or 'official' visitors such as a clergyman or landlord. All other access and regular domestic use came through the back door. This is why 'back-to-back' terraces and their occupants, which had but a single door because each side of the building was a separate house, were considered inferior in status to regular terraces and their humble dwellers. Author I.A. Watson can attest that this practice and the prejudices that went with it were still observed by elderly residents of Yorkshire as late as the 1990s.

"There he is!"

Chaffinch went even paler. He produced a grubby paper bag from his pocket and handed it to Holmes, like a guilty schoolboy caught smuggling treats into class. But his next words destroyed that cosy allusion. "Our Effie grazed 'er knee. I gave 'er a lump early for being a good girl."

The luxury had been reserved for the night's revels, then, but one lethal piece had already been distributed.

"The child," I called sharply. "Where is she?"

Chaffinch shouted his other children to locate their little sister. The urgent call alerted neighbours and other boys and girls to the crisis and the search became general.

Effie Chaffinch was found unconscious by the perimeter fence, half-hidden in a patch of dock leaves. She did not respond to calls to wake up or to shaking.

I took charge of the patient. There was no time to send for emetics so I simply forced my fingers down her throat to make her gag. I kept doing it, messy as it was, until she had vomited up as much of her stomach contents as I could get out of her.

"Brandy! Or whisky!" Holmes called to Dr Manfred. There is no cure for belladonna poisoning, so treatment is by emetic and then continual stimulation. While Manfred raced for a spirits shop I applied artificial respiration.

"I didn't know!" Chaffinch gabbled to Hoker. "How could I know? I thought no 'arm! I'd never, sir, never…"

"Your part in this was but minor, Mr Chaffinch," Holmes assured the distraught father. "The author of this is the person who mixed this hellacious confection with such deadly intent. And, tellingly, had it ready to use before the pavement artist called."

Effie Chaffinch lived. With proper care and time she made a full recovery. The Bell Lane Mission Board of Trustees decided not to take disciplinary action against Chaffinch for his benevolently-intended theft, but Dr Manfred's contract of service was not renewed when it expired.

Coroners' inquests confirmed Holmes's already-established conclusions about the presence of deadly nightshade and laudanum in the victims' stomachs. The verdicts were amended to murder by person or persons unknown. But of course Sherlock Holmes would not allow the matter to end at that.

He later estimated that he was one day too late in identifying the Bedford Park home of Mrs Cawdore-Farrington's lover. By then Major Sir Albert Cawdore was in the obituary columns, reported as having died in his sleep of heart problems. A police investigation that the Cawdore household had not expected discovered that the Major's last meal had included a desert of his favourite treacle toffee, and a court-mandated postmortem discovered the poison that had killed him.

I need not revisit the scandal of the murderer's confession, nor his public instance that he acted alone without the aid, knowledge, or consent of the Honourable Alicia Sophie Victoria Cawdore-Farrington; in any case the salacious reportage of Langdale Pike and others can supply details for the ghoulish. I understand that the widow has emigrated to Mentone and no longer receives callers.

For the thousands of destitute men, women, and children in our Empire's very capital there seems no solution, except that steady march of civilisation by which we must preserve the best of what we have created and improve the rest. That there is no easy answer does not excuse us from tackling a hard one.

"Good old Watson!" Holmes exclaimed when I expressed this view to him. "In a city of unscrupulous employers and venal landlords there is a Bell Lane Trust and a Salvation Army. Where evil men plot crimes are also the well-meaning bumblers of Scotland Yard. And where adulterous murderers stain our national character there is John H. Watson—and therein lies our hope for redemption. We shall hold the line a little longer, my friend. Indeed, you know we must!"

THE ANGEL

OF

TRUTH

"**J**ANE... I NEED you."

My heart lurched. It was a long time since Dr John Dee had said that to me.

I blinked sleep out of my eyes and peered across my bedchamber. My scholarly husband stood in the doorway, candlestick in hand, but he was not undressed for bed. Nor did his eye gleam with desire, or even droop with wine-lust. His face was pale beneath its greying beard. He looked scared.

I sat up quickly. "What's wrong? The children...?"

"Sleeping in peace," my husband assured me. "I... need you in my workshop, Jane."

I shuddered. It was nearly two years since I'd last heard those words from him. Those words had preceded the effective end of our marriage.

Yet I'd seldom seen John so white with fear as he was now; certainly not since that last shattering night in damned Trebona.[116] His hand trembled, quivering the candle to send crazy shadows spidering across the rafters.

I glanced across at the cot-bed where month-old Madina slumbered. The other children slept in a nursery under the attic eaves.[117] I looked back at John. I tried to keep my voice steady. "What must I do?"

He heard the tremor. "Nothing like that," he frowned. We never now discuss my part in his former experiments. "It is—Jane, I have *succeeded!*"

"Succeeded at what?" I began, but some nuance of expression in his face warned me of his meaning. "You mean you have *found* one? *Brought* one?"

My husband nodded. "At last. In greatest need. Perhaps that was what was lacking before—need. Need most dire!"

I misunderstood him then. I thought he referred to our reduced straits, near-bankrupt after our long sojourn overseas, returned four months since to a house burned and plundered by the ignorant and the jealous who thought Dr John Dee a sorcerer or necromancer. I even dared hope he was speaking of the parlous state of our marital relationship, so sundered

---

116   Dr Dee, his associate Edward Kelley, and their wives visited Třeboň, German Wittingau, in southern Bohemia in what is now the Czech Republic, intermittently from 1856-1859. Dee recorded in his diary the alchemical experiments and séances they undertook there—and their eventual conclusion.

117   This detail indicates a narrative date of early April 1590, since Jane's second daughter Madina was christened on 5th March of that year. Jane's older children at that time were Arthur, Katherine, Rowland, Michael, and Theodore.

that we merely staggered through the motions of matrimony. I did not yet know of the darker problem with which he wrestled.

His beard was matted, I noticed irrelevantly, and his garments were creased with many hours of uninterrupted labour. I reviewed when I had last seen John, and wondered that a time had come when his three days' absence from our board could pass without my notice.

"You're saying—claiming—that your experiments have worked?" I clarified. "That you have summoned..."

"An angel," John insisted. "I have summoned the Angel of Truth."

He swallowed hard. So even my brilliant husband had doubted whether his rites and calculations would ever bear fruit.

John pressed a night-robe at me. "Hasten. There isn't time for... for anything! He is come—*it* is come—but who knows how long the bindings will hold? I need your aid, to shore up the circle, to take notes as I question the being. Please, Jane... I really do need you. Please?"

As long as it was since John had come to my bed, how much longer since he had allowed me at his work? Perhaps he wouldn't have called upon me now had not our fallen circumstances robbed him of all other assistance.

I almost turned him down. Bitter words rose at the back of my throat. And yet—an angel! And John, shocked and vulnerable as I had not seen him for so long. John, needing me.

I dragged the robe over my shift. "Show me your angel."

John led down the narrow staircase to his workroom. A complicated chalk circle etched with seven names of God warded the door. The threshold was scattered with salt.

"John, these are serious precautions for an angel."

My husband winced. "We are beyond what we know here, Jane. Beyond aught I have achieved, even with..." He fell silent. He would not name his former associate in my presence. "What is in that room, inside a diagram of conjuration, is far from anything in our experience. Every precaution is necessary."

He did not mention his old experiments in an Essex graveyard, nor the Reichstein scryings in which he had involved our son Arthur. He would never remind me of the Uriel rites in Trebona. He did not need to. I knew how seriously he took precautions in his conjurations. I knew what happened when those precautions failed.

"He may try to escape," John warned me. "He may seek to beguile you to breach the circle that confines him. Remember that he is more than he seems. His mind is not as ours. He is dangerous."

I wanted to protest. Had John learned nothing? To bring such an entity into our home, where our children lay sleeping? To leash such a thing behind some flimsy line of chalk and salts?

My husband must have seen the criticism in my scowl. "There's good reason for this risk, Jane. I swear it. There are… matters of state, of high policy. Matters concerning the fate of nations."

I recalled the stream of visitors we had received these past bleak months at Mortlake. I had naively assumed that they were well-wishers, greeting our long-delayed return to England, perhaps bringing comfort and assistance in our reduced straits. I should have known that privy secretary Sir Francis Walsingham, England's spymaster,[118] would never call on the Queen's astrologer from mere courtesy.

"What matters?" I asked John.

He shook his head. "No time now for that. We must enter my workshop and reinforce the bindings. Paint an outer ring with tincture of hyssop, whispering the Paternoster—Greek, not Latin. Beware answering the creature's questions. Do not tell him your name."

We paused at the threshold. "An Angel of Truth, you said."

"Yes. And do we not know, Jane, that there are some truths which must be feared?"

He had the right of it. I nodded. He clasped my hand—his touch was cold and unfamiliar, a stranger's grip. He unlocked his workroom door.

There was light within. Five lanterns were positioned at the points of the pentacle drawn in the centre of the floor. A diagram was inscribed in careful detail across the polished oak, like the sigil upon the portal but much more complicated. Supplementary lines etched out to five smaller circles, each containing a small dish, variously filled with water, incense, flame, iron, and coal. John had bound his guest with the five elements and the secret names of the Creator.

I gasped. Right until then I had not really believed. A delusion, it might

---

118   Walsingham's titles do not immediately indicate the power this political insider possessed. As Privy Secretary he set the agenda for the Queen's Privy Council, her most intimate circle of advisors. He was also referred to as Secretary of State, in an era long before there was a role of Prime Minister. Walsingham effectively set the nation's foreign and domestic policies and ran its civil service. He was instrumental in thwarting several plots to displace or kill Queen Elizabeth I. It was his support that sent Sir Francis Drake on his circumnavigation of the globe. He was probably the driving force behind the 1586 entrapment for treason and subsequent execution of Elizabeth's Catholic cousin, Mary, Queen of Scots.

have been; John was well able to fool himself into believing his results more than they really were. Or a trick, to lure me back to his experiments and more vile degradation. But there, inside the magic circle on a high-backed wing-chair, sat a creature unlike any I had seen.

He seemed almost human. Tall he was, a head higher than most men, thin faced with sharp cheekbones, a hawk-hooked nose, hair drawn back revealing widow's peaks. His eyes glittered in the lantern-light, sharper and cleverer than anything I had ever seen in mortal man.

He stirred as we entered, looking up from a contemplation of his long delicate hands. His fingertips were pressed together, but it did not look like prayer.

He spoke. "Good evening," he bade us, "Doctor John Dee. And..." Those narrowed piercing eyes ran over me, "...Mistress Jane Fromond Dee."

John gasped. "An Angel of Truth," he breathed. "I did not tell him..."

The Angel tutted. "Come, come. If I'm to be plagued with hallucinations, at least allow that my deeper mind will provide me with signs and hints as to what vision I am to experience."

John's hand still gripped mine. It tightened as the Angel spoke. The creature's voice was deep, masculine, cultured. A scholar's speech, yet without deference or humility. A cold voice, devoid of emotion or humanity.

The Angel gestured around the workshop. "Construction, décor, and furnishings bespeak of sixteenth century, yet the items here are not of three hundred years vintage but new. The smell, I may note, is particularly authentic; and the stench, some dried clay upon that matting, and certain sounds beyond your house, suggest a Surrey location close to the Thames. The clutter of your study indicates travel and scholarly endeavour. I perceive you have lately visited the Continent—Nuremburg, Frankfurt, Prague, Cracow and elsewhere. The volumes on your desk..."

John looked to the content on his table. A new-printed copy of Hariot's *Brief and True Report of the new found land of Virginia* lay there, carefully bookmarked where John had reached in his studies.

The Angel made a wide gesture with those artistic fingers. "Those calculations on the chalk-board refer to a revision of the calendar in line with Gregorian principles, making use of the controversial Copernican theories of your correspondent Tycho Brahe. That partially-assembled device on the tool-bench is a replacement sea compass for one recently looted from this study during your European absence."

His gaze fixed upon my husband. John shied back a step.

"An Angel of Truth," he breathed.

The spirit leaned forwards. "Your hands display the callosities of a constant writer, a scholar given to using a goose-quill judging by the ink-spots on your cuff. Old acid burns on the backs of your hands suggest a practical chemist. Your dentistry and complexion speak of primitive medical practices. In short, my delusion insists that you are John Dee, Elizabethan mathematician, navigator, astronomer, and alchemist. Fascinating."

John gestured for me to begin my work reinforcing the circle. He picked up his hickory stave, to command the Angel if he could. "You know much that no mortal could," he told the spirit, "but I charge thee now to speak thy name!"

"Holmes," the Angel replied, without hesitation or chagrin. "William Sherlock Scott Holmes."[119]

"Homes?" John puzzled. No book I had ever seen, nor any of my husband's reading judging by his expression, chronicled an entity of such a name. And there had once been many volumes of angel-lore on the shelves of Mortlake, before our house had been plundered in our absence and damaged by fire. It was not only our personal relationship that was wrecked and gutted on our return to England.

"Sherlock Holmes," the Angel corrected us. "From the Old English *holm* and the Norse *holmr*, meaning holly tree. But this is irrelevant. I note from your easel that you are studying a manuscript which I have seen before—or later, might perhaps be a more accurate tense."

The spirit directed our attention to the vellum codex that John had left open on his writing slope. I had not seen this document before, but was amazed and enthralled by it. A fold-out triple page was rendered with beautiful depictions of plants and animals, accompanying a text in some coded language that I did not recognise.[120]

---

119   At no time in the Canon does Watson or Doyle record Holmes's full name. The information is revealed in W.S. Baring-Gould's definitive 1962 biography, *Sherlock Holmes.*

120   Jane describes here what would is known in modern times as the Voynich Manuscript, a mysterious tome "discovered" in 1912 by book dealer William Voynich. He claimed to have purchased the volume in a lot of books sold by the Jesuits from their great Collegio Romano library at Villa Mondragone. Carbon dating has placed the book's paper to the fourteenth century but doubt remains as to whether the content is authentic or a brilliant hoax. An accompanying letter claims its provenance from Holy Roman Emperor Rudolf II (1552-1612) then through the hands of Johannes Marcus and Athansius Kircher. Tradition has attributed the coded—or nonsense—volume to Roger Bacon (see next footnote), with Dee selling the book on to Rudolf. The manuscript is now in the care of Yale University's Beinecke Rare Book and Manuscript Library as MS 408. Reproductions of it are available online, or published in *The Voynich Manuscript*, ed. Raymond Clement, ISBN 9780300217320.

John's brows rose even further. "You... know this tome? I have only recently acquired it. It is said to be the work of Roger Bacon."[121]

"I am intimately acquainted with it, my dear doctor," the Angel replied. "Indeed, I suspect it to be the primary and immediate cause of my remarkable current delusion."

John brandished his hickory wand. "I charge you, explain!"

"I was retained by representatives of the Society of Jesus from the Villa Mondragone at Frascati, Italy.[122] This document had been extracted from their archive. They believed the thief had brought it to London, and therefore sought out my assistance in recovering the codex. This I did—the problem was elementary. Having recovered the tome I naturally inspected it in my Montague Street chambers[123] to verify that it was the stolen item and to study the remarkable cypher it employed."

John looked uncertainly at the thick volume with its narrow strange-charactered script. "You... decoded this?"

The Angel looked rueful. "I had scarcely begun when what I assume was some fungal toxin dusted onto the sheets took its effect and triggered this remarkable sensory delusion. I posit an interaction with other chemical agents which I have utilised of late to direct and divert my cognitive capacities. A fourteen percent solution of...[124] No matter. It seems the most rational response to my hallucination to treat it as real until my mind resolves itself to conventional reality once more."

I did not understand Holmes's words, though he spoke them as if they had sense and meaning. I am not sure even John followed, though his is the most acute mind I have ever known.

"I am John Dee," my husband admitted to the spirit in the circle. "Late

---

121   Roger Bacon (1214-1294), English philosopher and Franciscan friar, was accorded the title of Doctor Mirabilis—marvellous teacher—for his erudition and research. His 840-page *Opus Majus* covers optics, mathematics, alchemy, and astronomy. He may have been the first European to describe gunpowder. As with many middle ages scholars, he was also popularly attributed with occult learning and magical powers.

122   The Jesuits' distinctive, historical, and beautiful headquarters outside Rome housed their greatest library. The former papal residence was sold in 1981 and is now part of the University of Rome Tor Vergata.

123   Holmes's move to his more famous Baker Street address depended upon him finding some flat-mate with whom to share the cost.

124   In the Canon, Watson chronicles Holmes's occasional use of a seven percent solution of cocaine, then a legal drug. This is quite a mild dose. A fourteen percent solution used by a Watsonless Holmes bespeaks of a more serious addiction.

of John's College Cambridge and the University of Louvain, Fellow and Under-Reader at Trinity, Dean of Gloucester, Freeman of the Mercers' Company..."

"Yes, yes," the Angel interjected. "I am somewhat familiar with you and your work. *Mathematicall Praeface to The Elements of Geometry of Euclid of Megara* laid down some basic principles of calculation. *General and Rare Memorials Pertayning to the Perfect Art of Navigation* pioneered some excellent practical applications of science and mathematics. I was not so impressed with *Parallaticae commentationis praxeosque nucleus quidam*—too much superstitious astrological nonsense without clear evidence."

John frowned. "The work was well received in several European courts. Prince Laski, King Stephen Batory, Emperor Rudolph himself..."

"There will always be fools to admire foolish unsupported theories," Holmes snapped. "Your *Heparchia Mystica*—On the Mystical Rule of the Seven Planets—was confounded nonsense.[125] Your Paradoxal Compass, however, was an admirable advance in polar navigation. You should have confined your studies to the geo-mathematical and astronomical, where they would have been much admired."

John advanced as if to remonstrate with the Angel's brutal critique. I caught my husband's shoulder. "He goads you to cross the circle, John."

The spirit mused for a moment. "An occasional correspondent of mine even dedicated his volume *The Dynamics of an Asteroid* to you."[126]

"He is testing you, John," I warned.

My husband looked closely at the gaunt figure that regarded him across the enchanted circle. "Not testing me," John reasoned. "He is reading me, as a man might read a text. See how he scans the room, every book and paper, every instrument, missing nothing. If he provokes me it is to observe my reactions and learn from them."

"Most perspicacious," the Angel of Truth remarked. "However... our encounter, ephemeral as it might be, is clearly for some purpose. If one follows the logic of the situation as it presents itself, you have gone to remarkable lengths to obtain a consultation on some problem that perturbs and perplexes you, doctor."

---

125   This work, written "under the guidance of the angel Uriel" from a series of séances in 1582-3, contains diagrams and instructions for the summoning of spirits.

126   This would be the scholarly and controversial work published by Professor James Moriarty, "a book which ascends to such rarefied heights of pure mathematics that it is said that there was no man in the scientific press capable of criticizing it."

John raised his stave again. "Yes. I charge and conjure thee, Angel of Truth, to answer fully and freely in revealing the plot aimed against Her Majesty Queen Elizabeth."

The spirit snorted. "You don't require an Angel of Truth, then, Dr Dee. You require an Angel of Detection." He seemed amused.

I turned to John. "What's this? There is some conspiracy afoot against the queen? Is that why Walsingham came to Mortlake of late?"

There was a time when I would have recognised my husband's intense concern at some intractable problem. There was a day when he would have told me about it. Even now he looked a little shamefaced. "Walsingham came to me in confidence, to see if I could explain..." He paused, unsure how much he should tell me.

Holmes sat back in his chair, leaning on one arm to cradle his long forehead. "If I am to be presented with a case, Dr Dee, pray use that well-regarded intellect and impart the information as precisely and cogently as you are able. Spare no detail but include no editorial. Above all, let your account be interesting. Begin."

John looked at me. "You will record the conversation, Jane? Make notes as you used to?"

I stuffed down my first responses and assented. Most people assumed that it was for my looks that the widowed and eminent scholar had wedded a wife twenty-eight years his younger. I always suspected it was because I was literate and could record his experiments as he made them.

The Angel settled back in his chair, folding his hands on his lap and giving John his full attention.

My husband began. "This matter was brought to me by Sir Francis Walsingham, Secretary of the Queen's Privy Council. It is a matter of national security." He reached for a small wooden case and hinged it open to show Holmes the contents. "On Christmas day, one of these ornamental pins was discovered in Her Majesty's clothing, threaded into the fabric of her day gown."

I craned to look into the box. On a padded cushion lay six straight silver pins, three inches long with ornate moulded heads. They were the kind of fashion accessory that a lady might use to fasten hair, scarf, or veil.

"Little was thought of it," John went on, "until the first day of January, when a second was similarly discovered. That evinced some concern, for none were seen close by the queen to thread such a pin into her mantle. Indeed, one who was close enough to slide the pin into her dress was surely close enough to slide a dagger into her back."

I could see why Sir Francis, always Elizabeth's first protector, might be alarmed.

"A third pin appeared on Twelfth Night,[127] but this time on Her Majesty's night-gown. Her Majesty's lady-in-waiting, Lady Elsbet FitzHammond, was closely questioned but would not confess to planting it. Lady Elsbet is rumoured to have been a mistress of disgraced Sir Francis Drake.[128] In any case, she was removed from her position."

"Who undertook these investigations?" demanded the Angel.

"Walsingham himself, assisted by some gentlemen of the court. Depositions were taken, witnesses of high degree. Many were…"

Holmes waved John on. "The other pins?"

"This fourth on February 1st, discovered by Her Majesty's new lady in waiting, Jenet Hastings, when she disrobed the queen at night. It was threaded into some concealed undergarment, where none could possibly have placed it. The fifth appeared on March 16th on Elizabeth's pillow, stitched there as she slept. You will imagine that the sovereign of England is well guarded in these times of papist plot, and yet…"

"Who discovered this pin?" the Angel interrupted.

"Her Majesty herself. It was the first thing she saw when she awoke. There was a considerable stir."

"I imagine so," I interjected. A shudder ran through me.

John saved the most spine-tingling event for last. "This sixth object was discovered only two weeks ago, on Lady Day…[129] in Her Majesty's hair!"

"Detail," insisted our consulting spirit.

"Coming out of chapel, the item was noticed by William Cecil, Baron

---

127   The 6th of January, the twelfth night after Christmas, was the end of medieval Christmas revels, remembered now in vestige as the date by which trimmings and trees should be cleared away.

128   Drake (c1540-1596) was the archetypal English privateer explorer, second man to circumnavigate the world, wanted pirate to the Spanish fleet, second in command of the English force that had broken the invading Spanish Armada, and general swashbuckler. King Philip II of Spain placed a bounty on his head of 20,000 ducats—US$6.5m in modern money. Drake fell out of favour in 1589 when his mission to Lisbon to follow-up the English triumph over the Spanish Armada went wrong, costing 12,000 English lives and 20 English ships.

129   March 25th, one of the old English "quarter days" on which rents and taxes were due and wages were paid. The other quarter days were Midsummer's Day (24th June), Michaelmas (29th September), and Christmas Day. March 25th converts to April 6th under the current Gregorian calendar, and that revised date still marks the beginning of the British tax year.

Burleigh himself, the Lord High Treasurer of England. Good queen Bess[130] was much alarmed. As you can imagine there had by then been much gossip and speculation about the appearance of these talismans."

"Cries of witchcraft," I supposed.

"Most certainly, and of Papal devilry. Many observed that witches stab pins into poppet dolls to work malice on their enemies. Some hold it to be a work of vengeance for the execution of Scots Mary[131]—or even divine judgement for it. Accusations abound. A dozen great men have been arrested, questioned, their estates seized."

"Indeed," muttered the Angel. "And you, Dr Dee, do you attribute these pins and their appearance to some supernatural agency?"

John paused. He smoothed his beard as he often did when thinking. "I am loath to resort to crying deviltry until I have exhausted the possibilities of human agency. I have read the depositions that Walsingham took. There are still possibilities for mortal intervention. However, mundane or mystical, if the queen is in danger then nothing must be stinted to save her." He gestured to the circle where the remarkable creature he'd conjured listened to his account.

Holmes held out his hand for the pins. My husband shook his head. "Do you think me a novice, that I will break the binding circle? Make your observations from there, Holmes. I charge thee!"

The Angel growled. "Have you tested the pins? Analysed their composition, the silver content therein? Are all of them of the same minting, or are some created separately from others? What of the heads, those ornately carved decorations, each slightly different from the rest? Under a lens it might be possible to discern any meaning those imprints bear." He glared at John. "You can either be a sorcerer or a scientist, Dee. In this matter you cannot be both!"

A great hammering at our outer door interrupted John's answer. The thumps made us both jump. "Who could that be at this time of night?" I asked, trying to keep my voice calm. Had the ignorant fools who had

---

130   A colloquial term for Elizabeth I.

131   Mary Stuart, (1542-1587) Queen of Scots and dowager Queen of France, was Elizabeth's first cousin once removed and had a strong claim on the English throne. Elizabeth kept her imprisoned for eighteen years before Walsingham's entrapment garnered enough evidence to compel her execution. Baron Burleigh later criticised the Queen very strongly for allowing Mary's death. Mary's son became King James IV of Scotland and succeeded Elizabeth I to also become James I of England and Wales, uniting the kingdoms into Great Britain.

broken in and wrecked John's workshop in our absence returned to finish us too? Or did soldiers bear some arrest warrant to drag John away for diablerie or too-close association with Catholic scholars in Europe?

"Stay here," John instructed, passing me the hickory wand. He set the box of pins down beside the Bacon manuscript. "Keep watch." He hastened out of the room to attend the urgent knocking.

I turned back to guard the Angel—but he was gone from his chair!

Holmes was out of the circle. He had stridden across it to pick up the pin casket. Now the Angel was examining the items with a tiny lens from his pocket.

I raised the hickory stick faintly. A spirit escaped from its bonds can be cruel and dangerous. I knew that to my cost. Memories of that night in Trebona—when Uriel and Madimi had entered Kelley and convinced John that Kelley should lay with me—set me trembling again.[132]

"Your husband loves you," the Angel told me, absently. He continued his inspection of the pins as he spoke. "It is evident from your body language that the two of you have been distant of late, since well before the birth of your recent child. Your glances around this workshop indicate that you have been excluded from this place since your return to England. Your reaction to my simple perambulation across a scribble of chalk suggests some disturbing experience with Dr Dee's previous researches. I assure you, madam, that I mean you and your spouse no harm, and that your current estrangement is as avid a source of grief to him as to you."

"You... you know this?" I gasped.

"The signs are evident to any who will take the trouble to observe them." He laid a long hand on the illustrated page of Bacon's codex. "There is a subtle genius in this code. It requires certain modes of thought which predispose one to creative illusion. This is a most remarkable experience."

"If you will not harm us, will you help us?" I asked. "John is wise, and good, but not always worldly. He thinks Sir Francis Walsingham his friend, but Walsingham would sacrifice any man in service of the state. If John cannot solve this problem..."

"Sir Francis is first amongst those I must interview," Holmes declared.

"You... will assist? At what price?"

Holmes snorted. "The uniqueness of the experience pays for itself,

---

132   Dee's partnership with medium and alchemist—and convicted fraudster—Edward Kelley, ended abruptly shortly after Kelley relayed the spirit Madimi's command that the two men should lay with each other's wives. Dee records the "cross-matching" on 22nd May 1587; Jane's son Theodore was born nine months later.

Mistress Dee. The problem and context are sufficiently engaging to divert. And now, I suspect, comes a further complication."

He looked to the door as John returned. My husband was so pale and shocked that he did not even react to the spirit's escape. He clutched me and broke the news that had come so suddenly by urgent courier. "Walsingham... Walsingham is dead! He was discovered so in his bed—a silver pin pressed into his heart!"

I had not previously been to Hampton Court, that great cardinal's palace built by old Thomas Wolsey, stolen by Henry VIII, expanded to be the largest royal dwelling in England. At another time I would have thrilled at the barge-ride along tidal Thames, at our arrival through Anne Boleyn's gate—she was executed before the chambers prepared for her there were completed—at the great hall with its carved hammer-beam roof, at the sheer pomp and majesty and bustle and intrigue of Elizabeth's court, so well-remembered from my younger days at Windsor.[133]

John was familiar with the site. He paused in the inner court to point out to Holmes the astronomical clock that showed time of day, moon-phase, month, quarter-year, sun and star sign, and the state of the tide at London Bridge.[134] I was too concerned about the abrupt summons that had dragged us from Mortlake at dawn to take in the details.

We entered a royal palace in mourning for one of the queen's main-stays. Few could remember a time when Walsingham had not held a subtle and near-silent grip on the nation's governance. Yet already there were

---

133   Hampton Court remains one of the stateliest of all England's stately homes even today. Little of the complex as laid out by Cardinal Wolsey around 1514 or massively extended by Henry VIII from 1528 survives unchanged. The palace and grounds were thoroughly overhauled and rebuilt in the 1600s.

Anne Boleyn was the second wife of Henry VIII, for whom he broke England from the Catholic faith and instituted Protestant Anglicism. She was executed in 1536 on charges of adultery, incest, and witchcraft.

Hampton Court is now open to the public. A visit is recommended.

134   This massive 1540 timepiece, built into the gatehouse tower wall in what is now called the Clock Court, still functions. Its display of the tide's condition was a practical one at a time when most traffic to Hampton Court came by Thames; at low water there were dangerous rapids under the arches of London Bridge.

whispers, ambitions, changing allegiances, to fill the power void that Sir Francis's passing had left.

John and I were led into that court—and an Angel of Truth walked beside us!

Spirit Holmes might be, dragged by John's arts from some other place, but he strode as confidently as any man of mortal flesh, his odd quilted robe billowing behind him, his legs clad in cloth tubes over short boots, his shirt of odd design and material, stiff-collared and studded. His hands were rammed into capacious pockets.

Beyond the great hall were privy chambers, smaller but equally ornate. We were led to one such room where a dozen or more courtiers gathered round a table. The only one I recognised from scant acquaintance was sat in the tallest and most elaborate chair, at the centre of the huddle: William Cecil, Baron Burleigh himself.

The Lord High Treasurer looked up from the volume he'd been consulting as we entered. "Ah, Dee," he muttered. "And…?"

"My lord," John replied, "may I present my wife, Jane Fromond, formerly lady-in-waiting at court to Lady Howard of Effingham.[135] And this is my associate, Master Holmes of…"

"Mycroft," the Angel supplied.[136]

"I am consulting with him in my enquiries."

"Your *enquiries*," said Lord William. From what I'd glimpsed of him and heard back in my Windsor days he had always been a sour man. Years had not improved him, though his political stature had grown and grown. Surely it was he who would replace the late Sir Francis as Secretary of State.[137] If any had cause to celebrate Walsingham's death—or arrange it— then it was Baron Burleigh. "You are summoned here, Dee, to testify as to why Sir Francis Walsingham visited you some days ago."

My husband clutched the lapels of his court gown and addressed him-

---

135   Lady Howard was wife to Lord Admiral Charles Howard, who had commanded the fleet that repelled the "invincible" Spanish Armada. She remained a good friend to Jane and her husband throughout their lives.

     As a minor lady of court, Jane would have required royal assent to wed Dee, and Dee's diary describes his visit to court at Windsor at the end of November 1577 and several conferences with the queen and "Mr Secretary Walsingham", one of which must have broached the subject. Jane married Dee on 5th February 1578.

136   Again according to Baring-Gould, Holmes's birthplace in the North Riding of Yorkshire supplied the names of both Holmes's paternal uncle and his elder brother.

137   Cecil had actually already held the post from 1550-53 under King Edward VI.

self as if to a Star Chamber.[138] "Sir Francis has long been a patron of the sciences. On many occasions he referred some question to me, and found me to be of full use."

"He used you as a spy, you mean," one of the young men flanking Burleigh snorted.

"I am a loyal and patriotic Englishman," snapped John. "If I visit abroad, in company of kings, princes, and prelates, it behoves me to communicate any matter of national interest to the man entrusted with preserving our nation's security. It was in this vein that Sir Francis visited me at Mortlake a short time ago, to lay before me the problem of the silver pins."

"A sorcerer for sorcery," the youngster sneered.

"A scholar for a task not fitted to the ignorant," John barked. His glower quelled the bravo; perhaps the young toady had sought to please his master with his impertinence.

"That is a concern that has occupied much of our thought at court," the Lord High Treasurer admitted. "There have already been many accusations, some arrests, even duels over the matter. Superstition runs rife, and yet—when the Privy Secretary dies of such a tine to the heart, one begins to fear the devil's hand."

I noted the volume that the men were consulting. *De la Démonomanie des Sorciers* was French philosopher Jean Bodin's seminal condemnatory work on witches and witchcraft.[139] And we brought with us a spirit conjured by arcane art!

Burleigh suppressed a shudder at his own words then asked, "Have *your* researches suggested any conclusion, Dr Dee?"

John glanced at Holmes before replying. "Well, my first observation is that each of these pins is slightly different. See the embossed heads? Close

---

138   Jane shows some political naiveté here. The Star Chamber was a court convened from the 15th century in the royal palace of Westminster, made up of privy councillors and common law judges. It took its name from the painted roof of the court-room, which represented a night sky so the accused could look up and consider his place in the universe. Tasked with trying those deemed too powerful for conventional courts, it met in secret without indictments or witnesses, relying upon written evidence alone.

139   *De la Démonomanie des Sorciers* ('On the Demon-Mania of Sorcerers') by jurist, political philosopher, and French MP Jean Bodin (1530-1596) was a very popular tome, published in ten editions from 1580 to 1604. It cited cases of demonic pact, lycanthropy, and intercourse with devils, and argued for legal exemptions when dealing with witches from the usual judicial requirements of physical evidence, witnesses, and confession without torture. It was influential in developing the climate of inquisition which led to thousands of convictions and executions for trafficking with the devil in the years to follow.

examination under a lens of magnification reveals that each has a differ-ent sigil engraved upon the knob. This first is Venus, then Mars, Jupiter, Saturn—I shall return to describing the fifth—and the pin found in Her Majesty's hair carries the symbol of the Moon. In short, this set includes each of the planetary bodies that orbit our Earth excepting the Sun—un-less we choose to dare follow Copernicus and place Sol at the centre of our cosmology."[140]

"Have you the pin that was taken from Walsingham?" the Angel asked. Such was his authority that an attendant handed over a linen-wrapped object without question.

"What of the fifth pin, then?" Burleigh asked John.

"Closely examined, chemically tested, the silver is of a different mint," my husband reported. "Somewhat more mixed with tin, antimony, and bismuth than the others. The head appears to be copied from the fourth pin, representing Jupiter. In brief, this pin is not part of the set. It came from another source, for another reason."

"The dates!" I realised. "John, the fourth pin came on the first day of February, you said. There was a gap, a long gap, before that fifth one ap-peared in mid-March. Suppose someone felt that the scare was dying down? That Her Majesty was getting over her fright? Maybe someone took matters into his own hands?"

"Someone with access to the real pins to be able to mould a copy," John reasoned.

Holmes turned on us all angrily, waving the Walsingham pin. "This item has been cleaned! The blood stains are wiped away. It has probably been washed! How am I expected to deduce anything when idiots have tidied away the evidence and destroyed any clue?"

Baron Burleigh frowned. He did not like being barked at. "Of what use might a blood-crusted shaft be, sir?" he demanded gruffly.

Our Angel answered to no Earthly authority and feared none. "It might tell everything. Whether the victim was alive or dead when the pin punc-

---

140   The ancient Greeks knew of the planet Mercury, although they mistook its morning and evening appearances as separate bodies (the morning version was named Apollo). It was also part of ancient Chinese and Indian astronomical lore and was known to medieval Islamic stargazers. It was not recognised in the west until Galileo's 17th century observations. Uranus was considered a star rather than a planet until the 18th century.

      Nicolaus Copernicus (1473-1543) was the Renaissance astronomer and mathematician who posited a heliocentric model of the universe. The idea was not well received by the Catholic church on doctrinal grounds and was still a point of contention in Galileo's time.

"This item has been cleaned!"

tured him. Did he die of a pierced heart, or was this placed there afterwards? If the wound was fatal, what effusion of blood occurred to suggest whether the needle-point was withdrawn to let its puncture do its work and then replaced later? Useless to ask now. Where is the corpse?"

"It lies in state in the lady chapel here at Hampton," the Lord High Treasurer revealed. "Sir Francis had been unwell for some time and had repaired again to his own estates. When he died, Her Majesty attended on him immediately and had him brought back in her own cortege. There will be a full state funeral presently."

"And I suppose the corpse will have been washed and cleaned," Holmes objected. He turned to John. "Carry on, doctor. Sift what you can from these ignorant fools whilst I inspect this seventh pin with my lens."

My husband hastened to mollify the powerful men whom Holmes had insulted. "We can perhaps get to the truth of all this without having to resort to cries of witchcraft," he offered. "The fifth pin might be the key. The different pin. That was the one discovered on the queen's pillow. Who had access to her chamber that night?"

"Very few," Lord William deemed. "We can send for the waiting lady Jenet Hastings and ask her."

"Send for her," commanded the Angel, "but do not remain for the interview. I shall conduct that. What became of Elsbet FitzHammond, by the way?"

"After she was put to the question she was sent home to her father," John recalled from the testimony. "Whatever else she had done or not, she had disgraced herself over Drake."

Holmes dismissed adultery with a wave of his eloquent hands. "Was she put to torture?"

"No," insisted Burleigh. "There was scant evidence to warrant it. Even Francis Walsingham, anti-Papist terrier that he was, would baulk at using such cruelty on a noble lady without some cause."

The Angel of Truth paced the chamber. "I will see Lady Jenet first," he announced. "Then I must view Walsingham's body. Then speak to some other witnesses—*you* noticed the pin in Her Majesty's hair, I understand, Lord William? And after that I shall need to interview Elizabeth Gloriana Regina herself."

"That is not possible," Burleigh objected.

"Make it possible, Lord William," Holmes demanded. "If you want this murky business resolved, if you would not have it hanging over the court while Sir Francis is buried, if you do not want rumour and panic spreading like wildfire, accusation on accusation and suspected traitors everywhere, get me my interviews."

John interceded. "Her Majesty has always been pleased to entertain me before when I have something of import for her." It was true. Her Majesty even set the date of her coronation by Dr Dee's astrological calculations.

"Very well, I shall see what may be done," the Lord High Treasurer conceded.

"We shall take this chamber," Holmes told him. "Dr Dee will bring you a list of our requirements shortly."

I had never thought to see Baron Burleigh and his toadies hastened from a room as Holmes did then, yet swiftly the Angel was alone with John and I. He brandished the seventh pin at us. "The last of the set," he announced. "See the engraving on the head, doctor? A sun! The pins were placed in order from the centre of a Copernican universe, then moon and sun to finish all. A minor detail, except to tell us that our perpetrator is an educated person, who either believes in a heliocentric creation or else has a sly sense of humour."

"A nice detail," John agreed. "There are astrological significances to the celestial bodies and their corresponding metals and notes which have occult significance also. A practicing magician might elect to use such symbols in this progression for some malefic purpose."

I saw Holmes's expression sour at this suggestion of necromancy. I hastily intervened. "A man need not be able to perform magic to believe he does. The perpetrator surely knows that these signs will add to a general rumour that the queen is plagued with sorcerous malice."

"The progression was completed with *sol*," reflected my husband, England's greatest astrologer and celestial philosopher. "Certainly it is with that symbol that the supposed curse bit. Unless one assumes that *terra* forms part of the set too, and a worse final stroke is still to come?"

"The hint of occult trappings is significant," the Angel conceded without emotion.

"However, it cannot lead us to whoever placed these items, nor tell us how. Or why? There are so many suspects it is impossible to even guess. How many arrests did Walsingham make these last few weeks as fear mounted? How many loyalties have been tried? How many secrets betrayed? If these pins are indeed cursed, they scatter their malediction far and wide."

"They do," Holmes agreed.

The door rattled. A young girl peered timidly round the timber. She wore a sombre high-necked dress with no jewellery, court mourning garb. She was surely no older than I was when I first went to Windsor, a tender seventeen. "I am sent to Doctor Dee?"

The child was frightened. "Come in, Lady Jenet," I requested as kindly as I could.

"Yes, come in," Holmes told her. "Come and tell us why you slipped a fake pin into the queen's pillow that night. Or better yet, let me tell you."

Jenet's brows rose. "What? No. I never…"

"Observe the tiny bulge beneath this girls neck-hem," Holmes advised John. "The faintest rattle of muffled beads?"

John quickly followed the Angel's reasoning. "Lady Jenet conceals a Papist rosary under her clothes! The Hastings must be secret Catholics, I deem—and as such have ample reason to wish Protestant Queen Bess an uncomfortable fright with silver hatpins."

Jenet backed away. Her eyes were wide with horror at her discovery. Catholic plotters went to the gallows, the headsman, or the stake. "No!" she told us, desperately. "They never—they wouldn't! It was me that bethought of it, none other. Only me."

John accused her. "You forged, or had some helper forge, a copy of the genuine fourth pin you had discovered before as you undressed the queen. Why?"

The maid-in-waiting dropped to her knees. "I'll confess. Anything you want. It was me. I am a witch! I am possessed of a demon! No other helped. No other instructed. It was me, all me. Burn me—but blame no-one else!" She began to sob.

Holmes was relentless. "Mistress Jane, you hypothesised that our fifth, anomalous pin was planted after so long a pause to keep Her Majesty and the court disturbed, to fan fading rumours of divine displeasure against queen and administration."

"I was five years at Windsor Castle. I know how court gossip works," I replied.

Holmes stalked round the weeping girl, lunged suddenly, and hooked the concealed prayer beads from the girl's neckline.

"Give those back…!" blurted Jenet. She reached futilely for the confiscated necklace. It occurred to me how unwise and foolish it was to wear a rosary at Hampton Court, however well concealed beneath formal mourning dress. Surely the girl did not wear her talisman always? Had she donned it before her interview in the hopes of divine protection? To prevent its discovery in its usual hiding place if her chamber was searched? Or was I missing something?

Holmes lifted his lens to inspect the rosary clasp. "I see now that Lady Jenet had another motive for her deeds. Observe the engraving, doctor. *E F-H*. Might we posit Elsbet FitzHammond, this lady's predecessor-in-office, who was dismissed on suspicion of planting the pins?"

"How came you by this necklace?" John demanded of Jenet.

"A gift!" she whimpered, kneeling almost double now in her fear and distress. "Given to me as a remembrance."

"You claim to have this from Lady Elsbet?"

"I… no, of course not."

"Then how do you explain the inscription?"

Jenet reached the end of her resources. She lost all power of coherent speech and collapsed weeping, sprawled across the tiled floor.

"Lady Elsbet would only own such a dangerous item if she were Papist," my husband argued. "To pass it to you would be to deliver herself into your hands, for this rosary's discovery would betray her to those who hunt such secret Catholics—Walsingham, for example."

I had to intervene, to save the sobbing girl from her implacable interrogators. "John, Holmes, you don't understand how it can be at court. When a young girl comes to such a great household to serve a high lady, shyest and least at first amongst so many noble retainers, that newcomer can be overawed. It is easy—and common—for such an impressionable girl to develop an admiration, a devotion, to some older and more experienced courtier. As Lady Elsbet once did with Drake." I dared a glance at John. "As I did with the queen's astrologer."

My husband blinked and did not meet my look.

I went on. "As I think Jenet did with Lady Elsbet."

Now John stirred. "You think the girl had a passion-crush for the former senior lady-in-waiting?" John knew well that women can couple together amorously in their own fashion to the release of pleasure—another lesson we had learned at Trebona under Madimi-Kelley's malefic carnal guidance.

"Poor Jenet may have placed the fake fifth pin to 'prove' that her object of desire was innocent of the charges that had cast her from court," I reasoned.

Holmes regarded the quivering, hysterical mass that had been his suspect. "Nothing more can be got from her for now. We will return to this witness later. Let her be placed under watch, but say nothing of what she's confessed to Burleigh or any other. Our investigation has scarcely begun."

The Angel of Truth led us on to the chapel where Sir Francis's body lay. No sombre choir monks interrupted our study. In these Protestant days such indulgences smack of Papery. John, Holmes and I were left alone with the bier and coffer that held the fallen Secretary of State's mortal remains.

The spirit wasted no time in niceties but immediately stripped open the corpse's tunic and began an inspection of his wounds. To my dismay, John peeled down Walsingham's hose.

"Here is the pin mark," Holmes noted. "It penetrated the heart well enough, but as best I can tell—after these benighted fools have sponged and scented away the evidence—there was no great effusion such as a beating organ would have gushed from the lesion. A stiletto prick could kill a man, but with a three-inch pin it requires proximity and absolute accuracy."

"Here," John beckoned the Angel to the dead man's nethers. "Walsingham's balls. Feel them."

Holmes did so without demur. "A great lump," he found.

"Like unto a third testicle. When Sir Francis visited me at Mortlake he was much changed from the hearty man I had known before my Continental sojourn. He'd came to consult me on the witchcraft pins, of course, and to thank me for certain intelligences I had conveyed to him during my travels by means of coded letters. He brought a sum of gold to assist Jane and I in repairing our home after its vandalism and looting, and passed to me the names of certain men to whom I might look to find my missing books.[141] In return I consulted on his failing health. He confided that he was having gut pains and difficulty pissing."

"A testicular tumour such as this one could certainly impede his passing water," agreed the Angel. "One might wish for the opinion of a reliable modern man of medicine but... it is entirely possible that Walsingham's deterioration and death could be attributed to blockage and infection of the urinary tract. Or this growth might be one signifier of many other malignant tumours beneath his flesh."

"Caused by sorcery?" I ventured.

"Caused by nature," Holmes scorned. "If we could cut open the carcass..."

"I beg you not to try," John told the Angel hastily. There was a limit to

---

141   Thieves who benefited by acquiring books through the Mortlake villagers' arson attack on absent "magician" Dee's house included Dee's former pupil John Davis and Catholic polemicist Nicholas Saunder (or Sanders). Ironically it is Saunder's loot, now lodged at the Royal College of Physicians, which forms the majority of the surviving part of Dee's collection today.

the license we might claim. "Is there aught else to see here? If we are not to desecrate the flesh of England's spymaster and the queen's favourite?"

There was not. Holmes led us back to the room he had commandeered for interviews. Weeping Jenet had been cleared away to some annex. The Angel demanded, through John, conversations with an eclectic roster of men.

First was the Master of the Queen's Wardrobe. "Who had access to Her Majesty's gowns before she dressed? How were they stored? How were they guarded?"

The portly gentleman stuttered out his information. The monarch's gowns were very valuable, kept in locked storage in the privy wardrobe safe from men and moths. A guard stood sentry in the lobby outside. The Master and some few ladies-in-waiting had keys. When Her Majesty dressed there were always several ladies in attendance. It was these women's duty to see that Gloriana appeared immaculate. An unauthorised addition to her underclothes or outer mantle would most certainly be noted before she was allowed to leave. Her senior Lady in Waiting, formerly Elsbet, now Jenet, was responsible for a final check.

"It is impossible that those pins could have been there when Her Majesty left her dressing rooms," the Wardrobe-Master insisted. "The only feasible way would have been for her senior lady to affix the pin during final inspection, and Sir Francis—God rest his soul after his long labours—put Lady Elsbet to the question and found her innocent."

"Say rather he could not prove her guilt," John clarified, then thought again. "Walsingham was ruthless enough to wring the truth from any man or woman, though. If he released Elsbet FitzHammond he must have been satisfied."

Next was the Warden of the Queen's Bedchamber. I recalled this fussy little man's counterpart at Windsor, a sly grabby fellow we ladies took good care to avoid being cornered by. This specimen was altogether different; I doubt whether ladies interested him at all.

"The queen's private chambers are guarded at all times and points," this functionary assured us. "There are many plots against Her Majesty's life. Security is vital. None may enter without permission. Few have that privilege." He reeled off the names of ladies in waiting, some more common maids and footmen, and certain trusted guards who had permission to intrude.

"On the night when the pin appeared on Her Majesty's night-gown, the 6th of January, I believe, did the queen receive any visitor to her chamber by night?" Holmes enquired. "A suitor, perhaps?"

The Warden of the Queen's bedchamber spluttered at the suggestion that the Virgin Queen might receive a midnight caller in her bower. Yet even in my day at Windsor there were certain rumours repeated to me by Lady Howard that...

But this is not relevant to my present account. The Angel demanded and received assurances that no stranger had violated the monarch's room that night. Only Lady Elsbet and three other maids had attended her.

Walsingham's private secretary was a cultured well-spoken man with a fashionable forked beard. He never met Holmes's eye. The Angel questioned him on his former employer's business. "Sir Francis was said to be the best-informed man in England," our spirit noted. "What happened to his files and notes after his death?"

"All my master's papers were bundled together and dispatched to the Tower of London for the queen's pleasure."

"Nothing abstracted? Nothing burned?"

"In the last days of his illness Sir Francis disposed of certain documents himself, feeding them to his bedroom hearth."

"He was a knowledgeable man. Well read?"

"Yes. He corresponded with many of the great thinkers of our day." The secretary's shifty gaze flickered over John for a scant moment.

My husband chimed in with questions. "When was the pin in his heart discovered? At the moment of his death?"

"It was concealed beneath his outer jacket. It was only when he was stripped for his shroud that the item was first seen."

"There was not enough blood to betray the wound?"

"Underlinens were soaked, but the lining of Sir Francis's mantle had absorbed the effusion so it was not evident to the eye. The discharge was not great."

I remembered Holmes's earlier comments. "Not enough for it to have spurted from a beating heart?" I checked.

"I would have thought not," the secretary opined. "Of course, some thought the spirit that had murdered the Secretary of State might have feasted upon his blood."

"The stains were discovered after he had been laid out at his home and the queen and court had hastily visited to pay their respects?" Holmes checked.

"Yes. When he was brought to the chapel here and stripped in preparation for his shroud-clothes. Though even before that some cried poison and others cried witchcraft. Sir Francis Walsingham has been England's bastion against black magic and Spanish and French aggression for many years. Even in these last few weeks that Her Majesty has been tormented by the curse-pins he rooted out many traitors. He has cleaned England of those who seek our ruler's harm. Countless enemies would wish to see his death."

The Angel was tireless. He continued on until night fell and sconces were lit to illuminate his interrogation room. Humbler servants were summoned to add their testimony: guards, serving girls, footmen, coachmen, butlers, heralds, scrubbing women, sweeps. Each lady in waiting was questioned without knowing what the others had said. Even the scullions charged with laying out Sir Francis's corpse were called to speak.

As the night ground on I found a moment to break from taking notes and speak in undertones with my husband. "It's close now to twenty-four hours since you conjured the Angel of Truth. How long can he continue to manifest?"

John shook his head. "In truth, wife, I am still not certain *how* I brought him to us, or what I did differently from any time I have performed the rites before. You know that I have enjoyed some success in bringing forth spirits ..."

"Enjoyed?" I challenged the conjurer's choice of words.

"Well, Madimi was… You know I am sorry for Madimi, Jane."

"So you have said," I answered bitterly. "You have rarely shown it, though."

John swallowed. "I have taken Theodore for my own, raised him in my household."

"Theodore might be your own. Not Kelley's—or whatever demon he claimed rode him as he tormented me."

John glanced at Holmes as the Angel interrogated the Keeper of the Queen's Jewel Box. "This is not the time to speak of such things, Jane."

"No, the time was long ago, John. Before you avoided my bed. Before that one drunken night when you got me with child again. Before you closed me from your heart and counsel as a soiled thing unworthy of your regard—soiled by *your* consent and command, John, never by any will of mine."

I saw the guilt in my husband's stare. The rite of Uriel still cast its shadows over his heart.

I took a deep breath. "The Angel of Truth… Holmes… He said that you still had regard for me. Still loved me."

Dr John Dee looked away. "I will need to make a careful study of Bacon's manuscript. The Angel was somehow brought here by that."

There was to be no answer to my deepest question.

"I have surreptitiously appropriated certain artefacts from the Angel," John whispered. "A hair, a thread of his gown, a cup he touched which bears the grease-imprint of his fingertips. From these I can perhaps devise the alchemy to treat Bacon's codex so it will bring Holmes to me."

"Holmes is already here."

John rubbed his forehead. "This Angel comes from outside time. Outside our time anyway. If I prepare a summoning for him over the months to come then it may bring him to us last night." He reached out and touched my cheek, a gesture of affection that was strange and alien in our cold contemporary lives. "Keep careful note of everything he speaks and does, Jane. There is no other but you I can rely on for this... and none I would rather have at my side to rely upon."

We were interrupted. Holmes dismissed the jeweller and rose to stalk the room.

"Have you concluded your interviews?" my husband ventured.

"Not quite," the detective spirit replied. "There are three more people I must see, and such is their importance that I deferred their questioning until I was fully informed of the detail our minor witnesses could afford. Now I am prepared to speak with William Cecil."

It was perhaps a sign of Baron Burleigh's worry that he consented to meet with Dr Dee and Sherlock Holmes as the clock bell tolled eleven. He came alone and found my husband and our angel awaiting him at a writing table. I shall never forget that image of those two brilliant men, painted by candlelight, seated side by side in rapt attention. Holmes's gaunt hawk-like countenance and John's wise intent gaze both focussed on the Lord High Treasurer.

"What have you discovered, astrologer?" Lord William demanded. He may have sneered.

Holmes pressed his fingertips together. "We are close to revealing our conclusions, but some few anomalies must still be explored. You opposed the late Sir Francis's recent policies regarding the appearance of these pins, I understand."

"Of course," scorned Burleigh. "Any rational man must see that England's future depends upon a balance of interests. We are, and shall remain, a Protestant nation, but we *must* have relations with Catholic Europe. Perhaps, had Drake's foray prospered to punish the Spanish for their Armada, it might be different; but with religious war in Holland[142] and our queen expelled from the Catholic communion by the Pope we cannot afford to be so broad and blatant in our persecutions."

"Walsingham arrested several people these last few weeks, as concern for the queen's wellbeing mounted," John observed.

"And left me with the mess to clean," the Lord High Treasurer spat. "Sir Francis was apt to become so enamoured of his tangled plots that he forgot their wider consequences. He entrapped poor Scots Mary with his Babington conspiracy and had her head.[143] With one blade-stroke he inspired a hundred counter-plots against Elizabeth and her state. I do not wish to malign the dead, but the man was an adventurer—irresponsible and heedless of the collateral harm his exploits caused."

"Did you attend upon Sir Francis's body as he lay out at his estates before the queen brought him to Hampton Court?" Holmes enquired.

"When word came of his death my place was here, to ensure the smooth transition of responsibilities to other hands."

I well understood what those words really meant. No man would benefit more from Walsingham's passing than William Cecil.

"Were you present at the interrogation of Elsbet FitzHammond?"

"As if Sir Francis would allow any to contaminate his questioning! Look to Walsingham's smooth-tongued secretary for an account of that event— if you can get any word of sense from his conspiratorial lips."

Holmes deferred to John for a turn at the questions. "It was you who first spotted the pin in Her Majesty's hair, I believe," my husband began. "Please describe the occasion."

"We had heard an early morning service on Lady Day. Her Majesty was attended by her usual retinue. She bade me walk beside her as she left the

142   Burleigh's role in the Dutch Protestant rebellion was to finance it enough to continue but not so much as to allow it success. In this way religious concern was diverted from England and a potential rival nation was weakened and distracted.

143   Elizabeth I imprisoned Catholic Mary, Queen of Scots, also a viable claimant for the English throne, for eighteen years. Idealistic recusant Sir Antony Babinton was recruited into a poorly-thought-out Papist plot to rescue Mary and place her in power with military support from Spain and the Catholic League of France. One of Walsingham's double-agents uncovered the plan. Babinton was "turned", forced to lead on the conspirators on so that there was clear evidence of their guilt. This included corresponding with Mary until she wrote ordering Elizabeth's assassination. This final proof was enough for Walsingham to bring down the whole conspiracy. Sixteen principal plotters were executed. Babington was disembowelled before death. Mary was tried for treason (without legal counsel, access to the evidence, or the right to call witnesses) and eventually beheaded on 8th February 1587.

church. We progressed down the nave aisle and emerged from the eastern porch. A pale sun glinted off something in Her Majesty's hair. Not in her wig, but the natural locks that emerged beneath it, just below the left ear. I looked more closely, and there was one of those infernal pins, thatched into the queen's plait!"

"How did Her Majesty react?"

"She was much distressed. Each pin's appearance has alarmed her more. She must have heard by then the court gossip that the witchcraft was growing stronger, that each pin came closer to piercing her heart. She tore the item loose and hurled it in the mud. I retrieved it for Walsingham's investigation. I understand he subsequently passed it to Dee."

"That's correct," John confirmed. "Sir Francis, though ill by then and withdrawn from court, made a personal visit to Mortlake. You summoned me to ask about it."

"He wasn't there on Lady Day," Lord William declared. "Walsingham's malaise was already taking a grip by then. If… if there is some sorcery directed against Her Majesty and her principal ministers…"

"The truth will be discovered," the Angel assured him. "You may go now, my lord. You have been moderately helpful."

It was close to midnight when Holmes again summoned the unfortunate Jenet Hastings. The lady in waiting had endured long hours under guard, knowing that her secrets were discovered. She entered timidly, supported by two soldiers whom John dismissed.

"It is time to reveal the truth," the Angel warned her. "Dr Dee, Mistress Jane and I are not a court. We owe no duty to the Lord High Treasurer, or to Sir Francis Walsingham's faction. We are not here to catch Catholics nor to punish affections. But we *shall* have a full account from you before you leave this room."

There was no doubt in the spirit's voice. Jenet trembled and shrank back in her chair, but from Holmes there was no escape.

"The rosary. Did you steal it or was it given to you?"

"It was a gift. Truly, sir, it was given as a keepsake."

"From Lady Elsbet?"

Jenet squeezed her eyes shut and nodded.

"You were fond of her?"

Another nod, and a deep blush.

"You idolised her."

"Yes."

Holmes pushed the beads across to the young woman. "Pray with it now," he instructed. "Out loud. Show us how it works."

Jenet faltered. Her hands clutched the necklace. "H-hail Mary, full of grace…" she began.

The Angel shook his head. "The Lord's Prayer, then ten Hail Marys, then Glory Be To the Father," he corrected the lady in waiting. "You are no Catholic. That was Elsbet."

"She gave you the beads for affection," John suggested to the girl. "As a sign of trust."

"Or as a final coercion to carry out a task she was no longer able to perform," Holmes accused. "There are a strictly limited number of people who could have placed the pins about Her Majesty. Of them, her lady in waiting is the one who could have done so the easiest. Most often the logical suspect is the correct one. Catholic Elsbet was slipping those pins into the Queen's garments—until she was suspected and taken for questioning. Did she leave you that fourth pin to plant after she had gone, to suggest supernatural occurrence rather than human agency? To offer her an alibi?"

Jenet hesitated to surrender up her friend.

"And the fifth," the Angel persisted inexorably. "When no new instruction came from close-watched Elsbet did you decide by your own initiative to forge another pin, modelled upon the one previously left in your charge, to continue the deception, to protect your idol and further her plot?"

Jenet gasped. The spirit had hit upon the exact truth.

John saw the problem, though, and spoke it before I could. "Elsbet could have placed the first three talismans, and Jenet the fourth and fifth, but what of the sixth that appeared in church? Or the seventh in Walsingham's dead flesh?"

Holmes took up quill and scribbled some words on a scrap of parchment. "For that," he replied enigmatically, "we require one final testimony." He handed the paper to Jenet. "Take that and deliver it now. Go in haste."

The lady fled from the room, trailing guardsmen. John and I regarded the Angel of Truth with surprise.

"You see now how it came to be, and why?" Holmes asked us.

"I confess to still being puzzled," my husband regretted. "What have you seen that mortal eyes cannot discern?"

"Nothing that mortal eyes cannot perceive," Holmes snorted. "You are blinded by your training, doctor, by your prejudices and preconceptions. Free yourself of these things and you will excel. Your name will resound down history as a thinker, a scholar, a seeker. Merely *look* at what you see!"

John hesitated. "My name will be remembered? Is that prophecy or…?"

"Care not so much that it will be recalled as for what it will be recalled, Dr Dee," the Angel advised.

"Are we close, though?" I had to ask. "Close to penetrating this terrible mystery?" I missed my children, and my exchange with John earlier had left me raw, unsettled, hurt, as I'd not been since those weeks recovering from Madimi's ministrations.

Holmes interlaced his fingers save for two pointed indexes which he directed towards the door. The portal opened. Elizabeth Regina swooped into the room.

I had seldom seen the queen so close. She must have been approaching sixty, old King Harry's daughter who had reigned these twenty years with absolute power, who had survived her mad, bloody sister and executed her cousin, who had loved Dudley and destroyed him,[144] who had defied Spanish Philip and the Pope himself and forged a new England.

Holmes eyes sparkled.

Her Majesty held the parchment he had sent by Jenet. "What is the meaning of these words?"

John winced. Our monarch has a tendency to have men beheaded if they catch her ire.

"I believe the message was quite legible, ma'am," Holmes responded. "However, there are a few points I should like to clear up before I am satisfied that I have fathomed the case."

"A few points?" the queen repeated.

"Indeed. When did you first deduce that Lady Elsbet was placing the pins upon your person?"

An invisible contest seemed to be going on between ruler and spirit, some wrestling of mind and character beyond the outward show that we could see. Queen Bess elected to answer the question. "It was self-evident. The simplest explanation. When Elsbet was exiled and Jenet attempted the same ruse it became clear what was going on. Jenet is not so clever as Elsbet."

144   The other of Elizabeth's three greatest courtiers alongside Burleigh and Walsingham was Robert Dudley, 1st Earl of Leicester (1532 or 3–1588), who was widely rumoured to be her lover. When Dudley's first wife died suddenly of a fall downstairs it was bruited that he had murdered her to be free to marry the queen. The resultant scandal killed off any chance for such a wedding, but Dudley and Elizabeth remained close all their years. Dudley refrained from other marriage until very late in his life; the queen reacted badly when she learned of his secret wedding to Lettice Knollys, Countess of Essex, and banished the lady from court. Dudley died unexpectedly two years before our present narrative. Elizabeth kept to her chambers and admitted no-one for six days until Baron Burleigh had the door broken in. She retained Dudley's last letter to her in her bedside treasure box all her life.

John stirred. "You were distressed."

"I certainly appeared so. Why spoil a perfectly useful plot?"

Holmes face lit with admiration. "You also discerned, then, that Elsbet and her Catholic contacts were not the originators of the scheme."

"Of course. Elsbet is smarter than Jenet, but not so clever or well read as to devise the astrological symbol sequence on the pin-heads. It was clear that she had a backer."

"So there was a Catholic plot?" I blurted, then regretted it. "Um, Your Majesty."

"No, Jane," Holmes told me. "What value would there be in stirring up anti-Catholic sentiment by so public a resort?"

"Would Walsingham have allowed a secret Catholic so close a place in the monarch's intimate household?" John objected.

"He would certainly have known," Holmes confirmed. "That is presumably the hold he had over the lady, to force her to plant the pins?"

"And so alarm me and my court into allowing his Papist-cleansing?" the queen suggested. "Francis knew of his illness. He knew he had not long to finish his work for me and leave me a kingdom secured from treason and treachery. Hence his Byzantine plot to nudge my hand against my enemies, or potential enemies, while protecting me from opprobrium at court and amongst the general masses. Who objects to defending the queen from foulest black witchcraft?"

"You allowed Jenet to continue Elsbet's—Walsingham's work!" John exclaimed.

"And continued it yourself," Holmes observed. "No other could have placed that sixth pin whilst you were at prayer in church but you."

"I sent a trusted messenger to Elsbet in her exile," Her Majesty revealed. "At my letter the girl confessed all and yielded up the remaining two pins from the set that Francis had given her. One I used to complete Francis's plot; his weeding out of future threats was a useful last gift to me. I wonder if he realised by whose agency his pin was placed? I imagine he did. He was a subtle man."

"On this occasion he was mystified. For evidence I offer Dr Dee's involvement. Your ailing spymaster would hardly have made the journey to Mortlake to recruit Dee's help in discovering who placed the first five pins. It was that mysterious sixth that troubled him."

"And the final pin you reserved for Walsingham himself, Majesty," John concluded. "You visited him as he lay out at his estates. You paid your last respects there."

The monarch inclined her head slightly. "The old scoundrel had gone behind my back before, for my own good as he saw it. He and Dudley used a warrant of execution for poor Mary that I had signed on condition it would not be delivered without my further consent."

"His behaviour in the current matter was not uncharacteristic then," surmised the Angel.

"Characteristic but irking. His final gambit used even my own superstition to further his ends. I felt a little bit of posthumous payback was in order. I returned his final pin to him." Queen Bess snorted. "Perhaps the myth-makers will decide that Francis's last loyal act was to draw upon himself the supernatural end that would otherwise have befallen me?"

"Burleigh does not know," John realised.

"Burleigh is a fine man and a good servant. He does not need to know everything. England is *mine*, and only I keep all its secrets." Walsingham's papers had gone to the Queen's own Tower of London.

Holmes was satisfied. "Then the problem is solved. It was hardly a challenge once the obfuscations of royal etiquette were dismissed. Walsingham never prosecuted Elsbet nor put her to torture because she was his agent all along. You never confronted him because he was doing your business for you in a way you could forever deny.[145] The plot had just enough macabre touches to draw idle attention from the likely and correct solution. My congratulations, Your Majesty. A neat and professional gambit."

Elizabeth shifted her head in the barest motion of acknowledgement, of one master to another. Without making any other gesture she somehow caused her guards to re-enter the chamber.

"Now that you know the truth, you must also know that you cannot take it beyond this room," regretted the Queen. "I am sorry, Doctor Dee, Mistress Jane. You have never done me harm. You come to this end through your loyal endeavours to serve me."

I gasped. "We are... to die?"

John folded me in his embrace. "There's no other way," he recognised. "Jane—my beloved Jane—I am so sorry. All my arts and cunning have led you to torment and shame and... this."

"Not only to this," I assured him. "To enlightenment and joy and travel and the society of kings, to poets and wonders and our children. And to love!" I swallowed back sobs and clung to him. "I would not change the bad if it would also take away the good."

He held me tight. The dark spirit that had lain on us ever since the

---

145   One of Queen Elizabeth's mottoes was *Video et taceo*—"I see and am silent."

"We are… to die?"

Trebona rite could not endure that affection. I felt it lift from us, cast back to sinister shadow from whence it could not return.

"I love you, my wife," John told me. "*You* are my angel." In the end he too had discovered truth.

"Ah, angels," Holmes interrupted, rising from his chair to his full impressive height. "Remarkable things, those. Do you believe in angels, Your Majesty? You're not shackled by superstition, as is clear from your part in our recent conundrum. But do you believe there is a greater truth?"

The queen looked at John and I, together at the last, clinging to each other. She faced our detective Angel with a quizzical regard. "There's no trick can save you. I'll see that your ends are quick and merciful. Dee's children will be maintained."

Holmes chuckled then, the only time I had heard his mirth. "Dr Dee and his good lady wife will swear an oath to silence on this. Better, he'll pronounce the conclusion about Walsingham taking your supernatural doom on himself and so further cover your trail. He is a man adept at secrets, visionary, gifted, and loyal; and Jane is his true match."

"I am sorry," good Queen Bess mourned.

"Don't make an error now," Holmes advised her. "Watch." He turned to John and I. "Dr Dee, you conjured me here to solve your mystery. It is now revealed. My work is done. Release me. I need to rouse in my own rooms and return to the waking world."

Comprehension dawned on John's face. "Yes," he breathed. "Thank you." He raised his hand. "Sherlock Holmes of Mycroft, Angel of Truth, Spirit of Detection, your labours are done. I charge thee depart without malice. By rod and rood I dismiss thee! Avaunt!"

Holmes disappeared. Only a pungent scent of Virginian tobacco remained where he had stood.

Her Majesty saw him vanish in plain sight. "Remarkable," she whispered to herself.

John and I had the sense to stand silent.

"A spirit," the queen recognised. "Conjured by your art, John."

"At mighty need only," my husband cautioned prudently. "At unique cost."

Gloriana turned to us. She was England. "I will take your oaths and command your service as the Angel suggested. No man so clever as to associate with a creature of that kind should be wasted to the headsman's axe."

We made bow and curtsey. "He brought the truth," John acknowledged,

clasping my hand tight. The Angel had brought truth to us too.
John needed me.

AUTHOR

I.A. WATSON's first published fiction (as an adult and not ghost-writing) was a Sherlock Holmes story (in Sherlock Holmes, Consulting Detective volume 1). It was the second Sherlock Holmes story he had ever written (the first one was too short to fit the slot it was supposed to fill, and subsequently appeared in Sherlock Holmes, Consulting Detective volume 2). The tale was riddled with footnotes right from the start (brackets are an inferior alternative for "About the Author" paragraphs). It got nominated for an award. He was asked back to write more stories.

Eighteen novels, eight novellas, three compilation editions, sixty-odd short stories later (and counting), I.A. Watson is still writing Sherlock Holmes stories and still riddling them with footnotes. Holmes is a hard habit to break. Amongst those novels is HOLMES AND HOUDINI, which astute readers may detect is about Sherlock Holmes. Two of the compilations, SHERLOCK HOLMES ADVENTURES volumes 1 and 2, collect previously-published stories from the Consulting Detective series in a handy electronic format.

Escaping temporarily from Holmes, as Doyle also liked to do, I.A. Watson has ventured into Historical Adventure (The Legend of Robin Hood), Historical Fantasy (St George and the Dragon), Mythology (The Labours of Hercules, The Death of Persephone), Science Fiction (Two Blackthorn novels, The Transdimensional Transport Company), Urban Horror (Vinnie de Soth, Jobbing Occultist) and many other oeuvres. A full list of his publications is available on his website at http://www.chill-water.org.uk/writing/iawatsonhome.htm.

When asked about why he writes, I.A. Watson has all kinds of random answers ready. When asked why he sends his work in to be published, it is always because he likes getting a copy of his work to put on his shelf and then to read in the bath (Kindles need not apply).

I.A. Watson keeps going back to Holmes because Doyle managed to come up with an excellent and potent formula to deliver a certain kind of story. The tales themselves can legitimately cover a whole range of types from action-adventure to horror to human drama to fair-play mystery. The idealised Victorian world in which Holmes and Watson live and work is a rich setting offering so many interesting venues and situations. Dr Watson is one of the most useful literary creations ever, at once offering narrative, commentary, reader engagement, and separation of perspective. The Great Detective himself benefits from being the very archetype of gifted, difficult, fascinating investigators; it is quite hard to make him boring.

Even in the time since THE INCUNABULUM OF SHERLOCK HOLMES was assembled and sent off to the publisher, I.A. Watson has written three more Holmes stories. It may be an addiction.

COVER & INTERIOR ILLUSTRATOR

ROB DAVIS—began his professional art career doing illustrations for role-playing games in the late 1980s. Not long after he began lettering and inking, then penciling comics for a number of small black and white comics publishers- most notably for Eternity Comics, which eventually became Malibu Comics in the 1990s, on their book SCIMIDAR with writer R.A. Jones. Expanding his career he eventually began working at both DC and Marvel on likeness intensive comics like adaptations from TV shows like QUANTUM LEAP and STAR TREK's many incarnations. Primarily he worked on the DEEP SPACE NINE comics for Malibu. At Marvel he worked on the comics adaptation of Saturday morning cartoon PIRATES OF DARK WATER. After the comics industry implosion in the late 1990's Rob picked up work on video games, advertising illustration and T-shirt design as well as some small press comics like ROBYN OF SHERWOOD for Caliber.

Rob continues to do the occasional self-published comic book as well as publisher and designer for his small-press production REDBUD STUDIO COMICS. Rob is Art Director, Designer and Illustrator for the New Pulp production partnership AIRSHIP 27 collaborating with writer/editor Ron Fortier. Rob is the recipient of the PULP FACTORY AWARD for "Best Interior Illustrations" in 2010 and 2016 for his work on SHERLOCK HOLMES: CONSULTING DETECTIVE and has been nominated for the same award a number of times since. A collection of selected Rob's illustrations from Airship 27 has been published as PULP: THE ART OF ROB DAVIS available at Amazon.com and Barnes & Noble online with a second collection in the planning stages. He works and lives in Missouri with his wife and two children.